THE PRESENT IS PAST

Josh Rank

THE PRESENT IS PAST

1.

Mary Goes Dark

High schools smell like a basement. It doesn't matter how old they are. And it doesn't matter how long you've been in them. They say you start to go nose blind to certain smells after about five minutes. This is how people live next to slaughterhouses and sewage treatment plants without killing themselves. But for high schools, they always smell like a basement. Even after teaching for 36 years.

A dull *thwap* woke up the quiet room. Normally, the kids sit without more than a whisper until everyone's done writing their essays ("Symbolism of *1984*, Book 2 Chapter 1") but William Grey decided he was bored. A new pile of books lay on the floor next to him. Mary Weber had seen boys like him over the years. She wasn't impressed.

"William," she said in her loudest whisper. "What have I told you about that?"

The boy showed her his palms. "Oh you've told me?" he said full volume. "And what exactly did you tell me?"

He laughed. So did a few of the other students. Mary paused. She couldn't fathom why that was funny.

"Get up," she said.

"Oh *come on*."

"Let's go."

The rest of the students made their usual happy groans whenever she took someone out of class. Everyone likes a distraction.

William stood up loudly. Even after 36 years, Mary never really understood how they did that. He grabbed his backpack with a dramatic flourish and followed her into the hallway. She might as well have been in 1992 with Billy Prospect. Or 1998 with Craig Hilton. Or any of the other boys that acted out just enough to warrant the extra effort.

The teachers who taught the teachers said you should treat every student the same. That each student's education was as valuable as the next. Mary disagreed. Some kids gravitated toward schoolwork. They seemed to inhale assignments and exhale good grades. But then there were the others that either didn't care, didn't have the time to care, or didn't want anyone to know they cared. These students needed extra attention. And much like the attempt to fix a leaky pipe on your own without calling a plumber, Mary felt compelled to at least try to help them.

"The binding wasn't even broken, Mrs. Weber," said William. They walked along the empty hallway, pea-colored lockers lining the walls.

"What have I told you about picking on Bryce?"

William paused and looked out of the corners of his eyes. "Is that a real question?"

"You're not the only person in that classroom. I have twenty other students to think about. You think it's fair for me to be out here talking to you like a child instead of finishing the class with the rest?"

"I gotta pee."

"You what?" She noticed he wasn't next to her and turned around.

"I gotta pee." He nodded toward the bathroom door to his right. "Cool?"

"Yeah William. *Cool.*"

He stepped into the zig-zagged doorway of the boys' bathroom. The hallways of the high school were always a little amazing to her. They explode with locker doors slamming shut, laughter, and moving feet between classes. But once everyone gets settled in, they become meditative zones of silence. Whispers echo. Footsteps reverberate. A hallway to her right led to the gymnasium. A lobby area with doors to the parking lot filled in the space between.

36 years. And just about an equal amount of Williams. The clothes change but the kids—

And then the hallway started to dim. At first she thought maybe a couple light bulbs went out, but it was more than that. She looked at the fluorescent lights above and saw they were still lit, just dimming. Her footsteps echoed in the empty hallway as she glanced around the corner. It looked like someone was rolling a massive dimmer switch counterclockwise. She moved toward the gym. She expected shadows to stretch down the hallway from the doors leading outside. But when she got to the lobby she only saw the vague movement of autumn leaves blowing through the rows of cars.

She wiped her eyes but that didn't stop the dimming. Was there a solar eclipse? But how could that affect the lights in the school? Was she going blind? Did that happen all at once? She pushed through the doors to the outside and the brisk air ran through her shirtsleeves. It felt like daytime. It looked like daytime, except for the fact that no matter how much she searched the sky, she couldn't find the sun.

Darkness engulfed the school by the time she walked back inside. This didn't really matter since the parking lot was just as black. She stuck her hands in front of her like a mummy and eventually found the wall. *How has nobody else come out of their room?* she wondered.

The musty basement smell of the high school remained, but every image of the last 36 years was gone. The trophy cases that hadn't seen an addition since the 2002 men's basketball championship. The concession stand outside the gym that only opened during basketball games on Friday nights. The rows of tables where students ate their lunches. It was all gone. The images in her mind weren't strong enough to bring them back. She closed her eyes and tried to imagine the posters on the walls around her. And when she opened them back up, she saw a faint glimmer of light from the end of the hallway.

A second sun was rising, but this one didn't seem to have a point of origin. The lights slowly resumed their pale, white glow. Sunshine through the mostly-glass doors picked up right where it left off.

She felt rejuvenated—like she had taken a nap. Mary yawned even though she wasn't tired.

It was a short walk back to class. And when she got inside it didn't seem like anybody noticed every light in the entire world going out for at least five full minutes. Or at least they didn't say they did. She looked at the papers in front of the students and figured they had to be done with whatever they were doing so she asked them to pass them forward.

And that's when the sound of shattered glass exploded through the soft bubble of the afternoon.

Students sprang from their seats.

"Stay," said Mary.

She walked toward the noise, even though something that loud could only have come from the parking lot. People don't have the capacity for that level of destruction without some mechanical assistance. Other teachers and students filtered into the hallway with her, and they all moved past the bathrooms, through the lobby and mostly-glass doors, and into the parking lot.

The horizontal rows of cars ended in a vertical passageway that could've been called a path if viewed from directly above. But from the point-of-view of a person standing outside the doors, it looked like the cars were directing your vision to the driveway leading to Eastland Avenue. It wasn't a busy street unless school was either getting started or getting out. But at this moment, there was an obstruction in the driveway. The crowd advanced toward the smoking mess.

The door of the smashed car flung open and William fell from the driver's seat. He cursed as he hit the ground.

"Oh my God!" yelled somebody.

"Call 911!" yelled another.

Mary walked to the end of the parking lot as people began swarming the demolished car. Some students called out for help. People called for others to back up. More people called the police but an ambulance can only drive so fast.

Mary stared at William. A cut over his eyebrows bled down the side of his face. He looked around as if just waking up. She stood still as the crowd swirled around her. Was everything in slow motion? Or did her quickening breaths simply make it seem that way? She lost feeling in her hands and feet so maybe it was lucky that she couldn't move.

People went to check on the driver of the red pickup truck with the smashed headlights and grill. Mary simply wiped the sweat from her forehead that had grown cool from the persistent wind.

"What was he even doing here?" she heard someone ask.

Two ambulances, a fire truck, and a couple police cars would decorate the afternoon parking lot with their lights. But Mary only saw their reflection in the mostly-glass doors as she walked back inside.

The lights going out.

The bathroom.

William knocking Bryce's books to the ground.

It finally came back.

Mary sat in the principal's office. She kept her hands in her lap and her legs crossed at the ankles. William should've been in here. Not her. The fire trucks and the ambulances had left, but not the police cars.

George Caldwell sat behind his desk but didn't say anything. He got the job after Howard West retired ten years earlier. She had liked Caldwell immediately. Anybody would've been better than Howard West.

"Is he going to be okay?" asked Mary. She sat in the blue chairs that had been in front of this desk since sometime around the Vietnam War.

"Why wasn't he in your class?" asked George Caldwell. Students were terrified of him. At 6'3", that was understandable. His east coast accent made him an anomaly in the middle of Wisconsin.

Mary shrugged. "He was picking on Bryce Ballard again."

"Your students said you left the room with him."

She nodded.

"So how did you come back to the room without him making it here?"

She opened her mouth to tell him about the darkness. About how the lights sucked everything out of her. How was anybody expected to keep track of their day when something like that happened? But instead, as she had recently found herself doing more and more, she shrugged.

Caldwell stood up. It seemed to take a full minute for him to unfurl himself from the chair and fully extend every piece of his massive vertebrae. He walked around the desk and sat in the identical armchair with faded blue upholstery to Mary's left. He scooted it little by little until he faced Mary.

"I can't sweep this under the rug," he said.

She nodded.

"That boy is hurt and his parents are going to want answers."

She nodded.

"And when they find out this isn't the first lapse of yours, they're going to demand accountability."

She nodded.

"I'm sorry, Mary."

She looked up to the massive head floating above her and was surprised to see moisture in his eyes.

36 years.

2.

Two Years Later
Greg Finds the House

"It feels a little weird at first. Like you're on ice or something." Greg Weber stood at the top of the ramp in the second warehouse near the loading docks. Some new kid, Nick or Neil or something, sat behind the wheel of the paper mill's worst tow motor. An absolute piece of shit. There was only a little bit of the original yellow paint left toward the back. The rest was a Pollock-like smattering of paint streaks from walls, barriers, and other abutments that proved too difficult for a new tractor driver to avoid.

"But I still like, turn right to go right and stuff, don't I?" Nick or Neil would touch the wheel but held his wrists aloft like he thought it might fall off if too much weight rested on top. The lack of pressure allowed the nervous shakes to show more than Greg liked.

"Yeah. Turn like normal. But it's the back wheels that steer, not the front."

Neil or Nick looked behind him like he had never seen rear wheels. He was a legacy hire—his dad worked in the machine shop for the last two hundred years or so which meant anybody that shared a chromosome got a job as long as they passed the drug test.

Greg thought at one point he would inspire a legacy hire of his own. He was wrong.

"Alright. Fire it up." Greg crossed his arms and thought about the birds that kicked their babies out of the nest after a couple days. Fly or die.

Nick or Neil turned the key and let it rumble for a second. He looked at Greg.

"Push the pedal. Don't hit anything."

The tow motor crept forward. They usually gunned it right from the start, adding a new Pollock streak to the front end. But this kid acted like the world was about to come crashing down on top of him. Greg didn't have to break a casual stride to catch up.

"For Christ's sake kid put some weight on it, will ya?"

He nodded and sped up. A little.

"How long do you think I should wait?" A man walked up to Greg as Nick or Neil drove along the rows of gigantic paper rolls. But to anybody else, they would've looked like cylindrical columns wrapped in paper. Maybe pipes? Industrial insulation? The paper mill was itself a relic. Formerly the driving economic force that put the whole area on the map. In reality, it was a lucky intersection of access to highways, railways, and a river. And even though the majority of the industry in the region had cannibalized itself, the doors had yet to be padlocked. Greg liked to tell people he had spent more than half his life underneath this roof. He got the job before video games made their first appearance on kids' Christmas lists. He worked about every job there was to work before making the jump to management. But really, the only difference was that his paychecks were a little bigger than before. He still had to eat shit from his boss like everybody else. However, his boss wouldn't have nodded to Jim Rusch to go right ahead and shatter an OSHA regulation within the first twenty minutes of this poor kid's first day.

"You got it boss." Jim had become an expert at the delicate balance one needs with a water balloon. Throwing it too hard will rupture it before it ever leaves your hand. But you have to have at least a little force if it's going to catch up with the twenty-year-old dork that's never going to see it coming.

And just as it had every time for the last ten years or so, Jim's expertly crafted water balloon sailed down the path of Warehouse Two right around bays 15 or 16 where it caught up with the clumsily ambling tow motor driven by Nick or Neil or something.

"Goddamnit I'm good at this," said Jim.

The kid let out a quick scream when the water crashed through the slotted metal roof of the tow motor. He craned his head backwards to look at them.

Greg drew a circle in the air with his finger. "Doing great," he yelled. "Keep going."

The tow motor slipped a little on the wet floor but continued slithering along the aisles.

"Training's pretty tough, eh?" asked Jim.

Greg shrugged. "It's part of the job description."

Jim pulled a cigarette from a soft pack in the breast pocket of his green t-shirt and lit it. Smoking had been outlawed in the warehouse decades earlier. Anybody under 40 would be written up for it immediately. But after a few decades, you get some special privileges. He offered one to Greg, but he shook his head.

"The wife'll flip." This was most of the truth. The rest of it was that his breaths didn't seem to be going quite as deep lately. In fact, it had seemed this way for a little while now.

Jim nodded and took a drag. Greg always loved the smell of cigarettes.

"How's all that going?" asked Jim.

Greg just looked at him.

"The wife."

"Oh. Well, you know. She's got a lot of time to kill these days."

"Retiring will do that."

Greg shot out a quick breath. "You could call it that." They didn't say the word. Not much, at least. *Alzheimer's. Dementia.* Speaking its name brought it to life. Like Bloody Mary. It was safest to keep the words in your head.

His pocket jumped. He pulled out his phone. "Speak of the devil," he said to Jim as he put it to his ear.

"I'm not an idiot," she said.

"What?" Greg nodded to Jim who returned it before turning around. A trail of smoke followed him like a steam engine disappearing into the sunset.

"And it's not like I just moved here."

"What are you talking about?"

"But I turn and I turn and it's just not there." She sounded hoarse. The kid came around the corner and Greg waved him into Warehouse One. He turned around before he could see exactly how terrified the kid was.

"Mary. Stop. What's going on?"

Deep breaths pulsated through the phone. A dull static blanketed the background.

"Are you in the car?"

"I just needed two quick things from the store."

Greg pushed his forefinger and thumb into his eyes. Not hard, but not softly either. She wasn't supposed to be in the car. Not by herself. Not behind the wheel. First it was the highway that made her nervous. Everything moved too fast. Everything was too loud. There was too much going on. But it wasn't until the red light looked like, well only God knows how a red light can look like anything but a red light. But whatever the case was, she saw the red light but didn't stop. A carload of teenagers swerved up onto the sidewalk, but the only thing hurt was the front alignment of their Chevrolet Sonic. The cop didn't take that into account when he gave her the ticket. And as much as it made Greg feel like a dictator, he couldn't let her drive anymore. Realistically, it was a relief for Mary. But what it really meant was that she was trapped in that house unless someone came to get her. Greg felt the dull ache of guilt in his stomach every time he laughed when he was away.

"Where are you?" he asked. He released the pressure from his eyes, and it took a moment for his vision to clear. He looked up. Did a light go out?

"I—I don't know."

They bought their house when Ashley, their oldest, was still wetting the bed.

"Well, what do you see?"

A few breaths and another blanket of engine noise streamed through the phone.

"I think that's a school."

"Is it red? A white line around the middle like a belt?"

"Yeah."

Jefferson Elementary. The kids walked there even when it was snowing.

"Okay. Pull over. I'll be there as soon as I can."

He hung up and swung his head around, looking for smoke. Was it darker? He looked up and saw another light out.

"Jim!" he yelled.

The tow motor bounced up the concrete ramp between the two warehouses.

"Mr. Weber?"

"Not you. Keep driving." Nick or Neil exhaled half his body mass and turned right.

Another light went out and a small red dot could be seen by the garage doors of the loading dock. Greg started to jog but ran out of breath before he could set a steady rhythm. Shit, he needed some exercise.

"Jim, hey I gotta go."

"What's up?"

"It's Mary. She just—I just gotta go. Watch the kid. Keep him driving until he stops hitting stuff."

Jim's cigarette nodded.

Each step to the parking lot covered half the ground it should've. He burst through the access door and the explosion of natural light stung his eyes. He found his blue 2012 Chevy Silverado and tore out of the parking lot, squealing his tires as they made the jump from blacktop to asphalt.

Red lights took hours.

Every car was being pushed instead of driven.

All roads doubled in length.

It seemed to take a week and a half, but Greg finally turned the corner onto Greenview Drive and saw the red monolith with a white belt. He slowed the truck to a light jog until he saw their equally blue Chevy Malibu. He pulled alongside the curb behind it.

She was out of the car before he put his first leg out.

"Where is everything? It's not like I don't know where I am. I've been driving these roads for years. For years! So where did it go? Where—"

Greg jumped out and met her at the hood of the Silverado. Her arms shot pointed fingers in every direction. He wrapped his around her shoulders. She continued pointing at things that should've been there.

"I don't know where I am and I am where I always have been but it's different now and I can't figure out—"

Greg could feel the rapid rise and fall of her breaths through his arms curled around her back. Short. Choppy. Forced. Her entire body had become an earthquake. The air had a chill, but it was erased by the afternoon sunlight and a lack of wind. It was the shaking that would stick in Greg's mind as he tried to fall asleep that night.

"It's okay," he whispered into her ear on a loop. She hadn't stopped yelling since she got out of the car. He imagined her waiting for him. Every car was a threat and a possibility. Every movement was foreign. Stuck in a strange land that bears a slight resemblance to the world she at one point ran, Mary revolted. The tears spilling down her cheeks were as much from anger as they were frustration and fear. Greg held her tighter but the earthquake continued. She raged at the road signs. The new construction. She cursed the angle of the sunlight and every repaved driveway. It was all different and nobody sought her approval. Who made these changes? What right did they have?

Her words became slower and less forceful after three minutes that felt like twenty. Her arms went slack under Greg's. He rubbed her back and told her it would be okay. That it was time to go. And that he would come back for the car later.

He helped her into the truck and drove the two blocks that had previously been obfuscated by new houses and roads that were built decades earlier. The Silverado's tires crunched up their driveway in less than a minute.

"I drove down this road," she said as they climbed from the truck. She looked left and right. "I drove right past our house. Multiple times."

Greg followed her glance and tried to imagine seeing their house without recognizing it.

They walked in the front door where a tricolor beagle announced their return with a trumpeted howl.

"Hey hey, Al, that's enough," said Greg as he led Mary into the living room. She sat on the front of the couch cushions with her hands in her lap. Greg filled a glass of water from the tap in the kitchen and set it on the table next to her.

"That was terrible," said Mary, her voice soft and full of waves. She wiped her eyes with the back of her right hand and stared at a nothing spot in the middle of the floor.

Greg sat in the chair to her left and watched his wife of 39 years process the afternoon. He tried to find the words that could calm her down, but he wasn't sure if she'd be able to hear them if he did.

3.

Ashley and the Streetlights

The house was old. Built somewhere near the turn of the last century. Back when most of this town was still farmland. Around the time the entire world started fighting with each other for the first time. Darren Wolff had told her that it would be fine. He could fix the place up. And he could take care of any pop-up problems, too. Old houses seemed more dangerous to her. And with the prospect of a child in the near future, dangers were at the top of her hit list. And now all these years later, those repairs seem more impossible than ever.

"Why didn't Dad just follow us home?" asked Noah. He still wore the shiny green soccer jersey. His shin pads were probably lying on the floor by the back door.

She knew it confused him. But Darren, being that role model that he was, didn't want to miss his son's game. For some reason, he felt these games were more important than anything else. He coached the team the previous year, even after the separation.

"What do you think he's going to say when we get home?" she asked him a year earlier. The night all the promises of marriage came unraveled.

"What do you think he's going to say when he doesn't see me there?" It had to be around midnight. The kids went to bed hours before. Ashley made the mistake of mentioning something that had been on her mind for months. Years? Maybe.

Ashley sighed and put her forehead into her hands. Her alarm would ring in about six hours. That didn't matter. She didn't expect much sleep anyway.

Darren stood up and walked around the counter that separated the kitchen from the dining room. He rested against the countertop next to the sink and used his hands as a cushion behind his back.

"Are you sure this is what you want?" he asked her. So understanding. So goddamn rational.

Did she want him to get mad? To cry? To punch a hole in the wall and wake up the kids? She'd at least have something she could point to. A reason. A justification for shredding those vows she worked so hard on seven years earlier—for him, sure, but also for herself.

Do people really just fall out of love?

One day, maybe two years before, she chopped all her hair off. It hung past her shoulders when she left in the morning for work but would barely cover your fingers if you ran your hand across her scalp by the time she got home. Darren just stared at her as she took her shoes off by the back door.

"Here's where you say, *Looks good honey.*"

But he didn't. Instead, he asked her why.

She opened her mouth to respond, but the most honest thing she could do was shrug. The idea came to her two months before. She immediately dismissed it as crazy. But when she woke up, the thought was there. It followed her throughout her days. For two months. So when she saw the salon on her way home from work she didn't even really think about it more than, "Alright fine."

There had to be a reason she couldn't shake the thought. There had to be a reason it followed her everywhere. And then one day, after her hair had again reached her shoulders, she had another thought.

Do people really just fall out of love?

And now it had been a full year and she still wasn't sure. New questions took its place. Most of them came from the mouths of Noah and Sadie.

"Why didn't Dad just follow us home?" repeated Noah. Sunlight strained by the late afternoon shined off his green jersey.

She sighed. "Come on we went over this already." She'd gotten pretty good at making it through the day without sleep when Sadie was still in diapers. She didn't need more than a couple hours and a pot of coffee. People underestimated the power of momentum.

"He had to go back to his apartment." Ashley grabbed a green alligator from the floor. It squeaked. Darren was the one who realized their daughter liked to play with dog toys. It seemed like a great money saver at the time. But now it was just plain weird.

Noah turned away from her and said, "That sucks."

She knew she should've yelled at him. That's no language for a first grader to use. But what did she expect? Darren was great with the kids. Always had been. And Noah was right. It sucked.

She couldn't get used to the way his half of the bed looked when the sun finally rose in the morning. Cold. Empty. *Is this what you wanted?* it asked. *Do people really just fall out of love?*

She needed to get to the stack of papers sitting on the kitchen table. It was still close to the start of the school year, but if she expected the essays to be in on time, she should get them back on time.

She sighed and sat on the floor to grab the squeak toy from Sadie.

"Mommy no," she said.

The phone rang. Ashley let the alligator fall to the floor.

"I'll get it," she said to no one. She grabbed her cell phone from the short table next to the couch.

"Hey Dad," she said as she sat on the arm of the couch. The dull thud of music started in Noah's room. He was supposed to be getting into the shower.

"Hey Ash. How's it going?" He sounded tired. Like he had just run up a hill.

"It's okay. Noah won his soccer game."

"Oh *right,* the soccer game. Any goals?"

"Him? No." Ashley tried to remember if he'd scored any goals at all. Ever.

Ashley looked up to the stack of papers on the table just as Sadie tried to stand but screwed it up somehow. Ashley didn't see how it happened, but she heard the result.

The cry started as a slow putter but built itself to a wail.

"I, uh—" said Greg.

Ashley scooped the screaming child in her arm as she held the phone in the other hand. She was trying to be more patient these days, particularly with her father. His calls had been getting longer, like he didn't want to get off the phone despite having nothing interesting to say.

"I had to leave work early today," he finally said.

"Oh yeah?" Ashley noticed a car slowly driving past the front of her house. "You feeling okay?"

"Yeah. Yeah no it wasn't that," he said. A pause. "I got a call from your mother."

Ashley stopped the light wobble she hoped would calm Sadie.

"Is she feeling okay?"

"Well," an inauthentic chuckle, "that's all relative, I guess."

Two more cars drove past her house. There's nowhere to go down there but a dead end of more houses just like this one.

"She got lost," he said.

"Mom did?" More cars.

"She took the car to the store—"

"Oh jeez."

"—and couldn't find her way back. She's lived in the same house since 1985."

The alarm in Sadie's throat finally stopped so Ashley set her back down.

A few strands of a higher register bled through the leather of his voice. The same strands that infected her voice when she felt tears bubbling from their hiding places in her eyelids. A soft sound. Unsteady. Unsure. And coming from her Dad, it was one of the most upsetting sounds she could hear.

"She drove right past our house how many times," he continued.

She could feel her face contorting to the way her Dad's voice sounded. The bubbles in her eyelids moved to the center. She walked to the window to distract herself and saw even more cars in front of her house. What was going on?

"Is she okay now?"

"Yeah. Yeah she's lying down."

"Where did you find her?"

"By the school."

"Jefferson?"

"Mm-hmm."

"Jesus Christ." Mom couldn't find her way home from the school that both her and her brother went to for seven years.

"Ash, she was losing it when I showed up. She was shaking so much I thought her hair would fall out. It took almost two hours to get her to settle down."

"I'm sorry, Dad."

Noah's music continued and Sadie decided she wasn't hurt after all and went back to playing with her dog toy. Ashley glanced outside and almost forgot about her Dad on the other end of the phone.

Cars filled the road. Both directions. The sun was almost to the horizon now and the brake lights lit up the front bumpers of the cars behind them. A traffic jam? Here? Why would anybody come down this road? There weren't even many trees to look at. At most, she had seen two cars at the same time as neighbors went to meet each other for a beer to get away from their kids or spouses, or both. But there had to be at least thirty cars. What the hell?

"No, you know what, I'm sorry. I don't even know why I called to tell you this. You've got enough going on."

"Dad, don't worry about it."

He let out a deep breath. "Alright I'll let you go."

They hung up and Ashley scooped up Sadie.

"Put me down," she said. Sadie didn't speak much. She chose her words carefully.

"Nope. Come on." She walked to Noah's room just past the living room and kicked the door. The dull throb of music turned down.

"I thought you were getting in the shower?"

The door cracked open.

"Going."

As a high school teacher, she was better informed than most as to how unruly teenagers could be. She wasn't looking forward to the monster Noah would be in another ten years.

She walked outside, still holding Sadie. The early October air had more of a chill than it had any right to have, but they wouldn't be out there long.

The two-story house, white, a decorative fence that didn't guard anything from anything around a corner of the bushes by the front of the house—so many years and so many memories in that house and Mom drove past it like she was visiting the neighborhood for the first time. She'd heard people say stress or anxiety or whatever felt like a weight on your chest. But to her, walking out the back door and through the yard thinking of her Mom unable to recognize her own house, her chest just felt dead. A leaden mass of congealed blackness threatening to topple her over.

Good thing there was a traffic jam in front of the house to distract her.

But when she finally cleared the length of the house and walked down the driveway, all she saw was the same empty road she always saw.

"What the hell?" She carried Sadie to the end of the driveway and looked up and down the street. One by one, she watched as the streetlights kicked on until the wave of new light passed over their heads and continued down the street. Is that how they always turned on?

"Mommy I'm cold," said Sadie.

Ashley kissed her on the cheek.

"Me too, sweetie."

She stood in her driveway for another minute, just holding her daughter and staring at her house in the glow of the streetlights.

4.

Sam Finds a Dog

He liked scrubs. It felt like wearing pajamas to work. Granted, people don't consistently get blood on their pajamas, but Sam Weber prided himself on looking on the bright side of life. Or, at least, he tried to. Even now, walking out of the Emory University Midtown Hospital after twelve hours of pure shit, he was looking on the bright side.

"Oh great, it's raining again," he said to himself.

"Good thing you brought that umbrella there, big guy." Steve Campbell stood next to him. Twelve hours is a long time for strict focus.

Sam looked down. An umbrella hung lazily from his half-closed hand.

"Look at that," he said. Summer rains came with a thick blanket of humidity. But now that the heat had finally cooled to a point where bursting into flames in the middle of the afternoon seemed less likely, the air was approaching cold. Especially after sundown. "To tell you the truth, I don't want to go out there."

"Can't blame you," said Steve. "You worked all day to get those blood stains just right."

"I know it looks like a lot of work, but really, it was just that cyclist. He bled enough for everybody."

Steve drew in a deep breath and let it out slowly. "What a hero."

"Hero indeed."

"You know we have a locker room where you can clean yourself up, right?"

Sam shrugged.

And then they heard a light pattering of feet that sounded like raindrops hitting the pavement. The bright white streetlights reflected off the rain-soaked blacktop. Lines delineating parking stalls disappeared. In fact, the suggestion of a solid surface disappeared, leaving what looked to be a frozen lake. Cars driving through the pooled water created slight waves and the slurpy suction of tires on the moist asphalt below. Sam tried to ignore the mirage to see what had just run past.

"Right there," he said as if Steve had asked him what it was.

"Huh?"

"A dog. Over there." A black and white dog that might look like a border collie when it wasn't soaking wet had run past the entrance to the hospital. It paused near the handicap parking spots and did a great job of blending into the wet parking lot.

Steve shrugged. Sam stepped into the rain and opened the umbrella with a *fwoomp* in front of him.

"It goes over your head," yelled Steve. But Sam didn't pay attention as he carried the umbrella at his side.

"Hey buddy," said Sam. He shuffled forward and held one hand toward the dog while the other held the umbrella. Rain fully soaked his hair and dripped down his forehead. A slight chill ran through him. The dog had to be freezing. The temperature was around twice the actual point of turning water into ice. People back home in Wisconsin would laugh at what was considered cold, but numbers worked differently in the South.

People adjust. They adapt to their surroundings and reset their baselines. Sam spent the first few winters laughing at everyone around him. Two flakes of snow sent the whole city into a frenzy. Milk, bread, and eggs sold out at the grocery store as if the hinges on their doors would lock them inside until the spring thaw. He'd go out in a hooded sweatshirt while others wrapped themselves in thick coats, scarves, and gloves. He didn't consider himself a southerner and figured he never would, but things change.

People adjust.

He moved to the city in the middle of the summer after transferring his nursing license to Georgia. That was three years ago. Greg told him it was a mistake to move to a new city without securing a job first, but there were plenty of hospitals. What were the chances none of them needed an extra nurse?

Turns out, the chances were pretty good.

He walked out of hospital after hospital with the same words in his head—

"We'll keep your information on file."

The long list continually got shorter and he started to worry that the year-long lease he had just signed might condemn him to working fast food just to avoid eviction.

He allowed himself a night out. It felt deserved despite not having anything to show. He walked to a bar a few blocks from his house and felt his shirt stick to his back after maybe seven steps. He wondered why the hell he decided to move here anyway.

There hadn't been a lot of deliberation. He hadn't investigated the local economy or job market or potential recreational activities. His rubric for a new city was concise—no snow, and far from Wisconsin.

Won't you miss your family? people loved to ask.

No. No he wouldn't. Well, maybe the dog.

And when he finally sat down at the bar, he realized he had no one to talk to. Not having any friends will do that. So he sat back and watched the Braves game on the TV above the bar while he sipped on a beer he couldn't pronounce. A voice came floating over his shoulder.

"This sport sucks."

He turned around to see a woman trying to get the bartender's attention by waving a dollar bill back and forth. Her curly hair stuck out from her head in round balls. No makeup. Circles under her eyes. She wore purple scrubs which made her look like a character from a children's TV show compared to the rest of the garbage people in this garbage bar.

Sam scooted to his left to give her a lane to the bar. She stayed right where she was.

"It's all marketing, you know," she said. "That's why everyone thinks they have to like this game."

Sam shrugged. "I don't know. I don't think it's bad."

"America's pastime? You know why they call it that?"

Sam shrugged again.

"Because it's boring. Basketball and football, the real football, were invented by Americans, too you know. And right around the same time. But the baseball people had the great idea to label it America's pastime because Americans love it when you say America."

Sam spun a bit on his bar stool. "So what are you, like, on a mission to ruin baseball for everybody?"

A beer appeared on the bar and the woman tossed a collection of bills next to it.

"Listen, it sucks. I don't need an argument. It's inherent. Now if you'll excuse me—" She reached forward and grabbed her beer.

"Which hospital do you work at?"

"What makes you think I work at a hospital?" She continued standing right behind him and took a drink of the beer.

"Well I saw the scrubs and—"

"Oh so just because I dress this way means I'll clean out your bedpan? Dress your wounds?"

"No no no, I—"

"Relax. I'm fucking with you."

Sam turned back to the game. He liked this boring sport.

"Emory University Midtown Hospital," she said. "Just finished a twelve and boy are my wings tired."

"Huh," he said. "I haven't tried that one yet."

"It's not a restaurant, you know."

He shook his head. "No, no. I'm applying. Been trying to find a nursing job for a couple weeks now."

"Nothing?"

"Nothing."

"Janet Jackson," she said and stuck her hand out.

"Wait what?"

"Head of nursing at Emory University Midtown Hospital."

The bar stool squeaked as he put his feet on the ground. He accepted the shake and said—

"Sam Weber."

"You got a license?"

He nodded.

"You ever been sued?"

He shook his head.

"Stop in tomorrow." She looked at her watch. "Around noon."

He nodded. "Thank you. Thank you, Ms. Jackson."

"You know, I almost said no."

"To what?"

"My husband. It's Mrs. Jackson, by the way."

"So you married into being Janet Jackson?"

She nodded, sighed, and walked away.

And without Janet Jackson he wouldn't be standing in a shiny parking lot, soaked through his chest hair, with his hand out to a dog.

"Hey buddy," he said for the tenth time. And then a big white van drove past which sent the dog running. "Hey!"

Sam ran after the dog into the slight alley between the parking garage and the hospital. A dumpster stuck out from the hospital wall and the dog seemed to find a great scent just in front of it. It walked in a tight circle. He remembered the umbrella hanging from his hand and finally put it over his head. The soft thump of raindrops lazily hitting the nylon reminded Sam of camping.

The dog continued to circle, hunch its back, and circle more. This cycle happened three or four times before Sam realized what was happening.

"I gotcha buddy I gotcha."

He slowly stepped forward. The dog ignored Sam as he approached and shielded him from the rain with the umbrella.

A light jingle filled the air and he realized his phone was ringing. The dog didn't seem to mind.

"Hello?"

"It's Ashley."

"Hey sis. Nice greeting."

"Yeah well. Listen, I just thought you should know that Mom got lost today."

"She what?" His phone was getting wet. Weren't they protected against that now?

Ashley sighed. "She couldn't find her way home. Dad had to get her."

She always did this. It was going to ruin his whole night. He's however-many miles away. What the hell could he do?

"Shit," he said. He felt himself going up the emotional roller coaster. Muscles tightening. Heart pounding. Except he knew there would be no release.

"Yeah, shit," she said.

As if on command, the dog finally let loose. It was disgusting, but twelve hours in the ER easily eclipsed the horror show coming out of the stray dog.

"I really don't know why you call me with this," he said.

"You know what? Neither do I. Sorry I thought you gave a shit about our Mom."

"Of course I give a shit! But what am I—" He realized he was talking to a dead phone. She hung up.

Goddamnit, he thought.

"I don't see a bag."

Sam turned around, still holding the umbrella over the dog.

"What?"

Some dickhead with a long coat, umbrella, and gloves watched from the parking lot.

"The, uh—" He motioned toward the dog. "The business there. You gonna pick that up?"

Sam couldn't believe the dog was still underneath the umbrella, but everybody likes a break from the rain once in a while. A chill ran through his body. Is this how people catch colds? Shouldn't a nurse know the answer to that?

"It's not my dog. I was just helping him poop."

The dickhead laughed. "That doesn't happen."

A quick, but bright flash of lightning illuminated the parking lot. The thunder that followed felt like a gunshot going off directly next to Sam's head. The dog ran out from underneath the umbrella. The dickhead covered his head like a bomb had gone off. Two car alarms erupted. And Sam, sick of the conversation and unsure how it would play out, ran into the parking lot.

It wasn't until he finally climbed into the seat of his own car that he noticed the steady tone of his ears ringing.

5.

Mary and the Disappearing Salt

It's quiet.

It's always quiet.

The house had been quiet all day.

Mary didn't like to play music. She found it distracting.

She didn't like to watch TV anymore. They seemed to introduce new characters after every commercial break.

So she walked.

Not outside, unless the dog needed to go out. She stayed within the four exterior walls of their home of however many years. She never thought a trip to the grocery store would feel like a tropical vacation. But here she was, fantasizing about how the avocados looked in the produce section.

She'd been to that store about a million times. She used to go all the time back when she would cook dinners for her family on the weekends. Weekdays were too busy, of course, unless school was out. She was always so busy and now look at her: walking through an empty house in socks so she can't even hear her own footsteps.

I used to have a life.

People relied on me.

The most excitement she felt all afternoon was the comparatively loud sound of her sigh as she looked out the window to the backyard. The orange tint of autumn was starting to creep into the leaves of the cottonwood tree along the property line. It was getting tall. Too tall. It had been maybe a decade since she first saw it over the top of the house from the street out front, but now the height felt like a threat. One good soaking rain to loosen up the soil, a big gust of wind, and boom there goes the neighborhood.

Sam had thrown a rope over one of the branches to try to tie up a tire swing when he was eight or nine. Or was that Ashley?

Mary walked away from the window and tried to call up the image—Sam and his friend, what's-his-name from down the road, the kid that always peed the bed when he slept over. But she couldn't find the pictures anywhere in her brain. She tried again but put Ashley and the blonde girl from next door in the boys' place. Samantha. That was her name. Because it was so close to Sam.

Is it possible to be exhausted from doing nothing? She was wiped. Taking a nap felt like a sin.

I used to have a life.

People relied on me.

Back when she was a teacher. She loved holding the attention of the class. And not because of the power or anything weird like that. No, it was just exciting. There was immediate gratification in explaining things. Understanding nods from the class might as well have been a standing ovation. She loved it. So she pushed even further into it. Anybody can teach the kids that want to be taught, she used to say. But she liked a challenge. So every little asshole that crossed her path, every little prick that other teachers would complain about in the teacher's lounge, those kids became her focus. She chaperoned detention before and after school. And when one of these little pricks didn't have anybody to go home to, she'd stay with them. She never really had any of those movie moments where the school bully would break down and swear to change their ways. A couple of them cooled it on the classroom disruptions, but that was about it.

It made her feel good. She was doing at least a little good in these terrible kids' lives. So she kept it up.

And now she looked out the front window hoping a car would pull into the driveway. Surprise visits were rare. Linda stopped over every so often in the afternoon, but not much.

A truck pulled out of the garage across the street. Then a sedan crawled out of the garage to the right. Then another. And another. Soon, every house on the block in both directions had trucks, cars, and vans pulling out and driving away.

She was the only person in the entire neighborhood.

Maybe the whole world

I used to have a life.

She got off the couch and walked into the kitchen. It was late. Greg should be home by now. She opened the cabinet and pulled out a frying pan. The harsh clanks were downright refreshing. She thought about buying some water glasses to shatter in the sink every so often to make sure she was still alive. She set the pan on the stove, turned it on, scooped some butter, and flicked it into the pan. Al's collar jingled as she followed her nose into the kitchen.

She opened the refrigerator and heard the low rumble of an engine outside.

Greg was home.

It felt silly to get this excited, but she couldn't help it. She had said she was lonely other times in her life. But she was wrong. This was a pit with no ladder. And a lid.

She met him at the door. Al welcomed him with a series of what could be considered barks. But beagles don't really bark. They just say "woo" in either short increments (bark) or long increments (howl).

"Hey guys," said Greg. "Al, Al please shut up." He closed his eyes and blindly pawed at the dog's head.

"You're late," said Mary. It came out a little more forceful than she wanted.

"Yeah, there was…a, uh…a problem. It took forever." He walked into the living room and sat down without taking his shoes off. "How was your day?" he finally asked.

"Oh my day? Have you ever locked yourself in a closet for a whole day?"

"Wh—what?"

"Neither had I before now." She sat on the couch and leaned her elbows on her knees. "Greg. I'm going to go crazy." Where did these tears come from? "I can't take it. And then when you come home late, it's like—"

"Mary, shit I'm just trying to keep us afloat." He rubbed a hand over his face. "I need to work as much as I can. You know that."

Mary sat back and wiped her eyes. She hadn't meant to bring this up right away. She wanted to have fun for once in her life. And now she ruined it.

I used to have a life.

And then the smoke alarm went off.

Greg jumped from his chair and ran into the kitchen.

"What the hell is this?" he asked.

Mary followed behind him and watched as he turned around with the frying pan in his hand, smoke pouring from the burned butter.

Al resumed her version of barking.

She grabbed a towel and fanned the smoke detector. Another minute later, the oppressive quiet she battled all day settled over the house.

"I was gonna cook something," she said quietly.

"What? Why? Ashley's bringing dinner over tonight."

"You never told me that." Mary left him in the kitchen and walked back into the living room. And then more quietly: "You never tell me anything anymore."

A long sigh leaked from the kitchen.

The house remained mostly quiet besides the soft shuffling of feet until finally, graciously, a car pulled into the driveway. Mary opened the front door as the indistinct chatter grew louder.

"Hey Grandma," said Noah. He walked in the open door with a covered pot in his hands. Sadie strolled lazily behind him clutching a green alligator. It squeaked as she walked past.

"Excuse me Mom." Ashley held a large white crock-pot that seemed almost too heavy for her. "You're gonna have to move."

Mary stepped to the side.

"There they are!" said Greg from the kitchen.

Al ran quickly between rooms, nose in the air and tail wagging.

Mary followed the train of excitement into the kitchen where Sadie and Noah were trying to calm Al down enough for a pet, and Greg helped Ashley set up the food.

"What's this?" Ashley held up the frying pan.

"Experiment gone wrong," said Greg. He set it aside and put her pot on the stove.

Mary walked into the mayhem that erupted in her kitchen—it didn't even seem like the same house as the quiet coffin it was in the afternoon—and reached into the cupboards for the plates. But as she grabbed the stack all at once, the weight shifted and they began to splay out like a deck of cards. She quickly brought them to the countertop where they landed with a soft bang.

"Hey hey why don't you just take a seat?" said Greg. "We got this."

"I can set the damn table," she said quietly.

I used to have a life.

Greg nodded, took a step back, and smiled at Sadie who appeared next to them.

"Hey sweetheart," he said and picked her up.

It didn't seem like anybody in the whole room stood still in the twenty minutes it took to heat everything back up. She asked the kids about school (Noah hated it and Sadie was still a year away from preschool), Ashley told her the high school was getting a new paint job (a "puke green" color), and she avoided questions of how she liked retirement.

How did she like it? She hated it. But how did she answer?

"It's nice to have the time."

In reality, it wasn't an actual retirement at all. At only fifty-eight years old, Medicare was still a handful of years away. And being let go from the school wasn't exactly the same as retiring.

Finally they sat down to eat. Mary felt her stomach roar to life with hunger. Did she eat lunch? She must have, right?

A big platter of beef stroganoff sat next to a bowl of mashed potatoes. A bag of rolls had been emptied onto a plate. Salt and pepper shakers sat off to the side, an obligation of the dinner table whether anyone used them or not. Ashley scooped the stroganoff and potatoes onto her kids' plates and tossed a roll on there afterward. Greg passed his plate and she did the same. Mary passed her plate and she did the same.

"Alright, dig in," said Ashley.

Forks clanked against plates. Al circled the table trying to figure out who she could manipulate.

"This is good," said Greg.

Mary took a small bite. The table seemed like it was missing somebody.

"Where's, um…"

Ashley looked up, waiting.

Her memory clicked.

"Darren. Where's Darren?"

Ashley set her fork on her napkin, spotted with brown dots and streaks.

"He's not here," she said quickly. Her eyes darted between her kids.

Greg reached over and patted Mary's hand for some reason.

"Is he at work?"

"How'd that soccer game go, buddy?" asked Greg.

"Pretty good," said Noah. "We won, but like, I didn't do anything."

"Well, did you let anyone on the other team score a goal?"

"No."

"Sounds to me like you did something."

Noah smiled.

But why wasn't anyone answering Mary? The food was a little bland. She took a drink of water and scanned the table for salt. Where the hell did it go?

"I mean, I guess so," said Noah.

"Where's the salt?" asked Mary. Greg grabbed it out of nowhere and slid it to her.

She sprinkled it on her food and set it down. Tried the stroganoff again. Yeah that was better. She reached for her water glass, but it wasn't where she left it. The salt seemed to coat her entire throat. She went to grab her napkin but that was gone, too. Her hands started to shake a little. Where was everything going? Why can't she find these simple things she'd been using not only for the first few minutes of dinner, but her whole damn life? All she wanted was a small drink of water and to wipe her mouth, but nothing was where it was supposed to be. Nothing was ever where it was supposed to be anymore and it made her so damn mad and she knew there was no one to blame but herself so there was nothing she could do but feel the rage build inside her which only seemed to come out in a slight tremor to her hands but realistically came out in caustic comments to her husband who was only trying to help but sometimes—

"Mary?" Greg put his hand on hers again. "You good?"

"I'm thirsty," she said. He slid her water glass toward her. Where did it come from?

"Here you go."

I used to have a life.

6.

Greg's Last Stop

Football season was an absolute blessing from God. Greg hated leaving home because he knew Mary was just bouncing off the walls. But there was tradition at stake here, and even she understood that he couldn't miss going to the Overtime Sports Bar & Grill for the Monday night football games. Besides, Ashley and the kids had been over the previous night.

What was once an excuse to eat chicken wings and have a few beers had become an island of recreation in a week otherwise filled with obligation. Jim Rusch and Steve Shannahan had been meeting him every week since this place was still called The Finish Line and the TVs were big boxes instead of thin as a picture frame. Steve kept in contact even after he got caught up in one of the many downsizings at the paper mill.

A graveyard of chicken bones sat in red-checked paper trays, decorated with a tall pile of wadded napkins. Steve just finished telling the table how his daughter had gotten engaged to some asshole bartender. The guys gave their condolences.

The bar erupted as the Cowboys completed a long pass on the last play of the half. Should be a good pickup for fantasy football, but no real points came out of it.

"Hey, whatever happened with taking off from work the other day?" asked Jim. He took a drink from his half-filled glass of Miller Lite.

"Oh," said Greg. "It was nothing."

Halftime. The dead zone of football games.

"It was Mary, wasn't it?" asked Steve. As an electrician, Steve Shannahan mostly spent his time at the mill rewiring machines that should have been replaced two or three presidential administrations earlier. He wasn't worried when he got his walking papers at the mill.

"I call that a vacation until I gotta get back to it," he said at the time. As long as people can get electrocuted, they're going to need an electrician. He figured a new job wouldn't take more than a few phone calls and applications. He took the break in employment as an excuse to go up north. After that, he stuck around town and called Greg and Jim every day to let them know how much he enjoyed being unemployed.

"Got up at five today, did ya?" he'd yell into the phone. "Well I think I'm going to take a nap. They say sleeping for eleven hours just makes you more tired. Who knew!"

And he kept coming to the bar on Monday nights. Football season was the excuse, but that didn't stop them from coming in the middle of July. Habits die hard, especially when they're also excuses.

Greg Weber wiped his fingers with another napkin. It had been a few minutes since his last chicken wing, but it was almost impossible to feel clean. He usually showered when he got home.

"Yeah Steve," he said. "Yeah it was." Greg looked at his watch. It wasn't late. He thought of Mary shaking on the side of the road by the school—

I drove right past our house. Multiple times.

—the way her eyes shot back and forth between his, the frantic pleading behind her voice. His stomach felt sick, and it wasn't from the chicken wings.

"Shit guys, I gotta go," he said. He expected them to put up a fight, but they just nodded and said "Alright, man." He had told them too much about what's going on at home over the last year.

He flagged down the waitress, gave her his debit card, and closed out.

"Alright. I'll see ya," he said as he threw his track jacket around his shoulders. Not that he'd ever run track.

The cold night air puffed into his face as he walked out the glass doors. It was still fall, damn it. Winter would come soon enough and ruin just about every day until the spring thaw finally came in five years or so. The cool air didn't fill his lungs as much as when he didn't need to wear a coat—even if the coat was light. Each breath seemed like it only did half the job. He blasted the heat when he finally got in his truck. And maybe by the time he was halfway home it would actually be hot.

He shouldn't feel guilty for taking some time for himself. Right? He wasn't sure. Mary couldn't go anywhere. She couldn't call up her friends and meet them for chicken wings and dick jokes at the local tavern. But did that mean that he shouldn't either?

Maybe.

Probably.

He turned onto the four-lane road that took him almost all the way home. Calumet Street. He used to take the kids for bike rides down here to the Dairy Queen back when it was only two lanes. Mary too, when she wasn't helping some delinquent with his homework. It might have been dark, but the leafless trees looked like skeletons waving their fingers at him as he drove underneath the streetlights.

You shouldn't have had that many beers.

You shouldn't have talked about your wife.

You shouldn't have left at all.

He turned off the radio. He needed to focus on his shame.

Five minutes later he finally pulled into the driveway. None of the outside lights were on. He hopped out of the truck in the driveway and dared his lungs to breathe the cool air for maybe fifteen steps until he pulled open the front door and walked in.

"Mary?" The house was quiet. He kicked off his shoes and walked through the living room and into the kitchen. "Hello?"

He heard a moan from the bedroom. He walked in, flicked on the light, and saw her lying in bed.

"Hmm? What?" She wiped her hair off her forehead and looked at him, but she still had the fog of sleep clouding her eyes.

"Hey, sorry. Go back to sleep." Greg flicked the light back off and started to close the door when he again noticed the quiet. He leaned back in but left the light off.

"Is Al in here?" he asked.

Mary shuffled around in the bed. A response didn't seem to be coming so he pulled out his phone and flashed it along the sides of the bed.

Nothing.

He walked back into the kitchen and crossed his arms. Honestly, it was better if she just slept through the night. He checked the living room. The bathroom floor. The kitchen floor in front of the oven.

Nothing.

Was the garage open? The lights were off, so it was hard to tell. They used it mostly for storage and sitting in lawn chairs when storms rolled through, so he wasn't really paying attention to it when he came home. This time of year, when it got cold, the only reason they went through it was to take the dog for a walk.

A cold chill ran down his spine.

Each step creaked through the old foundation. Each breath became deeper than the last. And when he finally made it to the door leading to the garage, right next to the empty hook where the leash usually hangs, he knew what happened.

He burst into the bedroom.

"Did you take Al for a walk tonight?"

The light from the kitchen crowded around him and fell haphazardly onto Mary. The bedroom light stayed dark.

"What?"

"The dog. Did you take the dog for a walk tonight?"

Mary sat up. She looked at the clock and pushed her hair out of her face.

"I don't think so."

Greg stomped his foot and took a step into the kitchen before turning right back around.

"Were you *going to*?" He hadn't meant to yell. He didn't want to yell.

He yelled.

"Is she…is she not here?"

All at once, the lava that filled his veins hit the ocean. Clouds of steam erupted inside him as it flash cooled, solidified, and sank deep inside. He wanted to throw up. It was a child's question. Not childish, but as from a child. His wife. The woman he loved since the Carter administration asked the question of a child because he scolded her like an adult.

He wanted to throw up.

But he didn't have time. No time to reassure his wife, to tell her it wasn't her fault. No time to make sure she was okay.

No time to throw up.

An image of Al popped into his head. Shivering. Cold. Afraid. She had always been a timid dog. In fact, that was what he liked most about her. She was gentle. Kind. It made for a great companion, but a terrible survivalist. Each car would send her fleeing until she crawled inside a bush where she'd wait for help. Shivering. Cold. Afraid.

He had to find his dog.

He ran back outside and jumped in the truck. The deep breaths of anticipation had been replaced by tiny scoops of air, barely enough to feed his hungry lungs. He rolled down the window. Cool air surrounded him.

"Al!" he yelled out the window. "Al where are you buddy?"

He looked down and noticed he wasn't wearing shoes. They sat just inside the front door of the house.

The dog could have been in another county by now, depending on when this walk was supposed to happen.

"Al!"

He didn't give a shit if the neighbors heard him. He didn't care if he looked like a lunatic. His dog was out here somewhere. Shivering. Cold. Afraid. The image of Al crouched in a bush again flashed through his mind, her leash strewn through the branches.

He screamed the image from his mind. No words. Just the formless shout of frustration and helplessness that had been slowly building for the last year. It could have gone on for hours if his breath hadn't given out on him.

He tried to yell the dog's name again, but nothing came out. Cold air surrounded him and stuck to the sweat that had broken out all over his body. His breaths felt like they were being sucked through a thick blanket.

"Al," he said out the window but none of his neighbors would hear it. Nobody would think him crazy.

All they'd hear would be the sound of tires transitioning from humming across concrete to crunching through fallen leaves.

And then they'd hear the violent crunch of the truck's headlights shattering around a utility pole.

7.

Ashley's Bloody Nose

The familiarity felt strange. Was that strange in itself? Ashley and Darren sitting at the table they bought for fifty dollars off Craigslist. Ashley and Darren talking about nothing when they should be talking about something. Ashley and Darren simply enjoying being next to each other.

But even with the familiarity, something was missing.

Was it love?

Do people really just fall out of love?

Darren showed up a half hour earlier. He said he wanted to discuss something about the separation. Maybe he wanted the divorce to move forward. Maybe he wanted her to explain it to him again. What explanation could she give besides what she had said already?

Have you ever bit into a jelly doughnut to realize it has no filling?

She taught literature. She didn't write it.

But the kids did their usual "Dad's home" thing and ran in circles screaming for a while. She always thought of her parents' dog when Darren came by. Except the dog quickly calmed down. It took a full thirty minutes to get them to take consecutive breaths without asking questions, demanding attention, and asking more questions.

"When are you coming home?" was a big one.

And now they sat at that cheap dining room table that she just couldn't convince herself to upgrade, sitting not across from each other but huddled around a corner.

"You okay?" he asked. It was a strange first question now that everything had finally settled down.

"You said you had something you wanted to talk about?"

The separation's birthday would be coming up soon, but it hadn't graduated to a divorce quite yet. Divorces seemed messy—more like a fight. But they didn't fight. The only time Ashley could remember a fight between them was when she wanted to name their son Phoenix.

Darren never put his foot down, but he slammed it down on that one.

"I will not be naming my son after a magical fairy."

"It's a flaming bird."

"It's also a wasteland desert city. Do you want your son to be associated with the apocalypse?"

But that was it. Nobody ever slept on the couch. Nobody ever spent the night at their parents' house saying *I just don't know if I can do it anymore.* So why spoil their track record of civility with divorce papers and lawyers and dividing up their assets and child custody hearings?

Or maybe it was just laziness. If something isn't pressing, it gets shuffled to the back of the deck. Separating was easy. It was out of sight.

Darren sighed and glanced toward the living room. The kids quietly watched a movie about talking vegetables. Or maybe it was the one where animals had jobs.

"This separation hasn't been fun," he said. "But I know there's nothing I can really do about it—"

And then the smoke alarm shrieked from the hallway connecting the kitchen and living room.

The high-pitched beeps were met with equally high-pitched screams from the living room. Darren jumped from his seat.

"Alright, alright," he said as if speaking it would make it so. Noah came running into the kitchen and looked between his mother and father.

"Come on! Come on!" He ran out the back door without putting on shoes.

Sadie walked into view holding her hands over her ears. She calmly looked between her parents as if to say, *Okay maybe do something about it now.*

Ashley's phone bounced along the countertop. She walked over and looked at the screen. Her Mom was calling.

She walked into the hallway.

"Well?" she asked Darren, who stood beneath the shrieking alarm. He stared into it like watching an eclipse with his arms at his sides.

"I need the stepstool," he finally said.

"Where is everybody?" Noah yelled from the back door.

Ashley grabbed the stepstool from beside the refrigerator. She unfolded it and handed it to the man that was technically still her husband. Twenty seconds later he had the battery in his hand and the house returned to silence.

"Thank God," Ashley whispered.

"Why the hell did that go off?" said Darren. He stayed on the second step of what looked like a miniature ladder. "I don't smell smoke. Do you?"

Ashley and Sadie shook their heads.

"Has this happened before?"

They shook their heads.

He carefully put the battery back into the smoke detector.

"Is…was there a fire?" asked Noah.

Ashley walked toward the back door and noticed her phone ringing again. She kept walking and held her hand out to her son. He shivered. His socks left wet footprints as he stepped inside.

"Everything's fine," she said, and it was mostly true. The phone continued to ring as they walked back into the kitchen. Ashley sighed and picked it up.

"Hey Mom," she said.

"Your father! I have to go to the hospital!"

"Wait, what? What's wrong?" She looked over her shoulder to see Darren whip his head around.

"I don't know. Something happened. They didn't really say."

"Who?"

"The hospital called. Greg's there for something. I have to go but I can't drive the…*fucking* car."

Ashley could count the number of times she heard her Mom swear on one hand. Especially that one. It sent a sliver of electricity down her spine.

"I'll be there in a minute." Ashley slid the phone into her pocket and turned around. Darren held the stepstool in his hand.

"What's going on?" he asked.

"I don't know. Dad's in the hospital for something but Mom didn't say what. Can you stay here with them?" She walked toward the back door.

"No."

If she were wearing shoes, they would have squeaked as she stopped walking.

"What?" She turned around and he was already flicking off the lights and wrangling the kids.

"We're coming with you."

She opened her mouth to argue. To say something like they don't know what's going on so what's the point of everyone being there the kids are going to get bored and honestly they're going to be a liability plus this is a family matter and you're not really part of the family anymore but that would be unfair even if it was mostly true but really it'd just be best if she went alone although the thought of dealing with her hysterical Mom on her own was almost as bad as what they might find at the hospital but really it's best if you just stay here.

But there was no time for that. So she said, "Whatever," and walked out the door.

Ashley drove with Darren riding shotgun.

"But I don't want to go to Grandma's," said Noah.

If only he could be as quiet as his sister, who sat with her hands in her lap and allowed an occasional squeak from the green alligator clutched between them.

"I know sweetie." Ashley sped up to get through a yellow light. It turned red before they cleared the intersection. "I don't want to go either."

It wasn't a far drive between the houses. Everyone in the car leaned left as she turned right. And then right as she took a left.

The tires chirped as she pulled into the driveway and honked the horn. Mary came running out of the garage and clawed at the door of the car.

"The handle's up on the side," Ashley tried to yell through the car.

Mary continued pawing at the door.

Darren hopped out. "Here, take the front," he said. She took him up on his offer. He closed the door behind her and climbed into the back seat.

"Go go go," said Mary. Her shaking hands couldn't get the seatbelt to click. Ashley reached over and got it for her.

The streetlights blew past overhead in a fast strobe.

"Remember there are kids back here," said Darren.

"Your father. There was some sort of accident."

"I thought they didn't say what happened?"

"Something happened. Something happened." Mary rocked in her chair and rubbed her hands together. Her gaze remained locked on the glove compartment in front of her. The sound of her scratchy, deep breaths filled the car.

"Hey, hey it's okay," said Darren. Ashley thought he was trying to comfort her Mom, but when she glanced into the rearview she saw Sadie pulled close to him with tears in her eyes. She knew it was a bad idea to bring the kids.

Condensation fogged up the windows. She couldn't see out of any of the side windows and was in danger of losing the windshield as well. She flicked the thermostat all the way to red and blasted the fans.

Nothing was easy.

They finally pulled into the parking lot of Saint Elizabeth Hospital and screeched to a halt in an open spot outside the emergency room.

Mary tried to hurry out of the car, but her body didn't cooperate. The seat belt wouldn't unbuckle. The car door wouldn't open. And when Ashley finally freed her from both of those restraints, her legs wouldn't keep up with the others. Ashley grabbed her by the arm and hurried her along until the five of them finally walked through the automatic doors of the ER.

"My dad was brought in here tonight. An ambulance. Greg Weber."

The woman in the booth click clacked on her computer for a little bit and looked up.

"He's in room 1125. Down that way and follow the signs. Only family, though."

"Does wife and daughter count?"

She nodded.

"Jesus." Ashley led the train through two full-size saloon doors.

"I want to go home," said Sadie. Darren had her in his arms but that didn't stop the tears. She clutched the alligator tighter, letting out a slow, lazy squeak.

They followed a sign pointing them to the right, past another woman sitting at a desk, and finally to the rooms.

1122.

1123.

1124.

Ashley reached for the door of 1125 as it swung open from the inside and cracked her in the face.

"Shit!" she yelled and held a hand to her nose and felt it grow hot.

"Oh my God," said the doctor. Then over her bowed head: "Nurse!"

A short man in green scrubs told her to lean her head back as he pressed his fingers along the bridge of her nose.

"Where's my Dad?" she said. Her eyes filled with water, and she felt a trickle of blood leak over her upper lip.

"I'm so sorry," said the doctor.

"He's dead?" she screamed.

"No, no about the nose."

"Oh fuck the nose." She swatted her hands in front of her face until the nurse took a step back. He handed her a tissue which she pressed to her nose.

"It doesn't look broken," he said.

"Great." Then to the doctor: "My Dad?"

"He's resting. He's stable."

"Oh thank God," said Mary. She leaned against the wall.

"What happened?" asked Ashley.

"It's hard to say if the heart attack caused the car accident or the other way around."

Ashley: "Car accident?"

Mary: "Heart attack?"

The doctor nodded. "It seems your father had a mild heart attack as a result of the accident. Or, as I said, the other way around. We have some more tests to run but things like this tend to build up for a while and can be set off by some sort of catalyst."

Ashley reached for the door. The doctor put his hand out.

"He's resting. We can't let anybody in to see him."

Ashley took a step toward him and pointed to her face. "Doctors get sued all the time. Especially when they assault grieving women."

The doctor looked from her, to Mary, to Darren and the children. He then looked around the hallway where the nurse continued to stand awkwardly.

"He needs his rest. And he's a little beat up. So don't touch him and don't be loud. Just for a little bit, okay?"

Ashley pushed past him with everyone else trailing behind.

It was dark and smelled like a locker room. Various blips and bleeps sang from the monitors surrounding the bed. And in the middle, center stage, lay her father. A series of cuts ran along his forehead and cheeks. Small ones. They didn't look deep. A larger gash had been covered with gauze along his hairline. Tubes went this way and that, leading to either machines measuring something or bags containing something else.

"Oh my God." Mary's voice came out in a whimper. She walked up to her husband and put her hands along either side of his face. "I'm sorry. I'm sorry. I'm sorry—"

Ashley walked to the foot of the bed. Darren kept the kids near the door.

"We're going to go get a snack," he said.

"We are?" asked Noah.

They disappeared out the door. The bright white light from the hallway cut through the dim hospital room like a searchlight. The only things it found were mother and daughter hovering over the beaten shell of the man holding them together.

Mary stood up and wiped her hands across her own face.

"What are we going to do?" she asked.

Ashley opened her mouth to respond. To tell her everything would be okay. That they'd get through this. That Dad would be fine.

But she couldn't find words that didn't exist.

8.

Sam and Mr. Beef

Thwap.

Another bird hit the window.

"It was a heart attack. And an accident."

"Heart attacks aren't accidents, Ash." Sam Weber held the phone to his ear while looking out the window of his modest one-bedroom apartment. Where were all these birds coming from? And this late at night? Didn't they sleep?

"Jesus. Yes. *Duh.* Car accident, you asshole."

He took a step back from the window. "Is he alright?"

"Don't know. They have some more tests to run, I guess."

Sam ran a hand through his hair. He hadn't really seen many heart attacks in the three years he'd been at Midtown Hospital. Lots of homeless people in various stages of disrepair. Pregnancies. Drunks that seemed to be continually falling or fighting, much with the same result. But only a few heart attacks.

Thwap.

Another bird hit the window.

"What is going on over there?" asked Ashley.

"Honestly—" Sam looked out the window. He expected an assorted pile of dead and concussed birds below his window. There were none. "I have no idea. How's Mom doing with all this?"

"She tried to stay at my house last night."

"And?"

Ashley coughed out a breath. "Why don't you have her move in with you? There's no room here. I have enough going on with the kids and I still gotta go to work and—"

"Alright alright easy."

Thwap.

Another bird hit the window.

"That's not a bad idea," she said.

"What? Mom moving to Atlanta?"

"Well, no. Dad's going to be in the hospital for a little while. And Mom can't drive—"

"Doesn't she have some friends? Why doesn't Linda come over?"

"—and I've got a lot of shit going on."

"You think I don't? I work in a fucking hospital, Ashley."

"How many times have you come back to visit? In the three years you've been gone, how many times?"

"Every year!"

"For what? Four days at a time?"

Thwap.

"That doesn't even add up to two weeks," said Ashley. "In three years."

Sam ignored the smudges on the window and sat on the couch. The spring in his chest, tightly wound and ready to explode, wanted to hurl rebuttals and accusations. He wanted to tell her that he's got his own life. His own priorities and responsibilities. He can't just pick up and leave. He doesn't want to. Mom made her priorities clear a long time ago and he's just abiding by her wishes. He wanted to tell his sister that this wasn't his responsibility.

But the words weren't there.

Thwap.

"I've been here this whole time. Okay? I know you think I'm an idiot or whatever because I never left but here I am. Bringing the kids over there. Cooking. Talking to her. It's real to me because I see it and live with it every day. I can't hide behind a missed phone call when I don't feel like talking."

"I don't do that," said Sam.

Someone knocked on the door. He ignored it.

"I don't *hide behind a missed call,*" he said.

"Yeah. Yeah you do. You call Mom and Dad whenever you feel like it and ignore all the heavy lifting. Well you know where that goes? It doesn't just disappear. Dad's doing his best but even though it might be tough to hear: He's a person. Dad's just a guy and he's got a lot going on. I try to help out, but I have a lot going on, too. You're busy? We're all busy. And when we're not busy with work we're busy with family. What do you do when you're not at work? Play video games? Go to bars?"

The knock at the door grew louder.

Thwap.

"I'm sorry that everyone is busy but it's not like I do nothing."

"Yeah, Sam. Yeah it is."

He leaned his head back into the couch and looked at the ceiling. He tried to remember his retorts the last time this conversation came up. The specifics might have changed but the overarching themes were the same.

Sam, you're ignoring your family.

Sam, you're selfish.

Sam, you're an asshole.

But that was all bullshit. People move away from their hometowns all the time. Why does that make him an asshole? His Mom didn't seem all that interested in him when he was growing up; why would his absence suddenly be the biggest tragedy the world has ever seen?

The move hadn't exactly been planned out far in advance, but it couldn't have been a surprise to his parents. He hated snow. He always hated snow. If anything, it should have been a surprise that he didn't move out of Wisconsin as soon as he graduated college. But he didn't. He found work at Aurora Medical Center in Oshkosh and reported dutifully for five years. Five whole years of being a mere half hour away from Greg and Mary. And how often did they stop by? How often did they reach out to him? Why does the burden land squarely on his head now that he lives 900 miles south?

Thwap.

The knocking rattled the door on its hinges.

Sam sprang off the couch.

"How much is it to ask? How hard can it really be to come home and help your parents? If this isn't a time when they could use your help, I don't know what would be. Do you need one of them to die? Would a funeral be enough?"

"Jesus, Ash. Hold on a second."

"No. No fucking way am I—"

Sam pulled the phone from his ear and opened the door with his left hand.

"You in the shower or something?" A man that looked like a Pez dispenser come to life stood with his arms crossed. Thin, receding hairline, cream polo shirt tucked into his khaki shorts— phone sales representatives had always asked to speak with his parents. This man stood at the top of the rusted metal stairway that wound along the exterior of the house. A dim, yellow light cast shadows across his face. He looked like a jack-o-lantern. The doorstep acted as a tiny balcony where college kids might smoke cigarettes and play guitar.

He tapped his foot and tried to look over Sam's shoulder. This was his building. Mr. Beef. Seriously. Sam asked him to repeat it three times when they first met. But as much as Sam loved the name, it felt much more appropriate to address him by his first name.

"Hey Aiden. Listen, you mind if I come down a little later? I'm kinda in the middle—"

Thwap.

"That! That right there!" Mr. Beef stood on his toes to look behind Sam. "What the hell is that?"

Sam turned around as if he hadn't noticed. "Oh yeah." He turned back. "Birds."

"Birds?"

Sam could hear his sister's voice through the tiny speaker in his hand. He held up a finger to Mr. Beef.

"Hey Ash just gimme a—"

"I don't have all day to sit here and listen to—"

Thwap.

"Do you have pets in here? Is that a dog? You're not supposed to have pets up here, Sam."

"—just man up and come—"

"I told you it's a bird." Sam loosely held the phone to his ear and whispered to Mr. Beef.

"Birds are pets too, Sam."

"They're not pets!"

Thwap.

"Who the hell are you talking to?" asked Ashley.

"Mr. Beef!"

"What?"

Sam stomped a foot.

"Listen, Sam. While I'm here. We gotta talk about the noise."

"The noise?"

"I've warned you about this before. You keep me up all night long sometimes. You can't blast your TV at all hours of the night."

"The TV? I can't watch the TV?"

"Just do it at normal times of day."

"I work in a hospital! I don't have a normal time of day!"

"Is this really more important than your family? TV?" said Ashley.

Thwap.

"You know you're liable for damages if you break something."

"It's not a pet!"

"Just do the right thing. For once in your whole life just do the right thing and come home while Dad gets better. I mean my God it's not difficult."

"One more talk like this and I'm gonna have to ask you to move out."

Thwap.

"Alright! That's it!" Sam spoke into his phone. "Fine! I'm coming home." He threw the phone on the carpet behind him. Then to his landlord: "Shut. The fuck. Up. *Aiden.*"

The human Pez dispenser dropped his crossed arms and took a step back.

"I want you out of here," he said quietly.

"You got it." Sam slammed the door.

He sat on the couch and waited for another bird to slam into the glass.

9.

Mary Tries the Popcorn

Warm, morning sunlight poured through the hospital window. Everything was still. Quiet. Mary sat in a wobbly, vinyl-covered chair next to her husband's bed. The sporadic cracks in the otherwise smooth, shiny material caught on her jeans. Ashley had been nice enough to drop her off on the way to school. And with the kids in back, it almost felt like she had a full family again.

But now it was quiet.

Greg woke up at some point overnight, but not since she arrived.

How many people sat in this chair? Two thousand? Three? Just imagine the things this chair has seen. Births. Deaths. Rebirths. Hospitals always got a bad rap. She'd heard all her life about people that hated hospitals. That it stinks of death and all that garbage. But there's an equal amount of hope and possibility. This is where people come to get fixed. This is where prayers are answered. Sure, the odds are going to go the other way a certain number of times, too. And this was most people's problem that stretched far beyond their viewpoint on hospitals—they focused on the bad. Don't ignore it. Certainly don't pretend bad outcomes don't exist. That leaves you in a fantasy land of marshmallow clouds and eternal sunsets. But you also shouldn't fixate on the negative aspects. It isn't worth internalizing the bad if you don't allow yourself to acknowledge the good.

People also come to hospitals to get better.

That's what Mary thought, anyway.

She stretched her legs and looked out the window. The morning sun was still a soft orange, but that would change soon.

The door cracked open, and a nurse walked in.

"Knock knock," he said, looking down at a clipboard.

Mary sat up straight. His head didn't hit the top of the doorframe, but it came close. Young. Brown hair closely cropped. She wondered if he ever passed through one of her classrooms.

"How's he doing?" he asked. He dropped the clipboard to his side and finally looked up.

"You tell me."

"Well, in my expert medical opinion," he glanced at Greg, tied down with various tubes and wires. "He's asleep."

Mary nodded. "I think you're probably right."

"He'll come out of it soon. He's gonna be sore, but he'll be okay. What about you?"

"Me? I'm not asleep."

"Hey, easy. I'm the medical professional around here."

"Right, right. I'm sorry." She crossed one leg over the other and sat back in the vinyl-covered chair that had seen a thousand deaths. "I'm okay," she said.

The nurse smiled. "Good. Keep it that way."

She waved him off and he slid back into the hallway. The door hung open long enough for her to catch a glimpse of a familiar blur. The view through the open door only afforded a blink's worth of time, but it sure looked like Peter Schulke. She hadn't seen him since her last week at school—surely she had seen him at some point that week—but he couldn't have changed much since then.

She hopped out of the ancient chair and ran to the doorway. She swung her head around the corner and looked in the blur's direction.

Various people in various stages of walking moved in every direction. Why were there so many people out here? It was morning in a quiet part of the hospital. People weren't being battering-rammed through doors on gurneys surrounded by a gaggle of shouting medics like she saw on TV. Old men walked slowly while supporting themselves with poles on wheels that held clear bags of stuff. Nurses tiptoed from room to room to avoid waking the delicate patients.

Or at least that's how it should have been. For some reason the hallway was a hive of commotion as doctors, nurses, patients, and visitors moved this way and that when all she wanted was for everyone to shut up for a moment so she could see if a history teacher from Appleton East High School had just walked past.

Shouldn't he be in school right now?

Mary glanced back into the room. Greg snoozed as steadily as ever. She looked at the room number placard on the wall and burned it into her memory.

1125.

1125.

1125.

Please let that one stick.

She stepped into the hallway and a wave of nervous energy rushed through her like she was sneaking out or skipping class. It had been a while since she felt like she was getting away with something despite the fact that nobody told her to stay in the room. She simply assumed that was what was best.

She began swimming upstream against the flow of motion in the hallway. A moment later she caught another glimpse of the back of a head that might or might not belong to Peter Schulke—the man who once told her that his students not only hated his class, but that they hated him and every person that he ever spoke with.

He was prone to exaggeration.

Her target reached an intersection of hallways and took a right. She moved to the right of the hallway to position herself to follow his lead but the crowd had grown thicker. It pushed back. Mary Weber found herself losing ground, caught up in the momentum of others so she dug in her heels and crawled through the ever-expanding crowd until she finally got her fingers along the edge of the hallway which wasn't much of a grip but enough to secure her weight and give her something to pull until she finally broke free and stumbled into the empty hallway.

Silence.

A window at the far end of the corridor lit up the white tiles with soft, morning light. No shuffling feet. No bodies bumping into each other. Nothing besides the soft hum of the heating ducts. Schulke was gone, if he was ever there in the first place. Mary stood frozen in place, slowly acclimating to the church-like calm. A vague sharpness lingered in her chest, remnants of stress from the recent battle. But she breathed deep. She relaxed her muscles. And then the sunlight at the end of the hallway began to dim.

At first she thought it to be a passing cloud.

And then it seemed more like a solar eclipse.

And then it felt like midnight.

The hospital lights along the ceiling of the hallway should have carried the burden of darkness, but they didn't.

It wasn't so dark as to walk into a wall, but it was disorienting all the same.

Something felt familiar, but she knew she was in an unfamiliar place.

How long had she been gone?

What time of day was it?

What day was it at all?

…

…

Where was she?

She began feeling along the walls and moving toward the window that formerly held the sun. But now it held nothing but a shadow.

What was she looking for? No, *who* was she looking for? It was someone from school.

Ah, yes.

William Grey. No matter how many times he's told, he just thinks it's the funniest thing in the world to slap the books off poor Bryce Ballard's desk. He's not so bad, this Grey kid. She'd certainly seen worse.

Mary glanced into each doorway.

No William.

Nope.

Not there either.

Finally, she heard some movement behind a door and figured he's hiding out. Even the tough guys don't like getting in trouble. She straightened herself up, took a breath, and pushed her way into the room.

The sunlight blinded her.

Instead of desks and a chalkboard, she found a bed and a window. A television showed someone jumping up and down as a bright light flashed and bells dinged. Soft beeping from a monitor of some sort tried to keep up with the game show but lost. A Mexican woman—in her sixties, covered to the waist in a white hospital sheet, white hair that had been brown no more than ten years earlier—lay in bed. Two women sat in chairs positioned on either side of her. A man stood near a table by the window. All four of them stared at Mary.

"Hi," she said.

"You're not the nurse?" said one of the women with a slight accent.

Mary shook her head. She had grown somewhat familiar with finding herself in unfamiliar situations. Just nod, smile, and figure it out. She stayed near the door and crossed her hands in front of her. She noticed a bowl of popcorn on the table near the window. The woman followed her glance.

"Would you like some?" she asked.

The man next to the table read their faces and opened a hand in the direction of the bowl. He smiled and nodded silently in the way you communicate with the deaf—or someone that doesn't speak your language.

Nobody else spoke.

"I couldn't," said Mary.

"Oh come on. It's popcorn. It cost like three cents."

It wasn't really fair. Mary hadn't had breakfast.

She walked across the room, past the bed and TV, to the window. The sunshine felt warm on the exposed skin of her arms. The popcorn smelled vaguely of citrus.

"It's good," said the woman in the chair. "Try it."

Mary grabbed a modest handful and popped them in her mouth one at a time. She was right. It was good.

"What are you watching?" she asked.

"I'm not sure. These three can't understand it anyway. Lots of lights and jumping. Kinda feels good even if you don't know what's going on."

Mary walked over and glanced at the TV. Someone was hugging a car.

"I guess you don't see that on many other shows."

The woman in bed had fallen asleep at some point and the other seated woman held her hand. The man continued eating popcorn by the window.

"So if you're not a nurse—"

"I'm so sorry," said Mary. "My husband is in a room down the, well I don't know. Somewhere. And I got a little turned around."

The woman nodded.

"Abuelita gets turned around sometimes, too." She nodded her head toward the woman in the bed. "Lost her at the grocery store a couple weeks ago."

"Oh, I'm sorry."

A moment of nothing but shouts and dings from the TV passed.

"It's not all bad. She has her moments."

Mary threw another piece of popcorn into her mouth. She'd have to remember to ask what this seasoning was called.

"She can go away, in her mind you know, for a whole day sometimes. Doesn't know me or my sister. Doesn't even know her own son." She nodded toward the man by the window. "But she has her moments. Certain places. I don't know. They just activate her mind. Get it going like it used to. She was a teacher when she was younger."

Mary smiled. "Me too."

"And now she can barely remember her own name most days."

The smile faded. "What brings her in here?"

"Pneumonia." She patted the old woman's arm that lay on top of the sheet. Did Mary look that old? "She'll be okay."

"Good, good," said Mary.

People also come to hospitals to get better.

What was she chasing in the hallway? William Grey? No, before that. Someone else from the halls of a school she hadn't entered for two years. Maybe this room was one of those places the woman was talking about—did her abuelita think more clearly here?

"I'm interrupting. I should go."

"There's nothing to interrupt."

"Even so, I should get going."

"You know, she had trouble asking for help at the beginning. She could pretend sometimes like she didn't need it."

Mary wiped her hands across her jeans and just looked at the woman. She was in mid-twenties. Dark, shiny hair that spilled off the top of her head onto her shoulders. She continued:

"But she did. Things started to get better when she let us help her."

Mary walked slowly to the door.

"Thanks for the popcorn. It was really good."

The man munched on another bite next to the window. Sunlight continued to cover the room in an almost golden shine.

It felt like everyone here floated. The game show punctuated each thought with shouts and bells.

"Take care," said the woman.

Mary pushed her way back into the hallway and the darkness of the absent sun enveloped her.

10.

Greg Jogs His Memory

The radio stayed off as he drove home from the Overtime. Greg remembered that. He was worried that maybe he had a few too many beers. He felt bad for leaving Mary home all by herself. But that was the last thing he remembered—flicking off the radio in his truck as the streetlights flew past overhead. And now he found himself in a hospital bed with things stuck to his chest and other things coming out of his arms.

"H-hello?" The word scraped out of his throat. He needed a drink of water.

A large window to his left framed a beautiful day and cast bright light over the bed.

What time was it?

What happened?

He found a control pad on the side of his bed with a cartoon version of what he guessed was supposed to be him lying prostrate surrounded by arrows above and below his head and feet. He first pressed the button labeled *NURSE* and then the arrow above the cartoon's head. The door cracked open by the time he reached an upright sitting position.

"Neat toy you've got here," he said to the tall nurse.

"I'm a fan of putting the feet up and the head down. Get all that blood rushing to the eyes."

Greg chuckled. No one said anything for a moment.

"You don't know why you're here, do you?" asked the nurse.

Greg tried to scoot himself up in the bed a bit but everything hurt. You don't notice your muscles until they're sore, and Greg noticed every muscle in his body. His entire torso felt like it was wrapped in a flak jacket filled with weights.

He thought back and could only remember the radio.

He shook his head. "No. No I don't."

The nurse walked to the foot of the bed and put his hands on the plastic barrier lining the bottom.

"It's a bit of an interesting situation. We're not exactly sure the order."

"Why don't you give me the pieces and I'll fit them together myself."

The nurse nodded. "You were in an accident. Your truck versus a pole. I'd say the pole mostly won."

Had he slid off the road after turning off the radio? Did he have too many beers after all?

"That's piece number one. Piece number two is the heart attack."

"Heart attack?" Greg sat up which released the tightly coiled springs of pain hidden throughout his body. "I had a heart attack?"

The nurse nodded. "So we're not sure if the accident was the catalyst that set off the heart attack, or the other way around. These things happen in conjunction like this sometimes and really, it doesn't matter which one happened first. If there's something wrong with the heart it's going to go off no matter what. It's just a matter of time. This time it was a car accident, next time it could have been an argument. All it really takes is to get you all riled up."

"Jesus." Greg relaxed back into the upright bed. "So what's the deal? When can I get out of here?"

"Depends on what we find. If I were a betting man, I'd put my money on congestive heart failure. Pretty common for a guy your age."

"That doesn't exactly sound great."

"Depends." He started tapping on the foot of the bed. "We don't know when we caught it. Like I said, depends on what we find."

"Where was I?" asked Greg.

"Huh?"

"The accident. Where was the accident?"

"Oh I don't know. I wasn't in the ambulance. But I heard it wasn't too far from your house." He finished his little drum solo on the foot of the bed with a flourish. "You need anything?"

Greg shook his head.

"Alright. Just checking in with the living. I get it." He turned toward the door. "The doctor will be around soon to ask you some questions. It's pretty helpful when the patient is actually awake."

"Hey wait," said Greg. "I have to call my wife."

"Oh. She's here."

"No she's not."

The nurse glanced around the room as if he had just walked in.

"She must've stepped out." He opened the door to the hallway. "I'm sure she'll be back soon."

"Could I maybe just—"

The door swung closed behind the nurse.

An accident? A heart attack?

He needed some fresh air. Beads of sweat bubbled up across his forehead and his hospital pajamas were sticky. He hated knowing there was something he should remember but couldn't.

Your wife has this feeling every day.

His itchy panic stopped cold. His wife. Mary. A shadow of a memory hung around her. Where was she, by the way? Hospitals are confusing. The maze of repetitive hallways could get anybody turned around. He closed his eyes and tried to work backwards from the accident. Put yourself in the truck. Where's the moment of impact? He tried to adjust his shirt but the sweat stuck to—

There. The sweat. He had broken out in a sweat before the crash. He was in his truck with the window down because—

Al. Oh shit poor Al. He was calling out his dog's name.

It came flooding back. The neighbors were going to hear him yelling his dog's name like a crazy person. He was worried she was in a bush somewhere and wouldn't come out until she starved or froze to death. He was upset. Of course he was upset—his dog was missing. But no, there was more than that.

He yelled at Mary.

Greg groaned and sat up despite the shooting pain down his sides. He pressed his palms against his closed eyes until he could see white dots. A part of him wished his heart had simply exploded that night. He would have deserved it.

And that was the key that unlocked the evening. He came home from the bar to find Mary asleep. The one thing he didn't find was the dog.

And he yelled at his wife.

Goddamnit he lost his temper and yelled at her.

The door slid open and Greg released his hands from his eyes. His vision stayed swimmy for a moment, but he could tell two people had entered the room.

"Hello?" he said.

"You're awake!" Mary's voice cut through the murkiness and stabbed right into his chest.

He had yelled at his wife.

"Mr. Weber. Look who I found."

Greg's vision finally cleared up. Mary walked over and gave him a kiss on the cheek. The doctor flipped through a clipboard of papers.

"The good news is we can rule out kidney disease, anemia, and hyperthyroidism. The bad news is that negative tests don't tell us what happened. They just tell us what didn't happen." He slid the clipboard into a little shelf at the end of the bed. "How are you feeling?"

"Fine," said Greg. He cleared his throat. He still needed that drink of water.

"Come on, tough guy. You had a heart attack during a car accident. You're not fine."

Greg felt Mary rest her hand on his shoulder. He looked up at her and she smiled. Two bubbles grew inside him—one made of love for his wife and the other an intense shame. He loved her so much. You don't make it through 39 years of marriage without that. Sometimes he felt she deserved better.

"I'm thirsty," said Greg.

"That's a step in the right direction." The doctor walked around the curtain and came back with a pitcher and a plastic cup. "Here you go," he said.

Greg drank it in one gulp.

"Now what else?" asked the doctor.

"Well, I'm sore. Like my whole body. It hurts to move at all, pretty much."

"Yup. Car accident. Makes sense."

"And I'm out of breath. Even though I'm just sitting here."

"Has that been going on for a while?"

Greg nodded. "I guess so. I didn't really think of it before, but yeah."

"Okay." The doctor smiled at him and Mary. "We'll do some EKGs and a chest x-ray now that you're awake. We'll address the surgery question after that."

"There's a surgery question?" asked Greg.

The doctor shrugged. "We'll address that after the tests."

Mary grabbed Greg's hand as the doctor left the room.

"This doesn't seem like a great hospital," said Greg.

"Oh hush. It's perfectly fine."

A silence descended over the room. Breaking it seemed wrong. Sacrilegious. Greg nestled himself into the pillow that had probably been comfortable a year or two before but had now been reduced to a mushy pile of synthetic fibers. But when your entire body's sore, simply sitting still feels like a massage. The room dimmed a bit as the morning sun continued along its tour of the sky. The heating rays no longer directly cut through the window. Part of him was glad.

"Hey Mary," he said.

"Hmm?" Her eyes fell upon him with an innocent ignorance. Not stupidity. Greg didn't look down on his wife. Ignorance could simply be the absence of context. There's a difference between not understanding information and simply not having access to it.

"I'm sorry," he said.

She cocked her head to the side.

"For what?"

He sandwiched her hand between his. A proper apology meant he had to recall the night. The anger in his chest that he couldn't extinguish. The resulting flames that came out of his mouth toward his wife. A tear dripped down his cheek and he attempted a demented smile.

But ultimately there was no point. She didn't remember him raising his voice. The apology would only recreate the moment. So he just continued smiling and tried to stop the tears.

"Nothing," he said. "Never mind."

11.

Ashley vs. Shane Duplass

Mary had been drawn to the troublemakers. Ashley couldn't understand it when she was growing up. And now that she was a teacher herself, she understood it even less.

Take this kid for example. Shane Duplass. Such an asshole. He always had to have the last word. And he always had to do something that stood out, but not in a good way. He wasn't turning in mind-blowing papers dissecting classic novels. He wasn't interjecting illuminating viewpoints into the class discussions. No. He was turning in an analysis of some ska song about date rape from thirty years ago.

"I mean, if the paper deserves an F based on quality, that's one thing. But to just give it an F because you don't agree with the subject matter is tyrannical."

Shane stood next to Ashley's desk at the front of the room. Class was over but a few students lingered to watch the show. This wasn't the first time Shane tried to make a spectacle of himself.

"Would you turn in an essay about a song that talked about murdering people? Torturing them?" she asked.

"Maybe. It depends on the assignment." She wanted to smack the smirk right off his face. Shane wasn't a small kid, but he wasn't a football player either. He was right in the middle where he wouldn't stand out in either direction. In fact, there wasn't much about him that stood out, which is probably why he liked to make these little scenes. Mary would find this fascinating. She'd dig into his home life as if it were her business at all. She'd sit down with Shane and try to find some common ground. Try to find a way to connect with him.

Ashley didn't have any interest in common ground.

"That's stupid," she said.

Shane's eyes opened wide.

"Did you just call me stupid?" The righteous indignation was building. Why did teenagers love it so much?

"No. I called what you said stupid. There's a difference."

Shane paused and looked behind him. Only a couple stragglers remained.

"You're just censoring me," he tried.

Ashley laughed.

"Yeah," he said, gaining momentum. "Yeah this is oppressive censorship."

"You're in high school, Shane. This isn't a poetry slam at the coffee shop."

"Huh?"

Ashley sighed and grabbed her purse from the back of her chair.

"I'm hungry. Don't bring in anything that you wouldn't read in front of your grandma, okay?"

Shane again looked behind him. The room was empty. The air that had been puffing out his chest finally released and he deflated to the skinny jerk he was. He nodded, grabbed his failed paper off her desk, and walked out of the room just as Becky West turned the corner.

"Ready?" she asked. Becky. Mrs. West. The most feared social studies teacher in all the land.

"Yup."

Ashley followed her out of the classroom, down the hallway, through the parking lot, and into her mold-green Honda Civic. The fabric inside was just as dirty as the color outside. They drove down the street to Judd's, the local hamburger spot. Ashley had been coming here since she was little. Back then, it was the place to get ice cream cones. And then when she entered high school it was the place almost everybody in the world went for lunch. Luckily these days the high school enforced a closed campus for the lunch hour, which freed up local establishments to normal people. Swarms of horny teenagers vibrating with too much energy had terrorized the neighborhood for long enough. People got sick of cleaning up the never-ending supply of discarded soda cups, burger wrappers, and cigarette butts.

They ordered their food and sat down. Someone would walk it out to them when it was ready.

"Little extra-curricular discussion with Mr. Duplass again?" asked Becky. She'd had her share of run-ins with him, but she shut that down real quick. Turns out Shane doesn't respond well to being screamed at.

"It never stops with that one."

They sat on opposite sides of a booth. The tabletop was yellow. The seats were yellow. The walls were yellow. It felt like being in a giant ball pit.

A man walked out from behind the counter and set their food in front of them. They thanked him and he disappeared.

"I hear your Dad got banged up last night," said Becky.

"Where'd you hear that?"

"What is it, a secret?"

Ashley shook her head and stuffed a few french fries into her mouth.

"He'll be okay." She swallowed. "They're still doing some tests. His truck has run its last stop sign, though."

"What happened?"

Ashley shrugged. "I haven't talked to him yet. Kinda trying not to think about it until I can just go over there after school."

"You ever been in a car accident?"

Ashley shook her head.

"Me neither. I mean, I've hit stuff before. But never like a full-on smashing into something."

Ashley grabbed more french fries. The burger cooled inside its wrapper.

The song crackling through the speakers changed to an upbeat pseudo-country song. No one in their right mind would call it *good* but it was fun to listen to.

"Oh shit!" said Becky. "Friday night, isn't it?"

"What?"

"This is Georgia Back Roads."

Oh shit. The concert.

"The concert!" said Becky. "Friday night, baby!"

Ashley nodded, tried to smile, and reached for the burger.

"Wait, you're still coming right?"

"Well, I mean Darren's going to be working and the kids—"

"You said they were going to stay with your Mom! Come on, you *need* a night out."

She wasn't going to argue with her there. As if summoned by magic, her phone started to ring. She held up a finger and slid out of the booth.

"Hey Dad," she stood up and walked outside. "Are they letting you out?"

"Not yet. Not for another couple days."

"How are you feeling?"

"Okay. I'm okay.

"Dad, can I ask you something?" She leaned against the wall. The wind picked up a bit.

"Sure."

"Did something happen with Mom last night?"

"Have you been over to the house since?"

"I asked you something, Dad."

"Just answer."

"I dropped off Mom and picked her up. Haven't gone in."

"So you haven't noticed Al's gone."

"What?"

"I was looking for her. Your Mom was going to take her for a walk and then—"

Ashley waited for Greg to finish the sentence when she decided she'd just go ahead and take it to its obvious conclusion.

"Mom let the dog out?"

"Hasn't come back yet, huh?"

"Oh Jesus, Dad."

"Listen, I just wanted to let you know I wasn't dead. I know you gotta get back to work."

"I'm coming over right after I get out."

"Okay, Ash. See ya then."

Al was gone. Her Dad would never come right out and say it but he probably loved that dog more than her. Ashley knew that.

And now Al was gone because Mom thought she'd take her for a walk.

Friday.

The concert.

She found her Mom's number in her phone and pressed the green circle.

"Ashley! Your father's up!"

"Hey Mom. Yeah I just talked to him. I don't really have a lot of time."

"What time is it?" A brief series of muffled scrapes puffed through the earpiece. "Are you on lunch?"

"Friday night. I was going to go to that concert."

A brief pause. "Was?"

Ashley paced back and forth on the sidewalk outside the restaurant. Nobody had entered or left the whole time she stood outside. She noticed her heartbeat. Why was she nervous?

"It's just—I'm not going to be able to go anymore."

"So I don't get to watch the kids?" Mary's voice was the source of a lot of her power when she stood in front of a class. Strong. Authoritative. You listened to what she had to say whether you wanted to or not. Even her kids never got used to it. Ashley feared that voice her whole life. She still does. But this voice that came through her phone wasn't her mother's. It was the voice of a diffident adolescent being told to go to bed. High-pitched. Quiet. And it was all because of a lie. Ashley felt like she had been kicked in the stomach.

"Don't you think you'll want to be with Dad?"

"Oh—yeah. Sure. I guess so."

It wasn't much of a swap, but it was worth a try. She knew Mary basically sat at the house all day waiting for someone to come home. She didn't want to think of her Mom like a dog in a cage, but she couldn't help it.

They hung up and Ashley lingered outside for a moment. A few quick breaths to steady her nerves. Okay back inside. Time to break more hearts.

"It's not gonna happen," she said as she sat back down.

"What?"

"The concert. I just—I can't go."

Becky tossed one of the final french fries onto her empty burger wrapper. Ashley caught a glimpse of what it must be like to step out of line in her class. She didn't like it. Then Becky turned her head and smiled.

"You gotta be shitting me," she said.

Ashley followed her glance and saw Shane Duplass standing in line at the counter.

"There's just no common sense anymore, is there?" said Becky.

Mary's situation wasn't a secret around the high school. Becky had at least a vague idea of what was happening on the other side of those phone calls even if Ashley never explicitly talked about it. Becky was right. Ashley needed a night out. But Becky must have also had a good guess at the reason she couldn't do it.

Shane ordered, turned around to find a seat, and froze. Ashley waved him over.

"Come on, dummy."

Shane looked around as if they could be talking to anybody else. His shoulders again deflated, and he walked up to the teachers' table.

"Take a seat," she said.

Shane sat in the seat next to Ashley, his back straight.

"Jesus, relax. We're not going to smush your food in your face," said Becky.

He eased into the backrest.

"You don't like to think things through all that much, do you?" asked Ashley.

Becky laughed. Shane just looked between them without speaking.

12.

Sam Searches the Moon

Stupid Mr. Beef.

This had become a mantra. Much in the way people get songs stuck in their heads, Sam repeated this phrase with every box he took off the moving truck.

Stupid Mr. Beef. Of course I keep weird hours. I work in a hospital. You want me to tiptoe around my apartment and unplug my TV?

He'd never used a storage unit before, but it seemed like the best option. He was technically homeless but he still had stuff. Don't people live in these things sometimes? He stood at the edge of the 10x10 unit. A rolling garage door opened to an outdoor corridor which allowed access to the other weirdos that kept their spare couches, baseball card collections, and whatever else someone puts in a storage unit.

There really aren't that many boxes. Some dishes. Some books. It's the furniture that he's dreading. He'd asked some people from work if they'd lend a hand. He'd asked a few friends if they'd help out. Nothing. He'd have to start seriously considering finding a new social circle when he got back to town.

So he sacrificed his back and got it all off the truck on his own. His couch was disassembled. His dining table seemed to be made of hollow wood. It was manageable but exhausting. He sat on a chair and surveyed his belongings. His life's work. He kicked his feet up on a box in front of him and flipped open the box to his right. He found an old yearbook and spread it open on his lap.

He'd asked to transfer to the high school across town at the end of middle school. He knew his Mom loomed large in the halls of Appleton East and he didn't want to deal with that. High school was going to be awkward enough. He didn't want to have to figure out how to get through it under the ever-watchful eye of Mrs. Weber. And this didn't even take into account the constant barrage of jokes he figured he'd have to endure.

He didn't end up transferring.

And flipping through the yearbook reminded him just how right he was about the jokes.

Signing a yearbook is supposed to be fun—promises of continued friendship, inside jokes, and maybe even a little flirting if you're lucky. And sure there was a taste of that here and there, but Sam mostly saw references to his Mom.

Disgusting suggestions of incest.

Declarations of love.

Highlights of the fact that she paid more attention to the likely dropouts than her own son.

He expected a light-hearted romp through time when he pulled out the yearbook. Maybe he'd find a picture of some long-forgotten crush. Instead, he found himself back in the place he had run away from as soon as he graduated. His Mom never really cared about him. She was too busy playing saint to all the assholes in school. She was too focused on saving the lost souls to be a mother. She pushed him to get good grades, but that was just so her credibility as a teacher didn't take a hit. Ashley was the pride and joy. He was a chore. And his classmates didn't let him forget it.

He threw the yearbook back into the box and walked out of the storage unit. His shadow fell onto the haphazardly piled boxes and furniture. Hopefully it wouldn't be too long until he was back in Atlanta. Trips home drained him within days. The leave of absence would cover his job until he got back. If anywhere was going to be sympathetic to heart attacks and dementia, it was going to be a hospital. But putting his life on hold to play babysitter to a Mom that didn't afford him the same considerations wasn't all that attractive.

He pulled the door down its track to the concrete floor and clicked the padlock.

See you soon, he thought. Please don't get stolen.

Sam pulled out his phone, requested a ride, and soon climbed in the back of the black Mercedes ten minutes later.

"Mint?" asked the driver. He was around the age of Sam's parents. He wore a suit coat despite the Georgia heat.

"No, thanks."

They rode in silence. No radio. Just the soft whoosh of the tires on the road and the occasional horn honks of displeased drivers. Ten minutes later they pulled up to what looked to be an empty stretch of road with doors to nowhere.

Sam thanked the driver, stepped out of the beautiful car into the sunshine, and disappeared into one of the doors. He walked down a series of steps to wait for the train. The Atlanta transit system didn't go many places, but the train service to the airport was incredibly useful. He liked riding the train. It made him feel like he was in one of the bigger cities. New York. Chicago. Los Angeles.

A few high windows along the stretch of the platform provided punctuated streaks of light into what otherwise looked like a musty basement. A Mom, Dad, and presumably a daughter sat on a bench to his right. They didn't speak. The train station remained silent besides the occasional car passing overhead.

Essentially no job, no apartment, and no relationship meant Sam had nothing tying him to Atlanta besides his favorite restaurants and bars. Sure, he had some friends that he would miss. But social media meant you were never too far away from anybody at any time.

Untethered. Unattached. It had been a while. He hadn't operated without a schedule since first moving to Atlanta. He had a plane to catch, but other than that he didn't have anywhere to be. No alarm. No appointments.

He took a deep breath of the cool, damp air. It would have been much more refreshing if he was outside. It would have felt good if the obligations of his hometown weren't hanging over his head.

A puff of air came from his right, soon followed by the rumbling of an approaching train. Sam grabbed his bag and watched as it slid down the tracks until stopping in front of him. He walked inside, took a seat, and noticed the family remained on the bench. The doors closed. He watched them disappear out the side window, still huddled silently together.

Who hangs out at the train station?

After a quick trip underneath downtown, the train emerged onto exposed tracks which bathed the mostly empty seats in late afternoon sunlight. It would be dark within the next hour or so. The orange glow of the descending sun would soon turn red before extinguishing entirely.

A man—the only other passenger— sat a few rows in front of him. At this point he wasn't more than just the back of a head, but he soon started moving around. Music began playing from somewhere. The head started bouncing back and forth. And then the man stood up.

He scanned the train and locked eyes with Sam. He smiled. The phone dangling from his hand somehow produced enough volume to require a yell.

"My man!" he said.

Random people engaging Sam for no reason was nothing new. Not that he was special. That's just kind of the way things went around here. Sometimes it's good, sometimes it's bad, but to Sam, it's always annoying. He offered a quick wave in response before looking back out the window.

The music grew louder.

Sam glanced back and saw the man coming toward him.

"What's up my dude?" he said. Even seated, Sam could tell the man was short. He'd have to jump to touch the top of the train doors. Bright white teeth. Black beard. His shaved head reflected the orange sunlight and he wouldn't need those sunglasses for too much longer.

Sam shrugged.

"You must be an airport man." The music continued blasting from his hand. Sam couldn't recognize the artist. Someone who liked particularly loud snare snaps. "I know you ain't going to College Park."

The man sat down sideways in the row in front of Sam.

Sam sighed. "Yeah, I'm going to the airport."

"What for?"

The train turned a slight corner, causing them to lean to their left.

"Family stuff."

"Oh shit, I know all about that." He leaned back and wiped his hand down his face.

"You mind if I just relax, man?" asked Sam.

"What kinda family stuff? Someone sick?"

Sam stared into the man's eyes. What the hell was he trying to do? Why the hell would he give a shit?

"To tell the truth I'd rather not talk about it."

"Why? Someone got Alzheimer's or something?"

All of a sudden the music turned off. It was just the two of them and the rumbling of the train tracks beneath them starting to slow. They came to a stop but nobody else got on. The train kept moving forward.

"I said I don't want to talk about it."

"It's rough when your Mom gets Alzheimer's, man."

Sam looked up and down the empty train. Quiet. Sunlight filling the empty seats.

"Stop talking to me."

The man stared at Sam.

"It's gonna be okay."

Next stop, College Park Station.

"It's gonna be okay," the man repeated.

The train slowed down. He stood up.

"But how do you know?" Sam's voice was quiet, but not a whisper.

The train stopped. The doors opened. Twenty people pushed their way through the doors, a raucous mixture of laughter, yells, and shuffling feet.

"This is my stop," the man said before he turned around and stepped into the fading sunshine. Sam watched him walk down the platform as the train resumed its path down the track.

It wasn't long before the train reached Hartsfield-Jackson Atlanta International Airport at the end of the line. He walked through the airport, stood in line for security, and walked forever until he found his terminal.

The sun had finally set. It felt like midnight, but it couldn't have been past eight o'clock. He found an uncomfortable chair and dozed until his plane started boarding. It was a full flight. Good thing he only had a carry-on backpack and didn't need the overhead compartment. He settled into the window seat at the end of a three-seat row. A Mom and daughter combo sat next to him. They smiled and nodded as a greeting but didn't say anything beyond that. Sam was grateful. He burrowed into his seat as much as possible and fell asleep before the flight attendants had time to explain the seatbelts.

An amount of time passed. It's impossible to know how much.

Sam slowly opened his eyes. The plane was dark. This was to be expected on a redeye. Everyone was trying to time warp. But then he sat forward and noticed the two seats next to him were empty. In fact, the seats on the other side of the aisle were empty, too. He sat up and craned his neck to look around the dark plane. There's usually at least one person reading. There's usually at least a little bit of light that leaks out from the flight attendant area.

But there was nothing.

All the seats were empty.

No light shone from any section of the plane.

Sam pulled up the window cover and moonlight fell into his lap. But there were no stars. No clouds. A full moon hung in the sky and radiated like a mid-day sun.

Without any competing light to restrict the corneas, even a candle in the middle of a dark desert can look like a spotlight.

He should have jumped up. Asked if anybody was there. He should have been flooded with fear and felt his breath squeeze out of his lungs.

But he didn't.

He stared into the moon and analyzed the craters. The dimples. The imperfections. The dark side of the moon isn't like the dark side of the Earth. Our world continually rotates as we circle the sun. Our dark side is constantly evolving. But the moon rotates in conjunction with the Earth. We only see its face, never the back of its head. The dark side of the moon is always dark. It doesn't change.

Sam studied the face of the moon and tried to recognize the imperfections. Even just one. He had been looking at the same surface his whole life. He should be able to find a discernible crater.

But he couldn't.

13.

Mary Gets a Phone Call

Thank God Linda was over. Mary tried to stay at the hospital but you have to be injured or sick to spend the night. So here she was, sentenced to another day alone in her house. She could only pass so much time by eating and watching TV before she started to feel sick, bored, or a combination of the two. But Linda Brooks was there and they were talking about—wait, what were they talking about?

Linda stared at Mary, not speaking. She must have just asked a question.

"Yup," said Mary. She leaned forward onto her elbows. Two hollow knocks rang out on the empty kitchen table.

Linda looked around. "I don't see her."

"See who?" Now Mary was looking around.

"Al. The dog."

Mary shrugged. "I don't know. She's got to be around here somewhere." She stood up. "Do you want some popcorn?"

"No, that's fine."

Mary walked over to the stove. She clanged around in the cupboard for a moment and pulled out a pot.

"So how's Brittany doing? I haven't seen her since—oh gosh I don't know—probably the wedding."

Linda adjusted herself in her seat.

"You really don't have to go through the trouble of making popcorn. Honest, I'm not hungry," she finally said.

"I remember it was so cold that day," continued Mary. "I thought they were crazy for wanting to have a wedding outside. In May, no less. You just never know what kind of weather you're going to get around here, you know?"

"I—uh—I haven't talked to Brittany in a while. Remember?"

Mary turned on the stove and let the popcorn oil heat up. She dropped in a couple kernels.

Linda stood up and walked near the stove. She leaned against the sink.

"Don't you just love being retired? Every day I wake up and expect to hit an alarm. Did I tell you that I used to set one? An alarm. For the first couple weeks. Then I'd turn it off, laugh, and go right back to sleep."

Mary stood over the pot.

"I hate it," she said quietly.

"What's that?" asked Linda.

"I said I *hate* it."

The coil on the old stove cracked and popped a little as it heated up. Mary always thought it sounded like it was going to explode.

"You know, when I was working, I had something to do. People needed me. I served a purpose."

The first kernel popped.

"And now I basically just sit around and wait to go to bed. Nobody visits, not really. Greg just thinks of me as a burden—and I kinda am. I mean, think about it. I can't drive anywhere. When

I do I get lost. I can't remember what the hell I'm doing when I'm doing something—"

The second kernel popped. Mary grabbed the rest of the popcorn kernels and dumped them into the pot. She cocked the lid on the top and let the syncopated gunshots fill the empty kitchen.

"—I screwed it up. I mean, look at the dog."

Linda looked around the kitchen, even bending over to look under the kitchen table.

"I don't see her," said Linda.

"Of course not. I lost her." Mary wiped her eyes.

"Mary, come on." She put her hands on Mary's shoulder and pulled her away from the stove. "Just take a seat. It's going to be okay."

Mary allowed herself to be led. "No it's not," she said. Then she surprised herself by laughing. "No wonder nobody comes to visit me." She sat back in her chair at the kitchen table.

The smell of popcorn filled the room. Linda turned off the stove and moved the pot to a cold burner.

Mary shook her hands like they were wet and blew out a quick breath of air.

"Alright. Geez. Sorry about that." Mary set her hands back in her lap. "So, um. Does Brittany still play the guitar? I thought she was going to play at her wedding, but I don't remember seeing that. Well, I guess that doesn't mean all that much, does it?"

Linda shook her head and sighed.

"Did they say when Greg's going to come home?"

Mary shrugged.

"Last I heard they were waiting on some test. Or maybe it was—" She felt the words fall out of her head. What comes after the test? She could picture the doctor saying it. Reading them. Everyone waiting for what comes next. But what is that?

"The, um—" Mary waved her hand in a circle, trying to flush out the words. "After the test. The answers."

"The results?" asked Linda.

"Yes." Mary bowed her head and let out a deep breath. "The results. Yeah they're doing tests and waiting for the results." She sighed.

Mary was never much of a drinker. She hated it. The loss of self-control, the soupy feeling the next day, but most of all she hated the stuttering. Her mouth would rebel after a few drinks. Every time. She'd be halfway through a sentence and feel the problem word coming up. It'd hit like a roadblock. It didn't make any sense. Just all of a sudden there'd be this word that was impossible to form. All the momentum of the sentence would build a terrible pressure behind it. She'd close her eyes and try to focus, try to force it through while her mouth was posed for the first sound of the word. Sometimes it would come. Sometimes she'd have to give up. Shake her head. Try to say it a different way.

And maybe that was just a precursor. Maybe getting drunk was a numbing of her mental faculties that should've been a sign of things to come. However, the mental roadblocks she experienced now were a little different than when she had too many glasses of wine all those years before. She at least knew what word she had been trying to find back then. Now the words themselves seemed to be hiding just out of sight.

"I'm sure he'll be okay. Greg's a strong guy," said Linda.

Mary stood up. "I just hate talking about this. Thinking about this." She rubbed her hands together and crossed her arms. "I hate this." She smelled the popcorn. It smelled warm. How could a scent have a temperature?

"But I don't want to talk about that anymore," said Mary. "Let's talk about Brittany. My kids don't have anything interesting going on."

"Mary, stop."

She wasn't doing anything. Not even walking.

"What?"

"You know I haven't spoken to Brittany since the wedding."

"In two years?"

"Three. You *know* this." She raised her voice and it sounded doubly loud in the quiet kitchen. "You know this. So why do you keep asking? You know I don't want to talk about it."

Mary didn't know what to say. And not like the words were there but couldn't come out. And not like she had a point but couldn't find the words themselves. She just didn't know what to say.

The wedding had been on a Saturday in late May. Wisconsin springs were unpredictable, but they decided to set up a tent in the backyard. They wanted it to feel like a party and not a formal event. It was a lot of work. Setting up the chairs, putting out the decorations, all of it was done by the family. They saved a ton of money but they were ready to collapse by the time the wedding happened. It wasn't a traditional wedding. It was in a backyard, after all. But there was an aisle, and they said vows, and she had a beautiful bouquet—all of the elements of a wedding were there. So when it came time for the dances, Linda expected Brittany and Sean—Linda's second husband and Brittany's stepfather—to have the father-daughter dance. Brittany told Linda beforehand that she would only have the dance with her real father, but of course he had died when she was ten years old. Linda assumed Brittany would cave on the day of the wedding. She didn't. And that was that.

Mary knew all this. She did now, at least.

Linda stood in front of her with tears in her eyes. Mary had been waiting for a friend to come over. For someone to visit so they could talk and laugh and relive fun memories. But this memory isn't fun. And Mary brought it up multiple times.

"Listen, Mary. I'm sorry but I'm going to leave."

"I'm—I'm sorry."

"Tell Greg we're thinking of him. Me and Sean."

Linda grabbed her purse from the living room on her way out the front door.

Mary stood alone in the middle of the kitchen. It felt huge. As big as a city block. And there was a brick wall ten feet thick all around the outside. The only thing inside was Mary and all the chances she had wasted.

She cried softly. The sounds of her whimpers echoed off the cabinets. The loneliness was almost tangible. It squeezed her like a vice. The shadow of Linda's presence still hung in the kitchen. But now it only served as a reminder of her oldest friend's inability to stand more than an hour with her. Linda Brooks. Mother of Brittany. Their kids had become friends back in a time when they still relied on their mothers to pack their lunches. People always talked about how important it was for kids to meet people their age. But there's no age limit to its importance.

And now Mary chased her off because she couldn't keep her stupid mouth shut.

Stupid.

Embarrassment came out to battle the loneliness. It tore Mary up on the inside. She couldn't decide what was worse—how difficult everything was becoming, or how embarrassing it was to continually make the same mistakes.

She had to move. She couldn't just stand still any longer so she walked over to the stove—oh *right*, popcorn—before moving back toward the phone. The phone. It began to look more like a life preserver. She reached down, picked it up, and put it to her ear hoping to find a warm voice on the other end.

Dial tone.

She listened to the droning buzz for a moment and set it back on the receiver.

The refrigerator hummed, but not much.

She stared at the phone, hoping it would ring.

Ring.

Ring.

And then the phone started ringing.

The sudden blast of noise made her jump. Her heartbeat thudded through her chest and she took a slow, deep breath. She steadied herself and picked it up.

"Hello?"

"Hey Mom."

The voice was familiar. It wasn't Greg. It couldn't be Sean. Wait, what did he call her?

"Hello?"

"Sam?"

"Yeah, geez. How's it going?"

"Sam! Hey! Hey it's going—good. It's good."

"Hey I'm on a bus from Milwaukee. We're in, shoot I don't know. Maybe Fond Du Lac or something. I think we have a couple of more stops and then I'll be up there."

"Here? You're coming here?"

"Yeah. I'm going to bounce around a bit but I'll be there, maybe around this evening or so."

"Okay! Okay Sam that sounds great!" Had he told her he was coming? It seems like he would have, but she would've written that down. Or remembered it. Right? God who cares. She bounced a little bit on her toes. The remnants of dried tears clung to her cheeks and made the skin feel a bit tight.

They hung up and the kitchen regained its silence. Something was different now, though. It buzzed with energy. With excitement.

With hope.

14.

Greg Gets a Visitor

You'd think they'd make hospital beds more comfortable. They know people are going to be lying in them for days on end. Their whole business is based around the idea of comforting people. Making them feel better. Why would they exclusively offer near-solid mattresses and pillows filled with shredded paper?

Greg adjusted himself for the twentieth time that hour. His muscles cried out for rest even though they were resting. His mind cried out for sleep even though it wouldn't let him.

These last few days had been strange. A heart attack? That's what happened to old people. Sure, maybe he hadn't been feeling great for a little while but who's actually healthy? Eating right, exercising, getting enough sleep—do people do that? What kind of a lunatic takes perfect care of himself?

But of course whatever he'd been doing landed him here. In this terrible bed. Listening to the beeps of machines he'd never understand. Wondering if each number was supposed to be a different number. Too much time alone. Too much time in one place.

Mary wanted to visit for the entire day. Sun up to sun down. She hated this even more than him, and he hated it quite a bit. But the doctor said he needed rest. Then why not provide a bed that someone could actually get to sleep in?

He stared out the window like a convict, longing to feel the wind on his skin. A few birds hopped around on a power line swinging from an unknown height above the window to a pole out by the street.

Greg wiped his hands over his face and felt the pull of tubes and wires connected to his arms. He'd woken up to find himself on the shittiest chain gang in the state. Sentenced to a life of draining his blood through tubes and announcing every heartbeat with an audible beep. No more secrets. Nothing to hide.

Beep beep.

Beep beep.

Every passing stranger was privy to something that up until now, had been mostly unknown even to him. The heartbeat really only shows itself when you need it least—afraid, excited, sick. There are more important matters to think about than the mechanics of your blood moving through your veins and arteries. But here you are thinking *Wow my heart is thumping* when you should be focusing on what you're going to say next to the woman that will become your wife, or how to avoid the oncoming traffic accident, or how you're going to sink that game-winning shot.

Beep beep.

Beep beep.

He focused again on the birds. One was a robin. That's for sure. The other one? Some kind of finch or something? They hopped up and down the line. Going one direction then back the other way.

Beep beep.

Beep beep.

Two hops one way.

Beep beep.

Two hops the other way.

Beep beep.

Their movements fell perfectly in line with the heart monitor.

Beep beep.

Beep beep.

Each hop. Each beep. Synchronized perfectly like a pop music video.

Greg sat up in bed. Two hops one way, two hops the other.

Beep beep.

Beep beep.

Then the door opened. Greg slowly turned his head away from the window.

"Sam?"

"Hey Dad."

His son stood in the doorway with a backpack slung over one shoulder. The beeps from the monitor picked up the pace a little.

"What the hell are you doing here?"

"You think I'm going to miss your first heart attack?" Sam moved further into the room until he stood at the foot of the bed.

"Well come here. I don't have Ebola." Greg sat up. Sam walked around the side of the bed and gave him a brief awkward hug.

"How are you feeling?"

Greg shrugged.

"When did you get in?" he asked.

"What time is it now?"

Greg looked at his phone on the table next to him.

"10:30."

"I got here at 10:30."

Greg smiled and smacked his son on the arm.

"Take a seat." Greg leaned back into the slanted, rock-solid bed.

Sam sat in a wobbly, vinyl-covered chair between the bed and the window and set his bag on the ground.

"So how was the accident?"

"I've had better."

"Are you sore?"

"It hurts to sneeze."

Sam nodded.

"So what the hell happened?"

Greg adjusted himself and felt all the muscles in his core scream for mercy.

"I don't know. It's a whole—" He flipped his hand in front of him. "It's a whole thing. Have you been to see your mother?"

"She's on my list." Sam leaned forward. "Really now. What happened?"

Greg sighed. Images of light through the open door spilling across the bed flashed through his mind. Mary lying there with her clothes on. The open door. The rage that filled him and poured from his mouth. Just thinking about it made his eyes heavy. She didn't know. She didn't do it on purpose. But yet—

"I yelled at her." It was difficult to get the words out in one go but he managed. "And it just makes me want to die."

Sam nodded, resting his arms on his knees.

"You're dealing with a lot, Dad."

Greg wiped his face even though nothing was there.

"This is my job," he said. "For better or for worse, right?"

The door opened again and a nurse came in. Tall guy. Looking straight at the clipboard in his hands.

"How we doing?" he said as the door swung shut. He looked up. "Oh. Hey."

"This is my son. Sam. He's a nurse, too."

"Oh yeah? Hey Sam." He walked over and shook his hand. "I didn't know there was a son."

Sam glanced over at Greg but didn't say anything.

"You gonna start telling me what I'm doing wrong?" asked the nurse.

"That depends. You doing something wrong?"

"Wouldn't know it if I was." And then to Greg: "Alright how we doing today, Mr. Weber?"

The nurse ran through the same questions he asked every day. He checked the same machines and wrote the same scribbles.

"When's he getting out?" asked Sam as the nurse finished his checks.

"Depends on if the doc says we need a surgery." And then the nurse left.

Sam looked to Greg.

"Surgery?"

"Thank God for insurance," said Greg. "Help me up. I gotta walk around a bit."

It took a minute, but Sam got him out of bed. Greg grabbed the IV pole and the wheels quietly squeaked as they moved toward the door.

"It was maybe about an hour or so ago someone shit their pants. Or the bed. Probably both of them, I guess. I heard the whole thing. Honestly the whole floor probably did. It sounded like something out of a cartoon."

"You get used to it after a while."

Greg paused. "You shit the bed a lot, son?"

"No, other people. I'm one of the poor bastards that has to clean it up, remember?"

Greg opened the door.

"I just wanna see who it was." He walked into the hallway and peeked around the corner of the next doorway. The little window showed a person-shaped blob huddled underneath white sheets. "Ah nuts."

They continued walking down the hall. It felt great to move his legs but his breath just wouldn't catch the way it should. Different doors showed different people in different stages of disrepair.

"It's like an awful game show," said Greg. "Pick your door. Do you want cancer? Kidney stones? How about a laceration?"

"People always read into hospitals too much. Like they think they're looking into their future," said Sam.

"Well you're a little numb to it. You think someone working in the slaughterhouse gets queasy when they get a paper cut?"

Sam shrugged.

They reached the end of the hallway and turned around.

"You ever think about living in a place like this?" asked Sam.

Greg nodded.

"Your mother's going to need some help. Someday. Not yet, I don't think."

"Well, that's why I'm here."

Greg looked at his son and smiled. "Thanks. She'll like that."

A man in green and red checked pajamas rolling himself in a wheelchair passed on their left.

"But I gotta think about a permanent solution. I'm still a few years from retiring. And if it keeps progressing the way it has…"

The sentence hung between them but no one wanted to finish it off.

"It'd be one thing if I could retire, but that's just not going to happen. Get my pension. Medicare. But we need the insurance until then. We need the income."

They reached Greg's room and walked inside. It wasn't loud in the hallway, but it was even quieter in the room. Sam helped his father climb back in bed. He didn't sit back down in the chair.

"We'll figure something out, Dad."

Greg nodded and tried to look for the birds on the wire.

It was empty.

15.

Ashley Gets a Visitor, Too

"It's still weird."

"He's been gone for almost a year now," said Ashley.

She stood along the counter next to her kitchen sink. This way, she could lean her weight against the granite and keep an eye on Sadie in the living room at the same time. Paula Olson sat at the kitchen table setting the island as a barrier between them.

"I know. It's just—" Paula looked around the house as if she expected a ghost to climb through the wall. "I don't know. One year off doesn't balance out the..." She paused and silently counted on her fingers. "How long was it?"

"Marriage or dating?"

"Marriage."

"Seven years. Would've been eight this year, but I don't think you count anniversaries after a separation." Ashley heard a shout from the backyard, but that was normal. Noah always became twice as dramatic whenever he had a friend over. Every joke was the funniest thing he ever heard. Every fall shattered all of his bones. And every disappointment was the end of the world.

"Are you sure? Seven?"

"Quite."

"Jesus," said Paula. "We *are* getting old."

Ashley and Paula met just after they moved into the sleepy neighborhood which was, apparently, about seven years before. They saved all their money for a year to pay for their wedding. Rented hall. Full open bar. The whole thing. But six months out, when they should've been sending out their save the dates, he sat her down in the living room of their apartment.

"Don't freak out," he said.

"That's a weird way to start a conversation." She could hear her neighbors cooking. That's how thin the walls were. Simply removing the lid from a pot was loud enough to travel through the wall. She hated it, but it still wasn't worse than the apartment with all the cockroaches. One tried to crawl underneath her foot while she looked through the refrigerator. Barefoot. She'd take thin walls over insects.

"I don't think we should have a wedding," he said.

She missed a breath but was too shocked to start the whole process of crying. They'd been together four years at that point. They had the children talk. They were engaged for about four months. Packed bags and random bouts of crying and shattered feelings, fuck *hurt*, flashed through her head in an instant. She'd be able to unpack it later but just then, sitting there on the couch, it felt like she missed a breath.

"Still married! Still married!" he said quickly, but not quick enough. "Just no wedding. I love you. I want to spend the rest of my life with you and raise a stable of beautiful children and all that crap but—"

"But no wedding?" The tears had finally shown up even though they knew they weren't necessary. They rolled down her cheeks anyway.

"That's a shitload of money to spend on one night. On a party for our family and friends."

"We'll get to eat, too."

"Do you want to spend $20,000 on a dinner?"

They decided to keep saving, but for a down payment. And then they got married at the courthouse with their parents watching. And then they bought the house where they met Paula and William. Paula paired off with Ashley. William with Darren. And Bryce and Noah would become friends once they were alive and old enough to realize another person was near them.

"I've never met someone named Paula," was the first thing Ashley said when they met out front all those years ago.

"Well, maybe *you're* getting old," was what Ashley said as she stood in her kitchen and Paula sat at the kitchen table.

And then another yell came from the backyard. One that got both her and Paula's attention. One kid screaming was fairly standard. But not two of them. Synchronized shouts from both Bryce and Noah either meant one of them was missing a limb or they found a pot of gold. One possibility was more likely than the other.

Paula scrambled out of her chair but Ashley was already outside by the time she got around the intrusive counter.

It wasn't a pot of gold, but both kids still had all their limbs. Noah jumped around and Bryce seemed to simply join in the fun. A bewildered man stood in the middle of the chaos.

"I don't even know who that one is," he said, pointing at Bryce.

"Uncle Sam is here!" yelled Noah.

"That's still funny," he said. "After all these years."

Paula appeared next to Ashley. She waved.

"This one yours?" he asked.

"Yup." Then to Ashley: "We should get going. Gimme a call later." Paula gathered her son and walked down the driveway.

"Well well Uncle Sam," said Ashley. She walked into the yard where Noah peppered his uncle with questions.

"When did you get in? Are you staying here? Are you staying for dinner?"

Sam looked up to his sister.

"Give him a chance to breathe, will you?" She put her hand on Noah's shoulder and shepherded him away from Sam's legs. "Come on. I'm sure the other one would like to see you, too."

The three of them walked inside where Sadie gave Sam an underwhelming welcome. She was more interested in lying on the couch and watching a colorful, noisy television program. Noah, however, made up for his sister's lack of enthusiasm. He stuck to his uncle's side like an obedient dog. They moved into the kitchen and sat at the table. Sam set his backpack on the ground next to his chair.

"Didja hear about grampa?"

"Yup." Sam looked to Ashley. "Yeah I did."

"I heard his truck exploded."

"No you didn't," said Ashley. "Don't joke about your grampa getting into an accident."

"I wasn't joking!"

"Did his truck explode?" Sam asked Ashley.

"No!"

"Yes it did," said Noah.

"Stop it," said Ashley. Her voice rumbled through the kitchen. Bleeps bloops and shouts from Sadie's show filled the gap before Sam turned to Noah.

"I'm pretty sure it exploded," he said.

"Noah, go wash your face."

"But *Mom*—"

"No. Go."

He hopped down off the chair and walked to the bathroom in the short hallway.

"Listen to me. I know you're trying to be the fun uncle and all that, but you can't talk about Dad like that to him. And you sure as hell can't contradict me in front of him. I'm his mother. You got that?"

"Jeez, yeah." He held up his palms and rolled his eyes.

"Have you been to see him?"

"Dad?"

She didn't even nod.

"Yeah. That's where I just came from."

"And Mom?"

"She wasn't there."

"Have you been to see her?"

He leaned back and crossed his arms.

"You have to see her."

"I know."

"Like right now."

"I thought I'd see the kids first."

"Does she know you're here?"

"She knows I'm *coming*."

"Jesus Christ."

"Well, could you give me a ride at least?"

"How did you get here?"

"What, you think I rented a car? I'm the one taking time off from work to come here and—"

"Oh boo hoo you have to take time off from your vacation life on the other side of the country to come slum it with your family for a little bit."

"Vacation life? You think working in a hospital is a vacation?"

"Of course not. It's not easy being the hero all the time, is it?"

"You're the one who guilted me into coming here in the first place. If you didn't want my help—"

"Then you wouldn't have come. Would you?"

The bleeps bloops and shouts from the television in the next room again filled in the space where their voices used to be.

"Are we going to Grandma's?" Sadie appeared in the doorway between the kitchen and the living room.

Ashley looked between her sleepy daughter and her asshole brother.

"Yeah. Sure. Everyone get their shoes on."

Five minutes later, everyone climbed into Ashley's car—Noah and Sadie in the back.

It wasn't a far drive to her parents' house. She backed the car down the driveway and headed toward the main road.

It felt a little weird at first—she rode her bike down this street when she was a kid. Her brother moved to Atlanta and she hadn't made it much further than screaming distance from her childhood home.

They turned off her dead-end road and merged with traffic after the stop sign.

"Would you still have bought the house if you knew you'd be single again?" asked Sam.

"What?"

"Well, y'know. It's a lot of room. Plus you're right down the street from Mom and Dad—"

"I don't *mind* being down the street from Mom and Dad."

"No, of course not." Sam leaned forward and looked into the side mirror. "It's just, I don't know, I was just being kinda hypothetical."

Ashley swallowed a sentence: *You were just being kinda an asshole.*

Instead she slowly slid her right hand a little past the steering wheel and turned the key while Sam continued looking at something in the mirror.

"Oh shoot," she said. The car began coasting. "Oh, *shoot*," she repeated to herself when she realized the power steering went with the engine. She eased on the brake and leaned on the wheel to guide the car toward the curb.

"What happened?" asked Sam.

Ashley sat back and waved a hand at the dashboard. "This thing. It's just been doing this lately."

"Turning off?"

"It up and dies."

"What dies?" asked Noah from the back seat.

"Dies?" mimicked Sadie.

Sam looked back to them as if they had the answer, then back to his sister.

"So what, we gotta walk or something?"

"Well, it comes and goes. Momentum helps. Sometimes if I just get it moving a little the pistons or something get pumping and it fires up. I don't know much about cars."

"Yeah, me neither."

They sat quietly for a moment.

"So you wanna get out there and give it a push?" asked Ashley.

"Me?"

"I'll help!" yelled Noah.

"Well someone's gotta do it. It won't be bad. Noah will help."

"Yeah!" said a thin voice in the back seat.

Sam rested his head against the headrest and closed his eyes.

"Fine," he said.

Sam and Noah climbed out of the car and walked around to the back. Ashley rolled down her window.

"Alright, mush!" she said.

Sam mumbled something that Noah probably shouldn't hear, but Ashley couldn't make it out.

The car slowly began to creep along the side of the road. Fully functional cars zoomed by on their left. It was slow-going at first, but they eventually picked up a little momentum. Ashley watched through the rearview mirror as Sam grimaced with the effort, and Noah smiled while talking to his uncle. She couldn't see his hands pressed against the trunk below the window, but she was sure the pressure on his wrists was minimal, if anything.

They didn't have more than two blocks to go, but it would be enough to keep Sam puffing for a little while. She turned on her blinker well ahead of the left turn and took one more glimpse in the rearview. She smiled before steeling herself for the unassisted left turn.

16.

Sam Comes Home

Sam never pushed a car before that night. Had most people? Is that a shared experience a lot of people have? It couldn't be. He'd had cars break down, sure, but that's what tow trucks were for. He pumped his legs like Coach Parker taught him in 9th grade football. He leaned into it so's not to strain his back. He didn't need experience to know his form had to be perfect.

"What's it like being a nurse?" asked Noah.

"It's fine." His breaths came in short bursts. "Kinda hard. Sometimes fun. Pretty tiring."

"Is it harder than pushing a car?"

Sam glanced over and saw Noah's hands reaching toward the car but not quite touching it. He jogged in this strange arms-out zombie stance.

"This? This is easy." He wiped the sweat from his forehead.

"Yeah, yeah it's not too bad."

"This happen a lot?"

"What?"

"The car. Your Mom. Said this happens. A lot."

Noah paused and then shook his head. "Nope. First time." He ran to catch back up.

Sam tried to look through the car to see if his sister was laughing. This would be a weird thing to make up. What had he said right before the car died? Was he being an asshole?

"Almost. Almost there," said Sam.

The car grinded around a corner at a whopping eightish miles per hour. It would have been much easier if there wasn't a slight incline all the damn way there.

Finally, mercifully, the car coasted near the curb and the brake lights glowed off his jeans. The sweat running down his face picked up a slight breeze. His chest heaved. Someone working in the medical field should probably take better care of himself, he thought. When was the last time he went for a jog? Ever?

He sat down on the curb and hung his head between his shoulders. If he had looked to his right, he would've seen Noah doing the same thing, but without all the heavy breathing.

Car doors opened, then closed.

"Thanks," said Ashley. "I really gotta take this thing in."

Sam looked up and wanted to flip her off but decided against it. Noah already copied too much.

He turned his head to look at the house. It hadn't changed in thirty years, and why would it? The only difference was the trees that were at one point too small to climb now hovered above the gutters. But the white siding and black shutters were the same as when he used to think about sneaking out in high school. Of course he never did, but man it would've been cool.

His friends always spoke of their fathers in a much different way than their mothers. The father would be the one waiting for them if they came home late. Their mothers would be disappointed when they heard about it the next morning.

But the Weber house was different. Mrs. Weber. It's hard to imagine a teacher with a first name. It's even harder to think of your Mom by any other name, but Mrs. Weber commanded the same authority around the dinner table as she did in the classroom. The students didn't fear her, and neither did Sam, but they did their best to stay on her good side. But why? There was no threat of violence or even a raised voice. There was only disappointment that she would dole out like an uppercut should you fail to live up to her expectations.

She was a giant.

A titan.

Eight feet tall in a five foot world.

But now, sitting on that curb with a miniature version of his sister pretending to be him, Sam wondered what waited for him on the other side of the red front door. He had never even seen her limp. And now she had her legs cut out from under her.

Phone calls weren't the same as standing in the kitchen with her. That had been Ashley's argument to get him here. Like that would make it better. No. It would be worse. Far worse. He thought about running down the street if his legs weren't already rubber. The breath had returned to his lungs, but his heart continued to thump like he was still pushing that sedan down Gladys Avenue.

Noah hopped up.

"You coming?" he asked.

Sadie and Ashley were already opening the front door.

He nodded and put his feet beneath him just as the front door swung open.

"Hey!" came her voice.

Sam turned toward the house and saw his Mom, Mrs. Weber, bending down to hug her granddaughter.

"Hey Mom," he said.

Mary Weber lifted her head from her grandchildren and an almost comic smile stretched across her face. She stepped around the children and walked toward her son. Each step was slightly faster than the previous one. She held her arms in front of her about five steps before she reached Sam and wrapped them around his shoulders when she reached him.

"Oh my God it's so good to see you," she said, and began kissing him, alternating cheeks.

"Hey, hey okay," said Sam. He tried to lift his arms, but they were pinned down. She readjusted her arms every few seconds to squeeze him in a different position. Her movements were quick. Jerky. It was the frantic energy of a child finding their lost puppy. The chasm between this reaction and the stoicism he had grown accustomed to as a kid flipped Sam's stomach. Phone calls simply weren't the same.

"Mom, Jesus," said Ashley from the front door.

Mary finally relaxed her grip and took a step back.

"I'm sorry," she said and wiped a hand across her dry cheek. "Come on. Come in." She turned around but kept a hand on his shoulder. Sam followed his mother up the sidewalk that led to the front door he had eagerly left years ago.

The kids went running inside, temporarily forgetting the dog hadn't been seen in about a week.

The front door acted like a portal. Outside, Sam was a 34-year-old nurse visiting home for the first time in a while, but he felt the nervousness of starting 7th grade as soon as he walked in the house. The scent was the same. The brown carpet was the same. The furniture had been updated a few years earlier but the layout was the same.

His shoes were suddenly a few sizes too big. His shirt sleeves hung over his fingertips. His belt had become loose, and he struggled to hold up his pants.

Ashley was swimming in her clothes as well, but she didn't seem to notice. She walked over the ends of her pants and grabbed one of the kitchen chairs through the elongated ends of her shirt. Her head barely reached the top of the kitchen table. The kids must have run off somewhere because Sam couldn't hear their voices.

And then Mary walked back from the kitchen. She paused when she looked at him, smiled, and put her hands on her hips. Her wrinkles had disappeared. The grey in her hair had darkened.

"Are you just gonna stand there all day?" she asked.

Sam thought about asking if he should take his shoes off.

And then his Mom turned around and banged into the table. The salt and pepper shakers eternally sitting in the middle of the table—through breakfast, lunch, and dinner—clattered to the wooden tabletop.

"Oh," she said and reflexively brought a shaky hand to her mouth.

"I got it. It's okay," said Ashley. She reached to the center of the table, no longer drowning in her clothes. Sam looked down and saw everything fit just as it had as he walked up to the front door. "Why don't you take a seat, Mom?"

"Yeah," said Sam. He walked into the kitchen where he learned how to scramble eggs and make a grilled cheese.

"No, no," she said, waving them off. "Are you hungry? You must be. Traveling all that way. What about you? You guys staying for dinner?"

Ashley pushed a chair back under the table.

"No. We gotta go."

Sam swung his head to his sister. Alone? Alone with Mom?

"Kids! Come on!"

Noah and Sadie appeared from the hallway.

They hugged their grandma goodbye and walked to the front door.

"Don't you need a ride?" asked Sam.

Ashley paused. "Maybe. Let me try it again. Thing comes and goes."

They walked to the car, climbed in, and the engine fired right up.

Sam held his hands out to either side, palms up.

Ashley rolled down her window. She yelled, "Weird, huh?" and drove away.

The sound of her engine disappeared down the road and was replaced with a blanket of silence. The same silence after an evening snowfall, when the fresh layer of powder absorbs any chance of an echo or reverberation. Sam turned around and saw his mother wiping the spilled salt and pepper off the table and into her hand.

"You don't have to cook," he said. Sam walked into the house and closed the door behind him.

"Oh come on. I don't get to cook for my son every day." She walked to the sink and brushed off her hands.

"I'm not really hungry."

She paused over the sink before pointing to the table.

"Sit at least."

He did.

"How's work going?"

He gave her the elevator pitch—fine but tiring. It's nice to feel like you're helping but it's just another job, really. She listened as she opened drawers and closed them without taking anything out. What was she looking for?

"It's really good to have you home," she said.

He smiled at her and held her glance. Her eyes didn't match her smile. The skin around them creased with the grin but her eyes didn't share the spark.

"How are you doing?" he asked.

She resumed her search through the drawers. "I'm fine."

"Mom."

Another drawer slammed shut.

"*Mom.*"

She slid another drawer open, pushed the contents around, and paused. She didn't look at her son.

"How are you doing?"

She sighed. "Do you know where the can opener is?"

Sam stood up and walked to the drawer to the left of the sink. The silverware drawer. He pulled it all the way out and looked toward the back.

"Here you go." He handed her the can opener. "What do you need that for?"

"I'm going to make us some tacos. Just like you like."

"I'm not hungry, Mom."

She looked at him like he was lying. His heart sank. The lights seemed to dim. He imagined her hands turning to sand and blowing away in an unseen wind. Up her arms, through her shoulders, and along her body from her feet and her head like a candle with a wick on both ends. She disappears into the darkness and there's nothing he can do about it.

The silence in the house is overbearing. How does she stand it all day? With Dad in the hospital, she doesn't have much more to do than stare at the wall and wait.

And wait.

And wait.

"Let's go out," he said.

The light came back and Mary crossed her arms. No sand. No breeze.

"Where?"

"To dinner. Your choice. My treat." Going out to dinner wasn't about being hungry. It's an activity as much as it's sustenance. And tonight, it was also about escape.

Mary looked at the can opener in her hand as if it were some ancient instrument from a forgotten civilization and put it on the countertop.

"I guess we could just get some tacos at Marco's," she said.

"There you go."

He waited as she gathered her things before they walked through the door into the garage. Greg's truck would have been sitting directly outside the door if it hadn't been wrapped around a pole a few days before. Instead, an empty slab of concrete sat below one of the overhead lights. Mary's blue Chevy Malibu sat in the far slot.

"It's been a little while since I've driven it, but it'll work," she said.

Sam shrugged and took the keys. Soon, they were driving through the neighborhood and out to the main road. How many times had he circled these blocks on his bike? How many times had he met friends to do nothing at all besides waste time until they were old enough to leave? And for what? To fast forward and return when things were different but still the same, slightly older and slightly worse?

Mary flipped through the radio stations and settled on the oldies station. Bob Seger complained about something or other.

Marco's wasn't far. This new strip mall was a grocery store when Sam was in high school. He noticed a handful of repurposed lots along the way. Every trip home involved a game of figuring out what had been replaced, what had disappeared, and what had withstood the constant wear of time.

The sun had set. White, fluorescent lights covered every section of the parking lot with fake sunlight. Shadows were difficult to locate, even between the cars filling almost every parking spot. Wisconsin autumns kept you at the top of a tall pole that wobbled drastically from side to side. You could find yourself leaning toward summer or leaning toward winter in the same day. Tonight, the air had the brisk chill of an impatient winter.

The quiet parking lot gave way to a bright, loud, and lively dining area. Marco's was franchised by a local family but the chain's roots went to the Texas-Mexico border. Colorful paintings of sombreros and burros and maracas covered the walls. Mariachi music blared from the ceiling-mounted speakers. A short man with unnaturally dark hair smiled at them from behind a skinny, wooden podium.

"Two?" he asked.

They were shown to a booth near the back corner, giving them a view of the open room. A large group filled the center of the restaurant—most likely a birthday party. Groups of two and three and four lined the exterior booths. And soon, a bowl of chips and a smaller bowl of salsa slid in front of them.

"We'll need a minute," Sam told the waiter. Mary swung her head back and forth, scanning the room. "Everything okay?" asked Sam.

She leaned forward. "I have to use the restroom."

"Already?" He turned around and saw the signs in the opposite corner. "Looks like it's over there. Down that hallway."

She stood up and disappeared around the corner.

He tried a chip. It was warm.

She'd repeat herself on the phone. Not much, but she'd find something to repeat even in their brief, occasional check-ins. They were easy to ignore and honestly more annoying than anything. But now, reaching for another chip, he replayed his mother walking between the tables toward the bathroom. Her steps were short. She was uneasy. He expected there to be forgetfulness.

But he wasn't prepared for fragility.

He pictured her in that silent house, worried about falling, wishing someone would stop by, and he wanted to cry. No tears filled his eyes, but damn it they should have. It was easy to pretend in a different time zone.

But phone calls weren't the same as standing in the kitchen.

He looked down and noticed half of the basket of chips was empty. How long had she been gone?

Sam turned around and scanned the restaurant. The entrance was closer to the bathrooms than their table. Was it possible? Could she get lost in a place this small?

He stood up. The chair squeaked as it slid backwards. The couple at the next table glanced over as they bit into something cheesy. Sam ignored them and navigated the busy dining room until he reached the hallway. His mouth was dry. His heart raced. He looked back and forth between the bathroom doors and the exit. It was a straight shot. There was a chance.

He stood outside of the women's room and wiped his mouth. How much trouble would he get into if he opened that door? There'd be some shouting. They'd definitely have to leave. But didn't he have a good reason? Didn't he have an excuse?

And then the door opened and Mary walked out.

"Oh!" she said. "You miss me?"

Sam let out a long breath.

"No, I…" He was never good at lying.

She nodded and led him back to the table.

"You thought I got lost, didn't you?" she said after they sat down.

He ate another chip.

"You know," she took a deep breath and let it out. "I know what's going on. Of course I do. I'm the one who has to live with it." She took a drink of her water. "You wanted to know how I'm doing? It's a hard question to answer. Sometimes good. Sometimes not great. It's almost like it doesn't affect me as much in some places. I don't know. There are sometimes where I feel like my old self and other times…"

Her sentence hung in the air. Luckily there was loud mariachi music to fill the space.

She shook her head. "I hate it," she said quietly, but not quietly enough. "I just hate it."

Sam reached forward and grabbed her hand. She looked up.

"I'm really happy you're here."

He smiled and found those tears he was looking for. All those years. All that time in a different state. And now here they were.

"I missed you," she said.

"I missed you, too."

17.

Mary Pushes a Wheelchair

Back in the hospital. Mary Weber again sat in the chair to the left of Greg's bed. The wobbly, vinyl-covered chair had become quite familiar. As had the sterile, white hallway. The nurses were about as familiar as they could get. She knew she knew them, but she didn't know how she knew that she knew them. Context was easier than faces. Faces were easier than names.

Greg sat on the end of the bed speaking to the doctor. Mary gave up trying to follow along maybe two sentences into the discussion. He was leaving. She knew that. It had been almost a week of tubes and tests and wires and beeps but now he was finally coming home. He was excited. She was ecstatic. The house had become more of a home again once Sam had shown up, but Greg would bring it all together. He always did.

"How does it feel?" asked the doctor.

"Great. Gonna be even better when I get back to work."

The smile that had been a near-constant feature of the doctor's face began to fade. He kept the majority of the conversation in good humor, even when going through all the jargon that Mary didn't even try to listen to. But now, his smile was gone. He swallowed and shook his head.

"Greg, you can't be going back to the mill. Not right away, if ever."

"*Ever?*" Greg laughed. "You gotta be kidding me."

"I'm sorry, Greg. I mean, after some time sure, you can find a job that won't have you on your feet all day. But your arteries aren't operating at a hundred percent. Too much stress and we'll be back here. Again. And that time we might not make it to this conversation we're having right now. Even if you were to have the surgery—"

"I can't have the surgery. I need to work."

The doctor took a breath and paused before starting again. "You can't work without the surgery. But even after that you won't have the physical stamina you're used to. That you used to have."

"So how are we going to live if I don't work?"

"There are always options, Greg. I can get you a pamphlet about filing for disability, if you want. But your heart can't handle going to work."

Greg crossed his arms. He stared at a blank spot on the floor about four feet in front of him.

"I'm not going on disability," he said. "I'm not disabled."

The door suddenly swung open with a bang.

"Jeez, take it easy Bill," said the doctor.

The tall nurse shrugged and smiled. He leaned on the handles of the wheelchair in front of him.

"Sorry doc."

Mary stood up and walked next to the bed. She rested a hand on her husband's rigid shoulder, but he didn't move. He hadn't taken his eyes from the nothing spot on the floor even when the door crashed open.

"I think this is for you," she said, motioning to the chair.

Greg finally moved his head to the left.

"I can walk out of here," he said.

"Hospital policy, Mr. Weber," said the nurse. "Just lemme do one last thing for you and we're done."

Greg turned to his right and locked eyes with Mary. She tried to tell him just to go along with it. What could it possibly hurt to take a short ride in a wheelchair? But of course it wasn't about the wheelchair at all. And she couldn't convey the motivation and reassurance he would need with a simple look. So instead she tried to fake a subtle smile and shrugged one shoulder.

But what was even worse to her than the inability to convey an emotion with her look was Greg's ability to succinctly and thoroughly convey his. It poured from his eyes like an open faucet:

Fear.

She rubbed her hand in a small circle on that rigid shoulder. It was all she could do.

"Come on. It'll be over before you know it," said the doctor.

Greg climbed into the wheelchair, which squeaked in recognition.

The doctor looked at Mary and gave her a little nod.

"Thanks for everything," she said.

"Just doing my job," he said with a smile.

The nurse motioned toward the grips on the back of the wheelchair. She walked around and pushed her husband out of the hospital room. The hallway felt different than when she had come in. The same white fluorescent lights hung above. The same row of doors punctuated the walls. The same scent of industrial strength hand sanitizer hung in the air. But somehow, it was different.

The right wheel of the wheelchair squeaked at one particular point of its rotation. It was rhythmic. It was soft. And soon it began to hypnotize Mary while the nurse followed two steps behind.

Squeak.

Squeak.

Squeak.

She focused on the noise and tried to imagine what the house would be like when they got there. Sam was out visiting a friend but he said he'd be home when they got there. Ashley should be waiting outside to bring them home. The whole family. All together just like when they were young.

But something felt different.

Squeak.

Squeak.

Squeak.

It was his face. Greg's. That look they shared before he begrudgingly climbed into the wheelchair. His eyes shot beams of anger, but the skin around them trembled like a young boy before his first day of school. Nervous. Scared. Afraid.

Squeak.

Squeak.

Squeak.

The elevator ride was quiet. The nurse didn't say a word. Neither did she. Neither did Greg. Finally, they reached the ground floor, walked through the lobby, and reached the front door.

"This good enough?" asked Greg over his shoulder.

"This'll do," said the nurse.

Mary turned around and thanked him. It was strange to have such an intimate relationship with someone you'll never see again.

This man helped Greg to the bathroom. He checked on him when he woke up. He made sure Greg ate well and got his pills. And now he nodded to her, took the handles on the back of the wheelchair, and exited their lives.

The chair continued to squeak as he faded into the distance.

Automatic doors welcomed them to the world outside. It had only been a few days, but Mary wondered how the wind felt on Greg's skin. He probably didn't even notice. They looked back and forth around the entrance to the hospital. A short half-circle acted as the pickup point. One way in, one way out. The air was cool but not cold. The sun had to be around somewhere.

Ashley's sedan finally appeared in the pull-through drop off point. The passenger side window rolled down.

"What took you guys so long?" she asked. "Did you crawl down or something?"

Greg walked up to the car and climbed into the back seat. Mary sat in front. Ashley looked back and forth waiting for a response.

"Not now, please," said Mary.

Ashley shrugged, put the car in gear, and pulled forward.

At first, Mary fought the idea of not driving. Was it stubbornness? Was it self-pity? Or was it simply not wanting to let go of a part of her life? Probably a mix of all three. Of course, she understood a lot better once she got lost on the way home from the grocery store. The streets, the houses, even the elementary school that she had known for years looked different. *Were* different. There's a difference between not recognizing something and having it change form altogether. Of course, she'd never explain it to Greg this way, but that's what it was. She had to relearn what everything looked like every day. New associations. New representative lines of thought. Every day.

And now, as they drove home from the hospital, there were more differences. Where were they? It was a straight shot down Calumet, then to Taft, and then they'd be home. But every turn Ashley took with no more thought than you'd give to a sneeze seemed wrong. Mary wouldn't say anything. She never did. It doesn't feel good to be wrong, even if you're just reporting changes that are outside of your control. This didn't change the fact that generally accepted ideas of right and wrong were decided by the majority, not by personal experience. And she hadn't found herself with enough votes to prove herself right in these disagreements for quite a while.

More funny looking houses. More strange looking street corners. And then finally, they pulled up to a house that looked close enough to the one she shared with her family since long before they finally got access to cable television.

"Well?" asked Ashley.

Mary pulled her consciousness back into the car and realized the conversation was waiting on her. Had Ashley asked her a question? Had Greg? She looked between them as they sat in Ashley's car in their driveway. Better say something. There's really only one safe option.

"No," said Mary.

Ashley glanced in the backseat and then back to her mother. She shrugged.

"Alright. Suit yourself," she said.

Mary opened her door and helped Greg out of the back.

"I was surprised," he said as Ashley pulled away.

"What?"

"That you didn't want to go over there for dinner."

Oh. That made sense. Just roll with it.

"You need your rest," she said.

"I'm not a cripple," he said.

"I know, honey. I know."

Mary released her grip on her husband's bicep and let him walk up the two steps to the front door. She held a hand out behind him but realized babying him might hurt a little more than a fall right now. He opened the door and she followed behind. She started to whistle for the dog and then she remembered.

It felt so empty. This house. Even with Greg home. Sam obviously hadn't made it back in time. She had imagined it would burst with life as soon as Greg got home. Music would spring from the walls and color would shine through the paint.

But it didn't. Instead, it felt just as sterile as the hospital. The wind moaned on the other side of the windows. Greg walked to the table and pulled out a chair.

It squeaked.

She didn't want the fragility of the hospital here. In her personal space. She had to do something so she started to clean. She didn't know what else to do. She couldn't help her husband with his heart or his job or anything else but she could fold the blanket on the couch. She could grab the pile of mail from the small table next to the closet. So she did. And when she approached the kitchen table she noticed that these small tasks, even though they were as much as she could do, they weren't going to get her husband's head up out of his hands. So she set the mail next to him and hoped that maybe there was good news hidden somewhere in there.

He looked up at her after she stood back up.

"These have been waiting for you," she said.

He looked at her for another moment but she turned away. She couldn't see that face from the hospital room again.

Greg readjusted himself and sat up straight.

The chair squeaked on the floor.

He tore open a couple of useless envelopes.

Nothing.

Nothing.

And then he stopped.

"What is it?" she asked.

He continued reading it.

"What is it?"

He set the paper on the table and pulled himself up from the table.

"It's a fucking bill," he said.

This man that had been there for her when she wasn't there for herself. This man that took the livelihood of the house onto his back despite her efforts and inability to help. This man that kept a clear head and was her bright, shining light for years walked into the living room and cycled a series of deep breaths.

But she didn't look.

She didn't follow him.

She was afraid of seeing the inevitable culmination of that peek of fear she saw in the hospital bed. So instead, she walked into the bathroom, took off all her clothes, turned on the shower, climbed in, and cried as quietly as possible behind the shower curtain.

18.

Greg Orders a Cheeseburger

The steps outside the paper mill weren't always this steep. They couldn't have been. How many times had he run up these stairs just a few minutes late for a shift? How many times had he skipped every other one on the way down?

But now, today, a mere three days after getting out of the hospital, here he was taking his first trip up the incredibly steep, incredibly long set of stairs that replaced the ones he had grown accustomed to for the last four decades. His chest hurt. But not *that* kind of hurt. The kind of hurt that comes around when you go for that first jog after taking five years off. The kind of hurt that comes from sitting by the campfire for too long before trying to move the picnic table.

He paused at the top of the mountain and rested one hand on the rusty rail. He loved this big, blue door.

That fucking doctor. He lived in a world of *shoulds* when the real world was one of *have tos*. Greg didn't have the luxury of following medical advice. He didn't have the privilege of worrying about such trivial matters as the health of his heart or the capacity of his lungs. He needed money. Plain and simple. And if he couldn't do the job that he had been doing since he graduated from high school back before cars were invented, he didn't have a chance. What was he going to do? Walk to the grocery and fill out an application along with the 16-year-olds?

So all he had was this big, blue door—the damp scent, the complete absence of natural light outside of the loading dock, the numerous years of his life. This was it. What was he without the paper mill? What would he be without work?

He pulled the handle and walked into the sound of presses, rollers, tow motors, and winders all mixed together into a dull hum with occasional feverish pops. He breathed deep and let the big, blue door swing shut behind him. The sliver of sunlight quickly closed upon itself and he was left with the orange lights along the metal staircase.

He walked through Building 2 into Building 3 and went up another metal staircase. The orange lights gave way to bright, white lights hanging from the incredibly tall ceiling. It had been a while since he stayed away for a week. The mid-day mill operated much the same as it did in the middle of the night, except with the addition of salary-types clogging up the lanes. Sure, he had been offered his own office job years before. And he even thought really hard about making the switch. But in the end, this is where he belonged. This was him.

He looked around Building 3 and recognized every single person. All of them. There were about ten within his line of sight at any time and the movement replaced them every thirty seconds or so. He could probably get away with yelling, "Hey!" and having everybody greet him with a round of applause like a scene in a movie or something.

At the top of the stairs, he opened the door to an office held by one of those salary-types that disappeared every weekend and trusted people like Greg to not burn the place down.

"Hey Chris," said Greg as he poked his head in the door.

A large man, thick brown hair that had obviously been dyed for at least a decade sat behind a terrible desk. How long had they known each other? Probably since before Sam entered high school. Who knows how long ago that was.

"Well holy shit," said Chris Verhagen. He stood up and Greg could almost see his beltline behind the stack of papers, folders, and sloppily labeled blue binders that covered his desk. "I didn't think we let dead guys in here."

Greg walked forward and shook Chris' hand over the desk.

"Well the security isn't exactly tight."

"Take a seat." Chris pointed to the chair as if Greg hadn't worn his own, specialized ass imprint into it long ago. Greg walked around the faded brown leather chair and tried not to look relieved when he sat down.

"Good to see the place is still standing."

"The guys all spent the start of week crying, but they've pretty much forgotten you ever existed by now."

Greg nodded. "Right. Right. Good."

"Really though—" Chris leaned forward and some papers crunched under his forearms. "How are you feeling?"

"Have you ever had a B12 shot?"

"Nope."

"Yeah, me neither. But I imagine this is what it feels like. You should try spending a week in bed. Really charges your battery."

"Yeah I bet. While you were on your little yoga retreat we had a mill to run."

"Well you see, that's what I came to talk to you about. Figured it was time I take a little of that off your hands."

Chris sat back in his chair. He squinted one eye but stayed silent.

"Can't sit around anymore," continued Greg. "I'm going crazy."

"You had a heart attack."

"No shit? When?"

"Do you have a doctor's note?"

"Am I in grade school? Do I really need a letter from mommy saying I can play with the big boys?"

"Greg." His voice was softer now and Greg absolutely hated it. It was his first time hearing Chris' attempt at compassion. He imagined it was the same voice he used when he tucked his daughters in at night back when they were still small enough to be picked up without a groan.

"There are rules for this sort of thing," continued Chris. "Laws, probably. But as far as the mill goes, we can't have one of our workers stroking out on the floor."

"I didn't have a—"

"You know what I mean. Not only is it a liability for the company, it's dangerous. What if you have a 2,000-pound roll in the air and you lose control?"

Greg knew exactly what that would mean. He saw it back in 1993. Paper rolls were stacked end-to-end like soda cans out in the warehouses. These stacks were kept in rows. And when you needed some rolls in a stack at the back of a row, the only thing you could do was disassemble the stacks until you got to it. This happened all day every day. And doing something with this much repetition makes it almost an unconscious act. It's really easy to let your mind wander when you feel like you've done something a million times.

So here's Richard Greene digging his way through row A13 in the warehouse looking for two six-foot rolls of #5 paper. He's moving the ones he doesn't need into the aisle and thinking about lunch or his kids or the Packers game but he's definitely not thinking about Bill Wozniak walking along minding his own business. And when Greene swung around too fast and hit one of his quickly made columns of unnaturally heavy paper rolls, Wozniak didn't have a chance. Luckily earplugs are a safety requirement, so nobody heard the crunch. Greene only heard a short yelp through his temporary fence of stacked paper. Nobody ever discussed what they found when they finally got the roll off him. Nobody asked either.

"Listen, how long's it been?" asked Chris.

Greg shrugged.

"You get a piece of paper from the doctor that says you're good to go, then we're off to the races. But until then…"

The sentence hung between them unfinished. Neither of them wanted to take it to its end.

So instead, Greg stood up and stuck out his hand. They shook. Greg nodded. Chris said he was sorry. And Greg turned around and walked out of his office for the last time. Was it called retiring when you're told you can't come back? Does being three years shy of Medicare eligibility factor into that?

The hum of the mill welcomed him. It had no idea that it would never see Greg Weber again. Greg did, though. He tried to breathe the awful mill air deep into his lungs but couldn't make it past the shallows. And when he opened his eyes he noticed the crowd that had previously awaited his public address had dispersed.

The floor was empty.

No tow motors sped along the corridors.

No salary-types clogged up the lanes.

All the familiar faces, everyone he had worked alongside for years, none of them were anywhere to be found.

He descended the stairs and expected to see a familiar face around every corner, but nobody was there. The whole place emptied out in the five minutes he sat in Chris Verhagen's office. He'd made this walk countless times, but he had never done it alone.

But he was.

For the last time, he was completely alone.

He didn't even notice how hard he was breathing until he pushed through that big, blue door and back into the sunshine. He had hoped the next time he walked out of that door would be after the sun had set. After the end of a full shift. But the sun was essentially in the same position as when he walked in. And his chest hurt again, but now there was a different kind of hurt. Not *that* kind of a hurt. Not even a physical hurt.

He walked down those steep stairs to distract himself from himself.

And then his phone rang.

"Hey Sam," he said.

"Hey! You don't sound too excited to hear from your baby boy."

Greg looked back at the big, blue door at the top of the steps and turned toward the parking lot.

"What's up?" Greg tuned his voice up high. He thought it'd make him sound happier.

"You hungry?"

Greg opened the door to Mary's car and climbed in. He missed his truck.

"Sure."

"Meet you at the Overtime?"

"Sure."

Greg barely noticed the passing scenery as he drove. This would be his first time back at the bar since the night of the accident. It struck him that this should feel weird. But it didn't. Trivialities weren't a luxury he could afford at the moment. The hamburger he was about to order wasn't exactly something he could afford, either.

The parking lot was mostly empty. It's a rare breed that comes to a sports bar when there are no games being played in the middle of a weekday afternoon. People with no other choice. People with nowhere else to go. And as he just learned from ol' Chris Verhagen, there wasn't anywhere else he needed to be at the time.

Sam waved from a table in the corner when Greg walked through the double glass doors. It should be a crime to have a bar without windows. He didn't notice when visiting at night. But the difference between the parking lot and the inside of the bar was, well, night and day.

"How's it feel to be back?" he asked as he pulled out a chair across from his son.

"Honestly? Pretty weird." He spun a coaster with the Overtime's logo on one side beneath his forefinger. "It's always kinda strange but this time—well, you know." He flicked the coaster with his free hand and it spun on its edge.

"Yeah, I know."

A waitress appeared from nowhere and asked what he'd like today.

"Gimme the cheeseburger. Medium. And a Miller Lite."

"I'll get the wings," said Sam. "Extra blue cheese."

The waitress jotted something down on her pad and disappeared as suddenly as she arrived.

"Are you sure about that order?" asked Sam.

"What?"

Sam set the coaster next to his glass of water.

"Dad, you just got out of the hospital."

"Exactly. They don't serve beer and cheeseburgers in there."

Sam put his hands up and shook his head.

Greg couldn't believe the bar wasn't playing music. If you're not going to play the sound of a game, at least turn on the radio or something for crying out loud.

"So." Sam paused. He looked as uncomfortable as Greg felt. "How's it going with Mom?"

"It's fine."

"Dad." He wiped a hand over his mouth. "How's it going?"

Greg sat back in his chair and shrugged. "I mean, you know, not good." He looked up and caught Sam's glance. He shrugged again. "It's good that I can stay home with her now. She doesn't have to be alone staring at a wall the whole day. But I gotta work. You know? I don't have enough to retire."

"And the surgery."

Greg sighed. He looked over his shoulder and saw the waitress returning with his beer.

She slid it in front of him. He wrapped his hand around it like a gun. They sat in the unnatural silence for a bit.

"It seems to be going fast."

Greg looked up. "Huh?"

"Mom. Her, y'know, brain. It's a lot worse than when I saw her last."

Greg shrugged. "We just kinda take it day by day."

"Dad?" Another pause. "You're—"

"Here you go." A cheeseburger with a mountain of fries on the side slid in front of him. Steaming chicken wings slid across the other side of the table with an extra paper boat and two ramekins of blue cheese.

Greg thanked her and stared at the pile of hot, greasy deliciousness. His hand continued to grasp the cold pint glass of beer. He inhaled the steam and felt it enter his lungs. A week of that hospital slop. He had reheated better meals in the microwave at work. Sam seemed to either have forgotten what he was going to say or decided against finishing his sentence. It would come out if it needed to. Greg continued staring at the plate of food in front of him.

An image of Mary sitting alone at the kitchen table flashed through his mind.

"Ah shit," he said, and then slid the plate and beer over to his son. "Just lemme have a couple of those wings and we'll call it even."

19.

Ashley Makes a Couple Calls

Surely there was something better to sell grocery store meat on than Styrofoam. Like what? Cardboard? That'd just soak up all the blood and fall apart. Maybe just the plastic? Everything was in plastic these days. Well yeah, because it's reliable. And everything's bad for the environment when you get down to it. You kind of have to kill yourself if you really want to be eco—

"Well hey there stranger."

Ashley dropped the tray of ground beef back onto the refrigerated shelf and shot upright. She turned around, trying to catch her breath, to find Paula Olson standing behind a shopping cart of her own.

"You scared the shit out of me," said Ashley.

"You were really giving that meat a once-over."

Ashley nodded. "Yeah. Yeah I was kinda in a zone there."

"Trying to figure out its name or something? Some kind of séance?"

Ashley looked to her left where Noah examined the back of a bag of chips. Was he thinking about plastic, too? Sadie kicked the air behind the cart, her legs dangling from her seat behind the handlebar.

"I was just about to ask you what you were up to," said Ashley.

"You should've. Really go for that *dummy* vibe."

"Surely you're here for groceries and not just to roast me."

Paula looked down into her cart. A loaf of white bread sat lonely toward the front of the rolling metal basket.

A chill rolled off the meat cooler and wrapped itself around Ashley's arms, making the hair stand on end. A shiver ran down her back.

"I don't know, I—" Paula looked around the end caps as if the rest of her sentence sat on a shelf. Turned out it was just a difficult sentence to push out. "I just kinda thought you could use a distraction."

Ashley and Paula had paired off together. So had Darren and William.

"From what?" Ashley wrapped her fingers around the handle of the shopping cart in an effort to warm them up.

"Well, y'know." Paula glanced at Sadie.

Ashley followed her glance to her own daughter. Little Sadie. Three years old. Started sleeping through the night almost immediately. She was a dream baby, especially compared to the nightmare that was Noah's first few years. She sat quietly in the seat on the back of the cart, looking around and waiting for what happened next.

"No, I don't know," said Ashley.

Paula sighed. "Darren's girlfriend," she said quietly.

Ashley's fingers tightened around the handle of the shopping cart. His fucking *what*?

"His what?"

Paula's eyes flashed wide. "You didn't…?"

"Did you say his girlfriend?"

Paula nodded.

Noah broke his leg. Not there in the grocery store, but the previous year. Ashley wasn't there so she could only piece together what happened through Noah's rambling explanation and the story from Miss Cross, who shouldn't have let him on the monkey bars in the first place. The actual mechanics of what he was doing, how he landed, and who was around when his tibia just couldn't stand the pressure wasn't important. She had been more fascinated by what happened immediately after. As the story goes, he fell. He says he was upside-down, Miss Cross says he was swinging by his hands, but that didn't matter. He fell. He fractured his shin. And it hurt like hell.

But then he stood up. Miss Cross assumed he was fine because what five-year-old boy stands up on a broken leg? He took two steps before collapsing back to the wood chips and letting the tears roll.

Her little man. Walking on a broken leg. And when she asked him why he didn't just stay on the wood chips from the start, he said:

"I didn't want people to feel bad."

She still cried, a year later, when she thought about it.

And she thought about it now—standing next to the meat section of the grocery store. Paula had this look on her face like she expected Ashley to melt down, so Ashley did the opposite.

She smiled. Her clasped hands tightened around the handle of the grocery cart until her fingernails dug into her palms. But she smiled.

"Huh. How about that?" she said. Why would she be mad? She had ended it with him. It had been a full year. Sure, they weren't legally divorced and her driver's license still said Ashley Wolff—still had his last fucking *name*—but why would she be mad? She didn't have the right. And even though these thoughts flashed through her head and she knew every single one of them to be true, her hands squeezed around the shopping cart handle like she was hanging off the edge of a skyscraper.

But she thought of Noah. Five years old and trying to walk on a broken leg.

I didn't want people to feel bad.

So she smiled and said a few more sentences to Paula to put some space between the end of the conversation and the news. Who knew what they hell they were. Then finally, mercifully, she could say goodbye and go somewhere else to process the fact that Darren was with another woman and she couldn't really be mad about it.

"Alright then. I should be going," said Ashley.

Paula walked along to grab something to put on her bread and Ashley stumbled forward in a daze. How are you supposed to react when you don't even know how you feel? She knew that she felt *some*thing, but it was jumbled. One emotion mixed into another until it was unrecognizable.

She continued on like this for maybe thirty seconds until one of Sadie's swinging feet hit her in the hip and she suddenly became aware of the store around her. The bright white lights above. The soft music playing from invisible speakers. The other shoppers trying to guess their future moods by purchasing specific foods. And most importantly, the absence of her son.

"Noah?" she asked the general area. She turned back to where he had been inspecting chips, but who knows how long ago that was. The fingers still clutching the cart went numb. For all she knew, she might have stopped breathing altogether. She never understood irrationality until she became a mother. Irrationality is what told her that because her son was out of sight, there was a 100% possibility that he was wrapped head to toe in duct tape and rolling around the back of a conversion van going 100 miles an hour down the highway. And it was all her fault.

She worked to swing the shopping cart around but the cooler in the middle of the aisle, full of discount yogurts and cheese, blocked her way. The rage building inside her filled her muscles with hydraulic fluid which would have made throwing the cart through the wall surprisingly easy. But instead, she grabbed Sadie under her arms, lifted her out of the seat, and power walked back toward the chip aisle.

Her feet slapped loudly against the scuffed white tile. She swung her head around the display of on-sale tortilla chips that Noah had just been inspecting to see an empty aisle. Her chest froze over.

She called his name and didn't like the way her voice sounded. Strained. Scratchy.

Frantic.

She began jogging. Sadie bounced from her hip but didn't utter a single protest to what was undoubtedly an uncomfortable ride.

Cereal aisle.

Baking aisle.

Soup aisle.

They were all empty.

She looked back toward the meat section and didn't see anybody. No shoppers, no employees, no Noah.

"Noah!"

No longer a question.

Wolves don't howl to find their pack. They howl to tell the pack how to find them.

She started running. Her feet slapped even harder against the floor creating a war drum of panic.

Household cleaner aisle.

Toiletries aisle.

All completely empty.

And finally the freezer section. A small lump of a person stood on the far end of the aisle huddled against the glass door.

"Noah!"

He looked over. She could see his red cheeks from thirty feet away.

"Are you alright?" she asked as she ran up to him.

He rubbed his cheek and smiled.

"I'm fine, Mom." He stood next to a frosted-over freezer door. Bags of frozen peas, corn, and broccoli sat on shelves. She could see them through the face prints melted into the frost.

I didn't want people to feel bad.

Ashley swallowed her tears and forced a smile. She rubbed her free hand over the top of his head.

"Good. Good," she said. "Let's go home."

"Where's the cart?" he asked.

"Let's go home."

She took her son's hand in hers and noticed that Sadie was getting heavy in her other arm. She ignored it. They walked along the front of the store until they reached the checkout lanes. All empty. Every aisle empty.

She didn't have time to think about it so they walked outside and straight to her car.

It was all automatic. Her shaking hands buckled Sadie into her car seat in back. Noah climbed into the front. Ashley walked around her side, buckled herself in, hit two quick buttons and all of a sudden the metallic ring of a phone call played through the car speakers.

She realized what was happening after the second ring and tried to undo what her hands had done, but the shaking made her too inaccurate to cut the call off in time.

"Ashley?" came a voice through the speakers.

"Daddy!" said Noah.

"Hey bud! How's it going?"

"Good! We're at the grocery store."

"Is your Mom there?"

"Yeah," said Ashley. She cleared her throat. "Yeah I'm here."

"What's up?"

Goddamn these hands, she thought. Disappearing children. New girlfriends. Tangled emotions. And now the pressure of a weighted silence that gets heavier every second. Just say something. Just say something.

"We're having dinner," she said. She glanced to her right at Noah. Smiling. Waiting.

I didn't want people to feel bad.

"You wanna stop by?" she asked.

"Yeah!" said Noah.

"Oh man, that sounds great," said Darren. "But really, big guy, I can't tonight. I have some plans."

I bet you do, thought Ashley.

"Oh," said Noah. "Oh okay."

"Well hey Ashley, why don't you give me a call later?"

"Alright Darren next time," she said and ended the call. Her phone lit up the otherwise dark car. She could add disappointing her son to the list of tonight's accomplishments.

She should have put the car in reverse and gotten the hell out of there but she hesitated. Noah continued looking at her glowing phone. She could sense the disappointment. She could feel it.

"Do you want to call your uncle and see if he wants to come over instead?" she asked.

A slow smile grew across his face and he nodded.

20.

Sam Stands in the Spotlight

Your whole life becomes plans when you're in a different city. What are you going to do all day? Who are you going to see? What are you going to eat? And as Sam sat on the couch at his parents' house, he had no plans. It didn't really bother him. The whole point of coming back was to not have plans and spend time at home, he guessed. But that didn't help the fact that he wanted more than anything to get out of the house. To go see some old friends. But he didn't know where to start. So instead he sat on the couch with his phone on the table next to him. Just hoping it would ring.

And then it did.

"Hello?" he said.

It was his nephew. And he invited Sam to dinner. Boredom trumped confusion and he agreed before he remembered the broken car that started right up. Chalk it up to hometown weirdness.

So he requested a rideshare and was soon knocking on his sister's door.

"Uncle Sam!" yelled Noah when he opened the door.

"Hey bud. How's it going?"

"Dad couldn't come so Mom said I could call you."

Sam nodded. "Nothing wrong with second best. Where is she, by the way?"

"In here. Come on."

Noah led him by the hand through the doorway, past a pile of shoes, and into the kitchen. He expected to smell frying vegetables. Or melted cheese. Or some form of food in some stage of preparation but for all he could tell, the kitchen was just a normal kitchen. No food of any sort.

Ashley walked in from the short hallway to the right.

"Hey Sam."

He held his palms up and looked around the kitchen.

"No food?"

"No gift?" she replied.

"Gift?"

"It's customary for adults to bring other adults a small token of their appreciation when they're invited to dinner. Wine is popular. Some bring bread."

"Well I didn't realize we were having a formal dinner party. I'll be right back with my tuxedo before we eat. Hey speaking of which, no food?"

"No gift?"

They stared at each other for a moment. Sam slowly began to wonder what in the hell was going on.

"We didn't get anything from the grocery store," said Sadie. She peeked around the corner of the hallway.

"Oh hey princess. Didn't see you there."

"We had food," said Noah. He moved around and stood directly in front of Sam. "But we left it there. At the store."

Sam looked up to his sister. "Oh yeah?"

She shrugged. "Pizza should be here any minute."

And then the doorbell rang.

"Pizza!" yelled Noah before he ran to the front door.

"Does he have cash or something?" asked Sam.

"I paid online, dummy." Then over her shoulder, "set it on the table."

Noah did as he was told and helped his sister climb into a chair. Ashley grabbed a small stack of plates from the cupboard and dealt them out around the table like playing cards.

"Uncle Sam?" said Sadie, her head barely visible above the table.

"Yeah?"

"Why are you here?"

He grabbed a slice from the box and set it on the plate.

"Do you mean in this house? Or in a philosophical questioning of existence type of way?"

"Philos-phical?"

"Sam, don't confuse the kid," said Ashley.

"Well, honey, your brother invited me over for dinner."

"But you don't come over for dinner…before?"

"Well…" Sam reached over and snagged the slice of pizza from Noah's hands and took a bite of it. "Your brother never calls me anymore." He dropped the slice back on Noah's plate. "Kind of hurts my feelings, to tell you the truth."

"What?" asked Noah. He looked between his Mom and his uncle.

"He's kidding, honey," said Ashley. Then she slapped Sam across the shoulder.

Noah laughed, but Sadie kept looking at Sam. He leaned toward her.

"I live far away. It's not easy for me to come over too much. But I think about you little dudes all the time."

Sadie giggled and said *Dudes* to herself.

The pizza was cold as soon as they opened the box, but that didn't matter. They didn't stop digging into it until the only thing left was a large grease stain and the little plastic table that keeps the box from squishing the center of the pizza. Clean-up took approximately thirty-five seconds and then the kids were hypnotized by a TV show staffed exclusively by helium-voiced aliens.

She didn't say much throughout dinner. Ashley. Well, besides to give him some shit every once in a while. She usually held court over her family and dominated conversations. But tonight she chewed her pizza, and that was just about it.

"What's up with you?" he asked. They were sitting back at the table. A vague scent of tomato sauce and cheese hung in the air.

She sat back into her chair. Arms crossed. Legs crossed. Eyes on the table.

"Did you really invite Darren over tonight?"

She looked up. Opened her mouth. And then looked toward the living room.

"I'm here, right? I'm saying words out loud?"

She sighed.

"We broke up like a year ago," she said.

He nodded. That was old news.

"It was my decision. I thought it was for the best. Break it off before we get all resentful. It was going down that path. I knew it. We still loved each other but—I don't know. It just wasn't there anymore. Whatever it is, it wasn't there. And that's how it starts. First you lose that, whatever it is. And then you get annoyed. And then you get resentful. Can you imagine what it would've been like growing up if Mom and Dad didn't like each other?"

He couldn't. In fact, he had measured every relationship he'd ever had against his parents. Greg had lost his cool with Sam. And that's only because he had given him every reason to do so. But he had never seen his Dad raise his voice to his mother. Not once. He couldn't speak to this magical *It* that Ashley seemed to be fixated on, but his parents never grew resentful. Never became annoyed with each other. And if they had, it was buried between their bedroom walls. So instead of answering his sister, he shrugged.

"Me neither. But I'm sure it's not great. Two separate houses are easier to explain than resenting each other."

The high-pitched sounds from the next room continued. He could only imagine the colorful blasts of light that stimulated every section of their little, growing brains. But out here, in the kitchen, a singular light above the table cast a vaguely yellow tint across the room. Being lit from above—it made you look sick. Like your eyes were slowly sinking back into your head.

"Yeah," he said. "I mean, but this was a year ago."

"He has a girlfriend," she said suddenly.

"Okay."

"And I care." She dropped her arms to her sides and let them hang like dead meat. "I don't know why I care but I do. Like, a lot."

"Do you want me to kick his ass?"

She let her head fall back until all he could see was her chin.

"Ugh, I'm not kidding, Sam."

"Neither am I."

She dropped her chin and looked him in the eyes. "No, I don't want you to kick his ass."

They listened to the overwhelming sounds from the other room, slightly muffled by the wall separating them.

"Jeez that moon is bright," she said.

He looked over his shoulder to the back door. What looked to be a spotlight lit up the entire backyard. He heard a slight squeak behind him as Ashley stood up. He followed her out the back door.

"Jesus. Are there two moons or something?" he asked as he stepped through the door.

A small deck, only a foot off the ground, acted as a giant step to get you from the backyard into the house. She stood on the edge of it like a stage. The moonbeam cast a shadow behind her, dark as a moonless midnight. Gravity felt weak. He became slightly light-headed. It was too bright to be night and his body didn't know how to deal with it. He held a hand in front of his eyes and tried to steal a peek of the moon through his fingers, but his squint was essentially the same as closing his eyes. He gave up and walked around his sister so he could face her with his back to the moon. Her face glowed. His looked like death.

"What are we gonna do about Mom and Dad?" he asked.

"We? What are *we* going to do?" She waited for a reply that didn't come. "I've been here. For all these years. I've been doing something this whole time. So I don't know what the hell you expect from me beyond being the constant source of support while their wayward son rambles around the other side of the country living his life blissfully ignorant of the deteriorating situation at home."

That came out a little too perfect. It seemed a little too rehearsed for his liking. He wanted to respond. That was how conversations worked, after all. One person shits all over the other one, and then that person defends himself. But the words weren't there. The counterarguments didn't exist. Because deep down, he knew she was right. So instead he stood there with his back to the moon and watched his sister's face—tight lips, taut cheeks, rigid brow—as the spotlight shooting from the moon slowly dimmed until he could no longer see the disappointment. The anger.

He sighed.

She turned around.

He watched as she walked inside.

She closed the door behind herself, and he walked around to the front to call a ride back to his parents' house.

But instead he just kept walking down the sidewalk. It's not far. He had just pushed a damn car almost all the way there. Something extinguished the moon, but the streetlights picked up the slack. Orange light dug its way through claw-like tree branches, mostly bare except the few remaining dying leaves. A wind picked up. He noticed it had some teeth to it so he stuck his hands into his pockets. These trees weren't large enough to climb when he was a kid. Now they reached the streetlights.

And that was when he saw something move through the dead zone between two streetlights. The shadows draping off the trees combined to negate the orange light. Maybe a few properties up. It was larger than a rabbit and smaller than a child. It moved with a familiar abbreviated gait. Something hung from its head.

Ears.

The long ears of a beagle as it searched the ground for crumbs. A leash scraped the ground behind it.

"Al!" said Sam.

The figure stopped. Sam started to run.

The empty street exploded to life as the loudest car he ever heard blasted its way down the road. The headlights shined directly in his face and blew past as quickly as they arrived. And by the time his eyes had a chance to readjust to the darkness, it was gone. The dog that gave his Dad a heart attack because it had gotten out.

Sam spent a few minutes looking around where he thought Al had been sniffing but became quickly aware that he was digging through the bushes of a total stranger in a small town at night.

He returned to the sidewalk and walked back to his parents' house with absolutely nothing to show for the night.

21.

Mary Visits the Doctor

It's morning. Mary wrapped herself tighter into the blanket and rolled over. There's a lot of bed. A flash of concern ran through her before she remembered—Greg's at work. He's always at work. She almost laughed at how she could forget the most basic aspects of their lives, but it wasn't funny. You had to remember the start of the joke to get the punchline, and she laughed a lot less these days.

Sunlight fell through the windows and warmed the blanket at the bottom of the bed. It felt nice. At least it would be impossible to forget that.

What was the point in getting up? She used to drag herself out of bed before dawn. She liked to get to the school early. And this was even more of a trick considering she volunteered to chaperone early-morning detention more than any other teacher. In all honesty, it was the easiest one. The students that managed to make it in were practically dead in their chairs. The afternoon detention is where you saw all the fireworks.

But now, what was the hurry? To go sit in the kitchen in silence and crunch her way through a bowl of cereal?

And that was all it took. Any comfort from the morning sun and the warmed blankets was quickly eclipsed by a screaming hunger. So she pushed the blankets off herself. After a quick stop in the bathroom she opened the bedroom door and walked into the kitchen.

Someone stood by the coffee maker next to the sink and another person looked up at her from the table. There was something familiar about them.

But they had no faces.

She could tell they were men. And they sure seemed comfortable. But a vague blur covered their heads where their eyes, noses, and mouths should be.

What the hell were they doing here?

"Good morning," she said and walked around the table.

She stared at the man sitting in one of her chairs as she passed. He turned his head briefly toward her but made no other movement.

She walked to the cupboard and grabbed a box of shredded wheat. A clogged pipe let loose and it came back to her in a wave.

The dog. The accident. The heart attack.

"How'd you sleep?" asked the man by the coffee maker.

Mary smiled and nodded.

"Good, good," she said. She tried her best to sound casual. Mary paused briefly in front of the sink. Another brain clog hiccupped.

The hospital. His return. His job.

Mary turned back around and smiled at her husband, standing next to the coffee maker. The blur faded like blown steam.

Sam crunched his way through a piece of toast at the table and Greg sipped from his mug in the corner by the sink. Mary grabbed a bowl and made her way to the table where she sat across from Sam. Her surprise settled, the embarrassment was fading, and excitement at not facing another day of staring at a wall hoping for a car to pull in the driveway started to grow. She didn't care when she noticed she hadn't grabbed the milk from the refrigerator. The cereal would be dry, but that's okay. She had company.

"Well, what are we going to do today?" she asked.

Greg upended his mug and set it in the sink.

"I'm going to the social security office for some disability," said Greg.

"And we're going to the doctor," said Sam.

Mary started to ask the question spilling from her mind but closed her mouth. It was obvious the appointment wasn't for him.

"Bill next door's letting me take his truck. He asked if I still had my license," said Greg. "Can you believe that? Made me show it to him and everything."

Mary bit into a mouthful of dry shredded wheat and it sapped every drop of saliva from her mouth. She crunched and crunched and crunched.

Greg walked around the table and kissed her on the cheek.

"I'm sorry I can't go today. We gotta get some kinda income coming in around here."

She set her spoon down. "Don't worry about me. We'll be fine."

"Yeah," said Sam. "We'll be fine. Have fun at social security."

Greg put a finger to his head and cocked his thumb. "Yeah, can't wait."

Her husband walked through the living room and out the front door.

Sam stood up and took his plate to the dishwasher. He turned around and leaned on the counter. It was quiet. No, it was silent. No wind outside. No movement inside. It was as if the whole world had paused and the only things that could move were the eyes inside Mary's head. She quickly took a bite of cereal to make sure she wasn't right. The crunch erupted through the silence.

Another half hour later they were on the road. Sam drove her car and followed directions on his phone. The world was becoming so amazing. Perfect timing for her brain to slowly start backing out of it.

These roads were familiar. They had been there since she was a kid. She drove down them her whole life. But still, she didn't know which way to go. She couldn't remember where the grocery store used to be before it moved to somewhere else. She closed her eyes.

Eventually she felt the car come to a stop and heard the engine shut off.

"Here we are," said Sam.

Mary took a deep breath and climbed out of the car. They walked through the front door, checked in with the receptionist, and waited about ten minutes.

"Mrs. Weber?"

Sam stood and helped her up, but he didn't follow her into the door to the left of the check-in desk.

"How are you today?" asked the nurse. Mary wondered if they knew each other. They had to be about the same age.

"Good," she lied.

The nurse led Mary into an office. A large desk sat in the middle of the room, piled high with papers, a picture frame, and an unlit lamp. There was no scale, no sink, and no firm bed covered in paper. This was the doctor's actual office. Not an examination room.

"Take a seat," said the nurse. He'll be right in."

Mary did as she was told. This would be her third time seeing Dr. Lee in his office. It had been unnerving the first time—as if she had progressed past the need for a physical examination into something more serious. But now it was comforting. A conversation felt like a conversation in here.

The door behind her opened quickly.

"Mrs. Weber," he said as he swung around the side of the chair and offered his hand. She shook it without standing up and he retreated to his side of the desk.

"You weren't waiting long, were you?" he asked.

Mary shook her head.

"Good. Good. So, another year another meeting, eh?"

She smiled with half her mouth and nodded.

"So, how are you?"

"I'm good."

"Hey," he leaned forward. "I'm your doctor. I know that we always tell everyone we're good when we're asked regardless of how we're actually doing. But you can tell me the truth." He sat back and said quieter, as if to himself: "You actually *have* to tell me the truth."

She nodded.

"Last time we met you were getting confused. Forgetting things. How's that going?"

Everyone knew. It wasn't a secret. But saying it out loud made it more real, for some reason. Nightmares only exist in your head. And unless she spoke it, so did this.

"It's...it's okay."

"How's it going at home? Still quiet?"

Mary wrapped her hands around the opposite biceps and rubbed her thumbs over her shirt.

"I...uh—" She swallowed and closed her eyes for a moment. "I lost the dog," she said.

Dr. Lee nodded but didn't say anything.

"I was gonna walk her. Something happened. I don't know. I don't even realize it half the time. Still looking for her and all that."

He nodded again.

"I'm going to tell you three words," he said. "I'd like you to repeat them back to me, and then I'll ask you to repeat them again later. Okay?"

Mary nodded. Her eyes felt heavy.

Come on, you can't cry in the doctor's office.

"Couch, afternoon, apple."

"Couch, afternoon, apple," she said.

Dr. Lee smiled and nodded. Then he stood up and walked behind Mary to a filing cabinet along the wall. He pulled open a drawer, flicked through some folders, and pulled out a piece of paper.

"Here. Scoot forward," he said. He set the piece of paper on her side of the desk and returned to his. "I want you to draw a clock."

Mary leaned forward in her chair to the blank sheet of paper. He clicked a pen and set it in front of her.

"What kind of clock?"

"With arms. Draw it out and set it to 20 after eight."

Mary leaned forward and grabbed the pen. A clock? That was easy. She'd been looking at them all her life. She'd never been much of an artist but anybody could draw a clock.

She started by tracing the outside. She dragged her hand in one continuous motion until the line connected back to itself. Then she went through and wrote out the hours.

This is ridiculous, she thought.

She put the pen to the paper but didn't move it.

Which hand was supposed to point out the hour?

Large?

Small?

She froze in place as she stared at the clock. The numbers she had written were suddenly nonsensical. Not only were they not in order, they weren't numbers at all. Random symbols filled the drawing and began moving around the page. How was she supposed to tell time when the numbers weren't numbers and they moved to different parts of the clock?

She stared.

The numbers continued changing and moving.

"Mrs. Weber?"

Which hand was supposed to point out the hour?

Large?

Small?

"Mary."

She looked up.

"Let's see what you've got."

She looked down, quickly sketched two arms on the clock, and handed it over to Dr. Lee.

He studied it for a moment before looking back up to her.

"Can you tell me the three words I asked you to remember?"

A drop of sweat dragged along the side of her face. Her heart beat like she had run up a flight of stairs.

"I…umm—"

There were three of them. Words. One was food.

But what were they?

Which hand was supposed to point out the hour?

"Is your husband here with you today?"

She looked up. "What?"

"Mr. Weber. Is he waiting for you out there?"

She shook her head. "Oh, no. My son is here with me. Sam."

"Would you mind if I went to get him?"

"Not at all."

And then he disappeared. A minute later, two sets of footsteps approached from behind, but she didn't turn around.

"Hey Mom," said Sam as he sat in the empty chair to her right.

Had that been there this whole time?

"This is the third year we've been having these meetings," said Dr. Lee. He spoke mostly to Sam. "And these tests aren't conclusive, but they are our best window into the progression of Mary's condition."

He paused briefly and glanced at Mary. She nodded. Back to Sam:

"The ability to plan and carry out specific tasks is what we refer to as executive functioning. The clock exercise is a way to test that." Dr. Lee handed a piece of paper over the desk to Sam. "Improper placement of numbers, hands, or shape of the clock are indicators that executive functioning is compromised, and to which degree."

Sam glanced at the paper and then to his left at Mary.

"This, along with other memory tests, help us understand how quickly things are progressing," continued Dr. Lee. "Have you noticed a decline in her ability for recollection?"

Sam set the paper on the desk in front of him and scratched the back of his head. He glanced over for a moment before turning back to the doctor.

"Well, yeah," he said.

Mary stared at the drawing on the table as Sam and Dr. Lee continued to talk. The figures had stopped moving and again looked like numbers. She could see them there—one all the way through twelve—but there was no order. It was as if they had simply frozen after mixing themselves around and gone to sleep. She noticed the frame of the clock was hardly an oval, let alone a circle.

Did she really think that was a perfect clock when she handed it to him?

Which hand was supposed to point out the hour?

Dr. Lee's voice cut back into her attention.

"That's not the easiest process."

She looked up.

"What?"

"Sam here was telling me Mr. Weber's working on getting disability." He shook his head. "They don't make that as easy as it should be."

She shrugged. The two men stood up.

"That's it? We're done?"

Sam leaned over and put a hand on her shoulder.

"Yeah, yeah we're good to go."

How long had she been here? What could be accomplished in just a few minutes?

Realistically, she didn't care. It hadn't been much, but it was exhausting. She pushed herself from the chair and followed the doctor back into the hallway. Sam walked a few steps behind her.

Dr. Lee led them back into the reception area.

"And good luck with the disability. I know that process can be a long one," he said.

Mary nodded. "Thanks."

They walked past the reception desk and the young woman sitting behind the counter stood up.

"Excuse me, Mrs. Weber?"

Mary stopped and turned toward her.

"We tried running your insurance while you were back there and, well, it didn't go through. Did you get a new plan or something?"

Mary shook her head. "No, no it should be the same."

"Oh, okay." She sat back down. "Well, I'll give it another try but if it doesn't work we're going to have to send you a bill in the mail."

Mary nodded again and said, "Oh okay." But what she really wanted to say was *Shit*.

She was tired. She didn't like talking about her memory and she damn sure didn't like to have it on display. Discussing it in the open was like pulling the bandage off a wound and showing it on national TV.

Sam climbed into the driver's seat. Mary pulled on the handle on the other side and the door didn't open. She pulled again. Sam turned the car on and looked over to her. She pulled and pulled but nothing happened even though she could tell the damn door was unlocked. Energy built beneath her ribcage that wanted to cry out in the middle of the parking lot and release the tears and shouts and all the words of frustration that were being kinked in the hose of her mind that built more and more pressure until Sam leaned over and opened the door from the inside.

"I can get it my*self*," she said through the crack of the opened door. She didn't like the anger in her voice, but she couldn't control it. The car dipped in recognition of her sitting down. She closed the door and pulled the seatbelt around herself but it just wouldn't click shut. She stabbed around her left side, waiting for it to find its home but nothing was there. It just wouldn't secure.

Sam reached over and drove it home. The click reverberated through her head.

"I just couldn't find the, uh—" Mary snapped her fingers and rocked forward a little in her chair. "The holster thing. I knew where it was."

"I know Mom. I know," said Sam. He patted her gently on the leg and waited another moment before backing out of the parking spot.

22.

Greg Notices the Birds

"Do I have to be missing a leg or something?" said Greg.

He sat on the business end of a desk in the little cubicle of some asshole named Brandon Beadle. Greg could have done all this online, not that he would have done that anyway. He liked to talk to a person. To their face. That way, when they told him he was ineligible for disability benefits they couldn't just hang up when he told them they were wrong.

"I can't work my job because of a medical condition. Isn't that the exact definition of a disability?"

Brandon Beadle turned up his palms like he had done too many times during this convoluted and annoying process and said, "I'm sorry but the system just isn't approving your situation."

"My situation," said Greg as he stood up. "My situation is only getting worse and the system that's supposed to help during stuff like this doesn't approve of it. Well you know what? Neither do I."

Greg walked out of the cubicle and along the row of identical boxes of people trying to get the same help for different reasons. Were they competing against each other? Is that how it worked? One person with a broken back and six children gets precedence over the old guy with a bad heart and two grown children? Or was it a lottery? Everyone's name gets thrown into a hat and they pick out the people that get to buy groceries without draining their savings account.

He stepped through the door of the social security office down by the courthouse and walked to his car in the massive parking lot. Well, Bill's car. He climbed into the black Chevrolet hatchback and didn't put the key in the ignition.

His heart thudded beneath his old, flannel shirt. And as he had found himself doing more and more since leaving the hospital, he paid attention to it. The length between beats. The strength of each one. He analyzed it for differences. He pictured the actual mechanics of it sending blood throughout his body. Heartbeats were a lot like breath—you don't even notice them until they're hard to come by, or stop coming by at all.

Everything was kind of like that.

He drove home and left the car in Bill's driveway. He knocked on the door and gave him back the keys. Bill started to walk outside to investigate the car—to see if Greg had hit any poles but Greg just kept walking past it, over the grass, and through the front door to his house.

Sam sat at the kitchen table in the same chair as when Greg left.

"Hey Dad."

Greg walked into the kitchen just as Mary came out of the bedroom.

"How'd it go?" he asked.

"Fine. Fine," she said and looked at Sam.

Greg followed her gaze and saw something between them.

"What? What happened?" he asked.

"Nothing. How'd it go at the social security office?" she asked.

"Not great. Now you."

Mary sighed and again looked to Sam. He shrugged.

"They said we should expect a bill in the mail."

"A what?"

"Our insurance didn't go through."

It shouldn't have been much of a surprise. He wasn't at the mill anymore. Why wouldn't they cancel his health insurance? But a surprise isn't any less surprising just because it makes sense. He was so focused on getting everything together for the social security office that something as simple as insurance just didn't cross his mind. But now it did. It crossed his mind in huge, blinking letters and he didn't like what it spelled out.

No checkups for Mary.

No surgery for him.

No help with the most expensive bills that force people in bankruptcy every day.

His heart throbbed in his chest. Greg reached behind him, pulled out a chair from the table, and sat down.

"You okay, Dad?" asked Sam.

"Yeah. I'm fine." Greg leaned forward and buried his face in his hands. There would be no help. No way to pretend everything was going to be alright. And if his heart were to slip up again, it would leave them penniless. They'd have to sell the house just to pay for the sludgy meals that were supposed to give him the strength to recover from coronary bypass surgery. He looked it up. Forty thousand dollars. There goes a large chunk of his retirement savings. He was only two years out, but that goalpost slid further and further toward the horizon. He knew he'd never get there. Any accident would sink them. And now, when he needed it the most, there was no safety net.

Greg breathed a long breath of hot air into his cupped hands and opened his eyes. Mary walked up to him and put her hands on his shoulders. A bubble of anger and frustration was building. He could feel it. She could sense it. You just need to have one thing go your way every once in a while. Just one glimpse of hope would be enough to carry him through to the next day but sometimes the dark of midnight doesn't leave you alone. It was hard not to feel helpless. He couldn't find the motivation. You don't keep digging through the trash when you know there's no food at the bottom.

"I need some air," said Sam. He pushed his chair back and stood up.

Greg looked over at him. He felt his wife's hands on his shoulders but the bubble inside him boiled over anyways.

"You know, I don't understand what you're doing here anyway," said Greg.

Sam stopped and turned around. "What?"

"Some newfound obligation? Guilt? Or maybe some sick morbid curiosity? Help if you're gonna help. Otherwise…"

The words stung his lips on the way out, but he couldn't stop himself. He'd held in every form of disappointment for too long. Did he even believe what he was saying? Or was he just swinging blindly in the dark?

Sam opened his mouth but didn't say anything. Too stunned to speak.

Mary's hands remained on his shoulders but they stopped moving in slow circles.

No birds chirped outside. No cars drove past.

Just silence as Greg's words infected everyone in the room.

Sam turned and walked out the front door.

Greg closed his face within his hands once again and felt Mary leave the room. Being this wrong was uncomfortable for everyone.

Now alone, he found himself with nothing but a year's worth of sadness and regret. The last time he felt like this he woke up in a hospital bed with one less truck. He loved his son. But he sure didn't act like it just then.

The room closed in on him. His breath became short and he was painfully aware of the inefficiencies in his own chest.

Greg stood up. He needed to move around or he'd start ripping handfuls of grey hair from his head. He instinctively walked to the door leading to the garage and grabbed the spare dog leash. He paused and looked down at the black leash with a green, plastic bag wrapped around the looped end. There was always a chance Al would find her way home. He could just open the door one day and there she'd be. But that hadn't happened. Not yet, at least. And it added another layer of pain on top of the almost insurmountable mountain of grief that filled the entire house. So he wrapped the leash around his hand and walked through the garage.

He thought he might see Sam outside, but he didn't. He sighed and started walking down the street just as he had a million times before with Al on the other end of the black leash—straining against her harness and sniffing everything in reach.

But a missing dog was unfortunately a minor issue at the moment. He spun another question over and over in his mind: What the hell was he going to do?

He turned the corner at the end of the block and continued adding to the list of questions to which he just didn't have any answers. Nobody did. And that's why he didn't notice the first bird fall from the sky. He walked along the side of the road twisting and untwisting the leash around his hand, imagining more and more drastic scenarios of his and Mary's future. So when the first bird fell and landed three feet to his right, he just kept walking.

Same with the second and third birds. But Greg just happened to be looking in the spot where the fourth bird fell and he finally stopped walking. He looked around the street and watched as another one fell. And then another.

Soon, an entire flock of birds littered the road. Each one hit the pavement at terminal velocity, which luckily wasn't too fast. They simply plopped onto the pavement and recoiled with a slight bounce. And then they lay still. No longer flapping their wings, soaring above the rooftops.

Twenty. Maybe thirty black birds covered the road around Greg and more were being added every few seconds.

Plop.

Plop.

Plop.

Greg wrapped the leash tighter around his hand and let out a long, slow sigh.

"Goddamn it," he said to no one and stepped around the birds on his way back home.

23.

Ashley and Darren Go for a Walk

It wasn't a nice restaurant, but it was their favorite. Darren and Ashley had been coming here since they started dating a decade earlier. Buonasera served enormous portions of mostly pasta-based dishes and really, you couldn't go wrong with that. It was a poor choice for a first date all those years before—pure gluttony was not a good look for either of them, neither were remnants of sauce on chins and upper lips—but it was comfortable. The quantity balanced out the quality. Plus, Ashley liked the dark dining room. Red votive candle holders projected dancing shadows on the water glasses and tabletop. The red vinyl booths were fifty years old but only the occasional crack gave away their age. People spoke in hushed tones. The clanking of cutlery on plates punctuated the soft traditional Italian music that played through unseen speakers. Ashley didn't think they'd come back here. Not together. But here they were, sitting in one of the old booths, watching the shadows dance around the table and listening to the clanks of forks and knives on plates.

Darren got back to her the day after she called him outside of the grocery store. He wanted to take her up on that dinner offer that she hadn't meant to offer. She suggested they go out. And here they were.

She dug into the giant piece of garlic bread sitting between them in the middle of the table. It was cold, but it was huge.

"What do you think the chances are they get our order right?" asked Darren. He surprised her by putting on a shirt with buttons. A nice blue one.

"Somewhere between *I'll be surprised* and *probably not.*" She chewed a piece of bread and looked at her husband. Still her husband. Legally, anyway. She replayed the excitement in her son's voice when Darren answered the phone. The disappointment on his face when his Dad couldn't come over for dinner. Going out to eat without them was a strange way to make up for it, but she had other ideas.

"Wanna put some money on it?" he asked.

Ashley smiled and stopped picking at the bread. "Alright. They bring out exactly what we ordered and I'll pick up the bill. Any mistake. Any at all, *any* mistake, and it's on you."

"I mean I should get some odds here."

Ashley shrugged. "You wanted to bet. This is the offer."

Darren looked down to the candle for a moment and then back to Ashley.

He reached over the table and they shook hands. He sat back in his chair and looked into his lap for a moment. "This is nice," he said. "You know, I was a little surprised that you called yesterday."

Ashley shrugged.

"And even more surprised that you wanted to come to Buonasera tonight."

"Do you have a girlfriend?"

Darren rocked back in his chair and pushed his eyebrows to his hairline. His mouth hung open a little and he started to slowly move his head from left to right. The pause was long. Too long.

Finally, he said:

"Yeah." The word came out slow, like it had fifteen letters instead of four. He looked down at the table for a moment before again sitting upright. "But why do you care?"

"Darren," she said. "We're still married. You can't just go around dating every girl you meet."

"Are you ready to order?"

They looked up to a young waiter, still in his teens, obviously hating where he was standing.

"Shrimp Florentine and the spinach artichoke dip," said Ashley.

The waiter looked at Darren.

"That's gonna be enough," he said.

The waiter quickly disappeared.

"We're married by paperwork," said Darren. "Nothing else."

"I know. But there are rules, Darren."

"You're the one who ended it. You're the one who didn't want to be married anymore," he said.

"I know." They were dangerously close to causing a scene. The restaurant was quiet, but full of people. Anything louder than a near-whisper was the equivalent of a shout in any other establishment. She grabbed the garlic bread and tore off another chunk.

"So what's the problem then? I can't just stay unsuccessfully married forever."

"I know," she said. She continued crunching softly on the cold bread and looked up to him. "It's just so soon."

He sat forward in his chair with both arms resting on the table. "It's been a year."

Had they sat at this same table on their first date? It looked too familiar. A strange sense of déjà vu ran through her and for a moment she swore his shirt changed back to that terrible red polo he used to wear all the time. He thought it made him look wealthy but it really just made him look like an asshole. But of course she never told him that. And then she looked down and saw that her black shirt had changed to the silk blouse that felt a lot nicer than it looked. She hadn't seen that shirt since Noah was born six years earlier. And all of a sudden they weren't two people trying to figure out how to navigate a failed marriage. They were two strangers that found each other in the pulsating crowd of society. She took a deep breath and watched Darren's red polo fade like a cloud of smoke until he was back in the blue shirt with buttons and she was back in her black shirt.

It felt better to be back in that silk shirt, even if it was just a passing memory. Another thought formed in her head that had been nagging her since she ran into Paula Olson at the grocery store. It sprouted in the confusion of learning Darren's news. And then it was obscured by the anger she felt afterward. But now she could see it. She could see why they were sitting in the restaurant together that night.

They locked eyes over the red votive candle and the cold hunk of garlic bread.

And then the windows exploded as a car blasted through the front wall of the restaurant.

It plowed through two rows of empty tables and came to a stop before hitting the bar. The people sitting in the surrounding booths jumped up and screamed. The manager came out of the back and shouted at the person in the driver's seat. Nobody seemed hurt besides maybe the driver. The constant hum of traffic on the street followed the initial blast of sound, even though most cars were now slowing to get a good look at the carnage just on the other side of the sidewalk.

Ashley and Darren continued looking into each other's eyes.

"I don't want you seeing that woman," said Ashley.

"I don't want to get divorced," said Darren.

Sirens could be heard in the distance, slowly growing louder. Things continued to crash around them as if people didn't see the point of leaving their glasses and plates on their tables. The driver opened the door of the car and the manager could finally focus his shouting. A few people remained inconsolable. Some sobbed. Some screamed. The sirens continued to grow louder.

"I need you to do something for me." Ashley stood up.

She stepped over shards of broken glass toward the car. Darren followed close behind as they walked past the shouting manager and the shattered windshield of the errant vehicle and the smashed tables surrounded by bent forks and partially folded napkins. They stepped through the hole in the front wall and turned down the sidewalk.

The cool night air bristled the hair on the back of her neck. Ashley had a light jacket, but she left it in the restaurant. The sun went down an hour earlier and took every fragment of its warmth with it. There wasn't much of a breeze but the small amount that was there bit into Ashley's arms as she walked through the gathering crowd. Darren continued following behind her. They got through the semi-circle of curious onlookers. They didn't speak. She led and he followed. They walked north down College Avenue and soon he caught up to her as if he knew where she was going.

Ashley operated on instinct. Something told her to get out of that restaurant. Something else told her to turn right. And now she would just have to wait until something else told her she was there.

So they walked.

They walked in silence and in perfect step with each other like choreographed performers on stage. The road behind them became illuminated as red and blue lights danced playfully off the buildings. She was looking for something. She had to find something that would tell her what the next step would be. And it felt good to give up the reins for a moment. She knew she was embarking on an important decision. She could toy with her own heart all she wanted but she would not do that to her children.

And then she noticed her shirt sliding a little easier around her torso. The slight breeze had all but disappeared and the air felt thicker. Warmer. Almost like an early summer evening that was too hot to stay still. She glanced at Darren and saw him looking straight forward, slightly pumping his arms beneath a red polo shirt. She didn't have to look down to know her shirt had become a silk blouse.

The road wound along a small college campus before it funneled itself into a bridge that overlooked the river. It wasn't a beautiful river, but it was a moving body of water. Even the dam looked great at night when compared to traffic lights and empty school buildings.

They were going to the middle of the bridge. It was clear now. This is exactly where they had gone a decade earlier, albeit under different circumstances. It was summer then. It was autumn now. They were in the first stages of falling in love then. They were on the other side of a failed marriage now.

But what was the difference between now and then besides time? Weren't they still the exact same people? They walked side-by-side, not holding hands but not shying away from each other either. Sweat dotted her head as the air continued to warm in remembrance of that night so long ago. Darren made no mention of the change happening around them, if he noticed at all.

They reached the middle of the bridge and stopped without saying a word. Beneath a streetlight, they turned to look over the side. One direction led upstream toward the dam. The other led alongside a park and eventually to a paper mill that no longer employed her father. But it did ten years before. And this moment wasn't separated from that moment. Not right now. That moment and this moment were now *these* moments and Ashley turned to her husband on their first date.

All the promises of the last decade together floated between them. She closed her eyes and remembered the way she felt that first night so long ago—her stomach knotted in anxious excitement. There was something precious between them that she didn't want to break. Everything was so fragile in the first stages of a relationship. But even after years of promises kept and obligations fulfilled, that fragility never really went away.

She opened her eyes and looked at her husband ten years earlier, when he was still this great guy that she didn't want to scare away.

She wrapped her hands around his and took a deep breath of the summer air. It smelled faintly of grass and sunscreen.

"Come here," she said with a smile.

He continued holding her hands as he stepped forward and kissed her underneath the streetlight in the middle of the empty bridge.

24.

Sam Gets an Idea

Good ol' Steve Bauer. He was one of the few people from high school that Sam kept in contact with over the years. Each trip home, each infrequent trip, they got together for at least a burger down at Judd's. And when he walked out of his parents' house a day earlier—after his father told him what was on everybody's mind—he called Steve Bauer as he walked down the road.

"You back in town?" asked Steve.

"Yeah. You free? I need a ride."

Steve lived alone. He inherited a house when his grandfather passed a few years earlier. It was a surprise to everyone, especially his parents. This was the house his father grew up in, after all. And for some reason the will hopped a generation and Steve found himself with a three bedroom, two bath home on the outskirts of the city. Old trees had been allowed to grow to maturity instead of making room for new developments. The road was quiet. So were the neighbors. Steve was the youngest homeowner in the neighborhood by about forty years. And when he picked Sam up on the side of the road and asked what was going on, he simply answered:

"Just wanted to make a visit to your retirement home."

So that's what they did. Night came. He slept in what was once Steve's father's room. And now it was mid-morning the following day and he sat on the couch.

"I gotta head out," said Steve. "You're welcome to stick around if you have nothing else to do."

"You mind dropping me off at the IHOP?"

Steve smiled. "Classy breakfast, eh?"

It wasn't a far drive. Sam soon walked into the tall blue building and the overwhelming scent of maple syrup greeted him as the doors slowly eased themselves shut behind him.

He took a seat in a large booth. The empty bench next to and across from him made it seem even larger. A waitress took his coffee order and promised to return.

Sleep came in short bursts the night before. Greg's words echoed inside his head. What *was* he doing there? Did he think that his mere presence would be enough to fix everything? Was he really that goddamn self-important? And now here he was, waiting on a coffee at the IHOP trying to figure out what the hell he was supposed to do. Maybe he should have considered this before.

Maybe he should have just stayed home.

"Here you go." A cup of coffee slid in front of him. He looked up at a woman probably in her fifties. She smiled warmly. And not a fake smile either. She obviously enjoyed her job. "You ready to order?"

"I'm gonna just drink this for a minute if that's okay." Sam held up the cup of coffee.

She looked around the dining room. It was mostly empty. "Tell you what, you look like you could use this." She set the full carafe of coffee on the table in front of him. "Just go ahead and refill as much as you like. I'll be back in a little bit."

Sam smiled back at her. "Thanks."

She turned and walked away.

Simple kindness. It doesn't seem like much but you can feel it when it's nearby. Sam Weber sat back in the giant, mostly empty booth and took a sip of his coffee despite its extreme heat.

What *was* he doing here?

How was he supposed to help? It's not like he was going to restore her memory. It's not like he could afford to support them while his father was out of work. Sure, he was a nurse, but he couldn't perform coronary bypass surgery.

He sighed and took another sip of his coffee. It was cooling down.

He knew his mother didn't recognize him the other morning. He saw the confusion. And it felt like a kick through his stomach and out his back.

He wanted to help. He needed to. But how?

He pulled a ten out of his pocket and dropped it on the table. Whatever he was supposed to do, it wasn't getting done by sitting here. He walked outside and called a ride.

Fifteen minutes later, he was back home. He stepped out of the car and saw Mary sitting on the front porch. It had to be close to noon so it was about as warm as the day was going to get.

"Hello," she said as he walked up. There was no recognition in her voice and he felt that familiar kick taking out his torso.

"Hey Mom," he said.

She smiled. The kick lost a little power.

"Aren't you chilly out here?" he asked.

She held her face up to the sun and closed her eyes. "It feels good," she said. "I feel good."

She was there. Physically and mentally.

"What are you going to do today?" he asked.

She opened her eyes and turned to him. "Who knows? I'm just enjoying being here right now."

He stepped onto the porch and sat in the chair next to her.

"You should probably go speak to your father," she said.

"Well, to be honest, I think I'd rather sit here right now."

She nodded and patted his thigh.

"He didn't mean it, you know."

"What?"

"Yesterday. Those things he said. He's under a lot of pressure right now." Mary sat back in her chair and put her hands in her lap. "He's got a lot to take care of. I'm no pony ride right now," she said with a smile.

"Does he think I'm mad at him? I'm not mad I—"

"He feels bad. I think he feels bad about a lot of things and that's just thrown on top of the pile."

Sam looked toward the front door but didn't move.

"Just go talk to him. He won't bite. I promise."

You can feel simple kindness when it's nearby.

"Alright." Sam stood up, walked to the door, and paused. "You coming in?"

She shook her head.

"I'm just enjoying being here right now."

He nodded and walked through the door.

Sam smelled the soft sourness of mayonnaise as he walked into the living room. The coffee in his stomach bubbled in recognition of food. His footsteps reverberated as he left the safety of the living room carpet for the tile floor of the kitchen. Greg turned around with a sandwich resting on top of a plate in his hands.

"Oh, hi," he said.

"Hey Dad. Listen—"

"Do you want something to eat?" asked Greg.

They stood silent in the kitchen for a moment.

"Yeah. Sure."

"Here." Greg reached the plate forward and gave it to his son. "I'll just make another real quick."

Sam sat at the table and listened as Greg opened the bag of bread and dug through the refrigerator. Three minutes later, Greg sat across from his son but didn't pick up his sandwich.

"I don't know what I should be doing," he said.

Sam set the rest of his sandwich down, looked up, and said, "I feel like I missed my chance."

They stared at each other for a moment.

"Mom didn't know who I was yesterday. It was only for a moment, but I saw it."

Greg nodded. He picked up his sandwich and took a bite. Sam did the same. They sat across from each other, watching each other chew.

"She remembers things," said Greg. "Old stuff. Years ago. She reminded me the other day about when you zipped your balls into your pants when we were camping."

"How did that come up?"

"No clue. But it's not that the past just doesn't exist anymore. Those memories are still alive. New stuff seems to stick a little less. Words can be hard. But she's still your Mom. It's not like she disappeared. Not yet."

Sam nodded and shoved the rest of the sandwich into his mouth.

The front door opened. Mary walked through the living room and into the kitchen. She looked down at them and Sam could see the light that shone through her eyes on the porch was gone. She simply glanced around for a moment before pulling out a chair and sitting down.

"If you could choose anywhere in the world, right now, where would you go?" asked Sam.

Mary looked between him and her husband.

"Isn't there anywhere you've always wanted to go but just didn't make it?"

She wanted to say something. Her mouth moved as if words would spill out at any moment but nothing happened. Sam looked to Greg.

"The Grand Canyon," he said and put a hand over hers. "She's always talked about the Grand Canyon like it was some alien world. A big hole in the ground in the middle of nowhere."

Sam looked to Mary. She nodded a little but that might have just been a slight tremor.

"So what's stopping us? Let's do it!" said Sam.

Greg patted Mary's hand and shook his head.

"Settle down, Sam. That takes money."

And then Sam's phone started ringing in his pocket. He took it out and looked at the display.

"You can go ahead," said Greg.

"No, no it's just a telemarketer." He ignored the call.

"Isn't it amazing how people never stop asking you for money?" said Greg.

Sam paused and held the phone just outside of his pocket.

"Yeah, people do that a lot don't they?"

Greg nodded. "All the time it seems."

Sam slid his phone into his pocket and set his elbows on the table. He looked into his father's eyes.

"Why don't we?"

"Why don't we what?"

"Ask people for money? People do it all the time."

"You wanna draw up a cardboard sign and go stand on the highway off ramp?"

"No, no not like that. The internet. We'll make a video."

"No way. No way in hell."

"Dad. People do it all the time. These internet things are different. There was a guy that asked for beer money and people donated a million dollars."

Greg sat back and squinted one eye. "What?"

"Yeah. People love to donate to things like this. It makes them feel good."

"A million dollars?"

Sam leaned forward and pushed his plate out of the way. Mary sat with her hands folded in front of her and Greg continued pressing his spine against the backrest of his chair.

"This can work." He looked to his Mom then back to his Dad. "Let's show her an alien world with a big hole in the ground."

25.

Mary Tells Herself a Joke

Mary sat on a chair. It felt like a familiar chair. Can a feel be familiar? Yes, of course. Anything can be familiar—songs, people, scents, and chairs. All of it. So here she was in a familiar chair surrounded by unfamiliar people. They're all talking to her and they seemed to want something. Everyone always wants something, don't they? Mary wanted to lie down. Even readjusting herself in the comfortable chair was tiring. And that wasn't much more than shifting from one buttcheek to the other. God she was tired.

Someone asked her to look at something. How long had she been sitting here? Where the hell was she anyways?

It looked like the backyard. Yes, that had to be it. She was in the backyard of their house. Gosh, how could she not have realized it earlier? She had been here for, what? Thirty years? Forty? It was hard to say.

Time becomes relative once you stop working. It becomes next to pointless when your *brain* stops working.

She smiled at her own joke even though she knew it wasn't funny.

Suddenly the sun came out. Warm light spilled across her exposed forearms. The scent of grass flooded the air around her. She closed her eyes and focused on the warmth of the sun and the smell of the grass. It was beautiful. She was in her backyard. And it was beautiful. Mary Weber took a deep breath of the warming air that should have been left back in summer, but somehow made a reappearance here in the fall.

She opened her eyes and it felt like walking out of the mouth of a cave. She was indeed in her backyard. Sam stood in front of her, maybe five feet away, holding his phone sideways in his hand. Greg stood to his right. Even Ashley was there. She stood closer to the house with her arms crossed, but she looked at Mary just like everybody else.

"What's the big idea?" asked Mary.

The three of them exchanged glances with each other.

"We're…making a video," said Sam.

Greg walked up to her and knelt in front of the chair.

"How are you feeling?" he asked.

"The sun feels nice."

"We're just making a little video."

"Of me?"

Greg nodded. "Yup. Yeah. Right now it is."

Mary looked over her husband's head to Sam. He looked uneasy.

"You okay, Sam?" she asked.

He nodded.

"Listen, honey," said Greg. "This won't take long."

Mary turned her face to the shining sun and felt it sink into her skin.

"We just need you to talk about how you've felt lately. What's been going on."

"What's been going on with what?" she asked with her eyes closed, facing upwards.

There was a pause.

"With your memory."

She opened her eyes and again saw her son standing about five feet away, except the hand holding the phone now hung at his side. Ashley walked over to his left. And Greg continued to kneel in front of her. She looked into his eyes and nodded.

"Sure. No problem."

"You sure?" he asked.

She nodded again.

He gave her a quick squeeze above her knee, stood up, and walked next to Sam.

"You ready Mom?" asked Sam. He raised his arms and held the phone as he had before.

She nodded.

"Alright go ahead."

Mary began speaking. She looked at her son as she recited her name and former title. She explained how hard it had become to keep track of items around the house and the words she hoped to say. She explained there were good days and bad days, good times and bad times, but that she feared these were her first steps down a one-way road. And the only place this road could end would be a steep cliff with nothing on the other side.

"I was supposed to go to the Grand Canyon once. A long time ago," she said. "I was a little girl. I don't know, maybe like five or so. My parents had told me for years about this great place. A gigantic hole that was whittled from a tiny stream after years and years and years. It sounded magical. A river made of knives or something. I dreamed about it every night. We'd pull up to the park in my father's station wagon. They'd stay in the car while I got out and walked up to the edge. I had seen pictures. I knew what to expect. So I'd walk up to the edge in my dreams and climb over the railing. There was no one to tell me not to. So I'd climb over and lean forward over the edge. I didn't jump. I never fell. But I'd have a viewpoint of the canyon without the ground beneath me. It was like flying. And it felt like the place I should be."

Mary glanced up to the sun and again felt the warm light across her face.

"But when the time came, I was sick. The flu. We drove all the way out there and it was the last day we could stay before my father had to come back to work. I stayed back at the hotel with my father while my mother and sister went on without me. I told them to. It would be a waste to get all the way out there and have nobody go. On the long drive home I continued to dream about the Grand Canyon's beautiful shades of red and orange—and I continued to fly over it. I always meant to make it back. To see it in real life. But unfortunately sometimes we get caught up and dreams just stay dreams."

Her arms grew cold as a grouping of clouds slid in front of the sun. Even the scent of grass disappeared. Mary suddenly found herself in a fog with no idea where she had gone. Or where she was. A few moments went by and it seemed like someone was trying to get her to do something.

How long had she been sitting here? Where the hell was she anyways?

It looked like the backyard. Yes, that had to be it. She was in the backyard of their house. Gosh, how could she not have realized it earlier? She had been here for, what? Thirty years? Forty? It was hard to say.

Time becomes relative once you stop working. It becomes next to pointless when your *brain* stops working.

She smiled at her own joke even though she knew it wasn't funny.

26.

Greg Visits the Hospital

And just like Greg thought, this handout campaign wasn't getting shit. He sat back in the stiff chair they crammed in front of the computer. It was the worst chair in the house. That's why it was in front of the computer.

"Nothing?" asked Sam.

"Well lemme see." Greg again leaned toward the computer screen for a moment before sitting back. "Thirty bucks."

"Well, it's only been a couple days."

"A couple days of people ignoring it. You put it on Facebook and all that?"

Sam nodded.

"So that's all but buried by now."

"These things take time, Dad. Everyone's not going to just unload their bank account right away."

Greg stood up. It's stupid to get your hopes up for something that's completely out of your hands. He knew that. But he couldn't help imagining the look on Mary's face when they pulled up to the Grand Canyon. It was reckless. There were more important things to focus on than fantasies.

"We gotta get a move on," he said.

Greg and Sam Weber walked into the living room. Mary sat on the couch leafing through a book. She'd only pause a few moments on each page before flipping to the next.

"You sure you don't want to come?" asked Sam.

She looked up.

"Do you really think they'll let you go back?" she asked. The good part of this cruel joke was that Mary wouldn't remember the video. You can't be disappointed if you don't remember your hope.

Greg shrugged. "I hope so." And there was that damn word again.

She returned her attention to the book in front of her and flipped another page.

Sam sat in the passenger seat as Greg drove to the hospital. He needed a chaperone in case the doctor wanted to get all worked up about who drove. Technically, it wasn't recommended that Greg get behind the wheel of a vehicle. One little mistake like totaling his truck into a pole and everyone suddenly loses complete faith that he can drive safely. But he was fine. He could drive. And he could work.

If they'd just let him.

And he had no choice but to hope for that to happen. This online charity thing sure didn't seem to be playing out in their favor.

So here they were, walking back into the hospital on the off chance that he could talk the doctor into letting him go back to work. The worst news he could get wasn't that his heart was about to fail and he'd be lucky to make it to sunset—it would be that he couldn't go back to work anytime soon, if ever. In fact, given the two options, he'd almost rather take the first.

It was a quick trip through the initial security checkpoint of the hospital and up to the third floor.

"Greg Weber. Here to see Dr. Craig," he said to the woman sitting behind the giant desk to the right of the elevator.

She clicked a few keys on her keyboard and looked up.

"I don't have an appointment or anything," he said. "I was here a couple weeks ago. Heart attack. He was, uh, well he was real kind to me and I just wanted to talk to him for a minute."

She nodded and put a phone to her ear. It wasn't more than thirty seconds before she looked back up to him.

"Take a seat. He'll be right out."

Greg looked at Sam and shrugged.

"That was a lot easier than I thought it would be," he said.

And just like she said, Dr. Craig came walking out in just a few minutes.

"Mr. Weber," he said and stuck out his hand.

Greg grabbed it and gave it a shake. "Good to see you, doc."

"You just making your rounds here or what?"

"Well, it's a little complicated. I'm here on business, actually. Just kinda makes it more tough that my work's insurance dropped me after they found out I wasn't exactly an employee anymore."

"Ah jeez," said Dr. Craig. "That's a tough situation."

"Tell me about it."

They stood in the hallway just ten feet from the reception desk. Nurses walked back and forth. Visitors tried to figure out where they were going. And even with all the commotion it was still quiet. Greg could hear the footsteps. He could tell people were speaking, but he just heard their movements. The fabric of pants and shirts rustled against themselves. Footsteps clicked on the tile floor all around him. But what he wanted to hear most of all were a few words from Dr. Craig. He'd settle for just one. *Yes.* He'd even take *sure*. Just one word from this man in the white coat could make it all better.

"I need you to write me a recommendation," said Greg. "For the mill. I need to go back."

"Mr. Weber…"

"Listen, I can work. Okay? I've been doing it longer than most of the people in this room have been alive. And not only can I do it…" He paused. It felt too close to begging. Asking for money on the internet was one thing. That was gross enough. But to grovel to a younger man? To ask for his livelihood and ability to provide and everything that he needed to prove his worth as a goddamn human?

"I have to," said Greg.

"Listen, Mr. Weber, I have obligations—"

"*So do I*." He didn't mean it to come out as a shout, but it did.

Dr. Craig sighed and dropped his arms. He looked Greg Weber straight in the eyes.

"I'm sorry Mr. Weber. But not now. And to be totally honest? Probably not ever. At least not until you get the surgery."

"Oh bullshit."

"Answer me this," said Dr. Craig. "Just now. On the way up here. Did you get out of breath?"

"Nope."

"You don't get short of breath? I get short of breath walking up half a flight of stairs. You still have a blockage. It's not going to work itself out. You still run a high risk of another heart attack. I'd be inclined to write a recommendation for you to go back to work if you sat behind a desk. The only risk would be that you drop a letter opener on your hand should your heart seize up again. But not at a paper mill. Not with those hours. Your need to go back to work doesn't trump the need to keep others safe. And even though you don't take this into account—it's important to keep you safe, too."

"What's the point of staying safe if it means we don't have food to eat?"

"What's the point of buying food if you're not going to be around to eat it?" Dr. Craig stared into Greg's eyes. "And what's going to happen to your wife if you're not around?"

The anger that filled Greg's veins—that made him feel like a spring about to release—began to cool. This son of a bitch was right. Goddamnit he was right but it didn't make Greg feel any better. There was no relief replacing anger. Just more disappointment. That was apparently the theme of the day: Useless hope replaced by disappointment.

Dr. Craig waited for Greg to speak. He knew he had a checkmate and didn't seem interested in rubbing it in.

But Greg didn't speak. Not at first. Instead, he just nodded. Words would be followed by other words and he didn't like the ones he had on-deck.

So he just nodded.

 Finally, Dr. Craig broke the standoff:

"I'm sorry Mr. Weber. I really am. But it isn't my job to tell people what they want to hear. In fact, a large part of my job is the exact opposite."

Sam appeared next to Greg.

"Thanks doctor." He put his hands on his father's shoulders.

"Yeah. Thanks," said Greg. He tried to drain any form of annoyance from his voice. He was mostly successful.

They shook hands and the doctor apologized one more time before turning around and disappearing back into the melee of the hospital. Greg and Sam rode the elevator to the ground floor and walked back into the parking lot.

And as if directed by the doctor himself, Greg noticed his breaths weren't as deep as they should have been and were coming much faster.

"Here," he said and threw the keys at his son.

They didn't speak until they got home.

"God I'm such an ass," said Greg.

Sam turned off the car and dropped the keys back into his father's hand.

"That was nothing," said Sam. "People lose it all the time in hospitals."

Greg forced a smile and nodded. He tossed the keys to himself and caught them with a light chime.

"Thanks."

They climbed out of the car and walked in the house. It was quiet when they left. But it was somehow even more quiet now.

"Mary?" The living room was empty. Greg walked into the kitchen. Also empty.

"Mom?" Sam walked through the kitchen and ducked his head into different rooms.

"Mary?" Greg's voice was a little louder now. A little more strained. He hadn't been out of breath before they walked into the house, but he was puffing now. A dull ache grew in his chest.

The house wasn't that big. They searched every room within a couple minutes and now they were back in the kitchen staring at each other.

"What do we do?" asked Sam.

Greg pulled the keys from his pocket and walked toward the door.

"Come on," he said over his shoulder.

Greg backed into the road and the tires gave a quick squeak in recognition that he didn't come to a full stop before flipping the car into drive. They each rolled down their windows as if it would help them see out the window better. This was too familiar. Greg had been here before. And he didn't like how it ended.

Sam pulled out his phone and put it to his ear. He sat for a moment before looking at his father.

"She's not answering."

Greg just nodded and kept looking around the neighborhood as they drove.

Sam hung up, hit a few buttons, and put it back to his ear.

"Ashley? Yeah I know you're at work. Listen. Have you talked to Mom today? Shit. *Shit.* Alright. No, she's not home. We don't know. Yeah. Yeah I'll let you know."

Sam slid his phone back into his pocket and hung his head out the window.

Greg pulled around another corner. He felt the sweat on his forehead. His chest heaved. This was too familiar. Greg had been here before but he knew what to watch out for. This wasn't going to end like last time. God damn it this couldn't end the way it did last time.

27.

Ashley and the Teachers' Lounge

Ashley kept her cell phone tucked safely within her purse in the drawer of her desk when she was at school. It would be damn near impossible for her to discipline any students for staring at their phones if hers were sitting on the edge of her desk. And that's why she was so thankful when Sam called between classes. She forgot to set it to silent and was sure to have received a chorus of sarcastic *oohs* from the students as she fumbled to turn it off. But she didn't. Because Sam called between classes.

This relief didn't last long.

Her mother was missing.

And Ashley had no choice but to hang up, take a moment to compose herself, and greet the students that started filling the room.

She set her phone on the corner of her desk, near the mug from her favorite coffee shop in college filled with pens, and the name placard Darren got her on the last day of student teaching. *Mrs. Wolff,* it said. They wouldn't be engaged for another few years. His idea of a joke. She knew keeping the phone out was a bad idea. Not because of what the kid's thought—she was past worrying about that—but because there wasn't much point beyond curiosity. What was she going to do? Run out of the room if they found her? She'd have to stay at least until the end of the period. There was no choice about that. So what kept the phone on the desk?

Desperate curiosity.

"Alright," she said after the bell scared everyone in the room. "Pass your papers to the front." Ashley—Mrs. Wolff—passed a glance over the class but didn't go long before looking back to the phone sitting next to the coffee mug and name placard.

The sound of ruffling papers filled the room like a hundred birds taking off at once. There were groans from those that didn't have anything of their own to contribute. But again, Ashley was past worrying about that.

She stole another glance at her phone before walking along the front row of desks.

"Thank you," she said to each student as she took the stack of papers. Some were thicker than others. Soon she had somewhere around twenty papers that were to discuss the island's treatment of Piggy in *Lord of the Flies*. She turned around and again glanced at her phone. Was she hoping it'd be lit up? Did she want there to be news? There was an equal chance of it being on the good or bad side.

Maybe it was better left blank.

She looked again as she walked around her desk.

"Is that a cell phone?" asked Shane Duplass. Of course this had to happen right before his class.

Ashley ignored him.

"Alright. Let's open it up. Who'd push Piggy around if there was nobody to tell them not to?"

"I mean, I thought cell phones were against school policy."

Ashley looked over the top of Shane's head but sparks of energy flashed through her fingers. She didn't want to engage him. There was too strong of a chance she'd throw him through a wall.

"I know you have an opinion on this. You just finished a three-page paper." She looked around the room at a collection of heads. Students seemed to think they were invisible if they didn't make eye contact. She chose one at random.

"Eric. Was it inevitable they'd treat Piggy like, well like his name?"

Eric Thompson looked up but only for a moment. His gaze quickly returned to his desk like he hadn't just handed his paper forward a couple minutes earlier. She could tell panic was building behind his pale skin and pimples. His hands searched his desk aimlessly.

Ashley briefly diverted her eyes from the implosion of Eric Thompson to look at her quiet phone in the corner of her desk.

"I'd be sent to the office if I did that. But I guess that doesn't really matter does it?" It wasn't the voice Ashley wanted to hear. A nervous squeak of a half-formed opinion would be far better than the fully formed but uninformed opinion of Shane Duplass.

Ashley returned her attention to Eric Thompson. He squirmed beneath her gaze.

"Those are the rules," continued Shane. "You should know them. Unless you forget everything, too."

The class shifted. Every one of them. The only person who became more comfortable was Eric Thompson as the spotlight shifted off of him.

Ashley's eyes flicked over to the blond-haired asshole sitting in the third row on the right side of the room. Her head slowly followed her eyes until she looked directly at him.

"What did you say?"

Shane buried his chin into his neck. He opened his mouth but shook his head in place of offering an explanation.

Ashley grabbed the phone from her desk, slid it into her pocket, and walked toward him.

"Let's go. *Now.*"

She continued past his desk and toward the door in the back of the room.

The class shifted again and someone murmured the standard *ooh*.

"Stop it," said Ashley, enunciating her point with an abrupt pause in her step. Silence sat heavy over the room.

Finally Shane Duplass stood from his desk with an exaggerated laboriousness as if gravity had kicked up tenfold.

"Now. Let's go." Ashley Wolff stood by the door and the class watched as Shane slunk past her into the hallway. She looked back and forth and noticed a janitor pushing a rolling garbage can along the side of the hallway.

"You," she said.

The janitor looked over.

"Watch my class for a minute, would you?"

He stopped walking but kept his hands on the rim of the garbage can. "What?"

"Just for a minute. I'll be right back." She turned down the hallway as the janitor abandoned the rolling can and tentatively stepped toward the classroom.

"Mrs. Wolff," said Shane. "I—"

"Save it."

Her footsteps clicked off the granite floor and reverberated along the lockers lining both walls. Shane followed her into the stairwell, down to the first floor, and back into the hallway leading to the office. And that's when she heard her mother's voice.

"No, no I just had to walk. I'm not usually this late."

Ashley turned the corner and saw Mary Weber standing outside room 132. This was the room in which she attempted to talk countless children out of acting the way Shane Duplass had acted mere minutes earlier. And now she was speaking with Greg Grabowski, the algebra teacher that took over the room two years earlier.

"Mom?"

Mary turned her head.

"Hello?" she said.

Ashley felt the anger in her chest turn to ice.

"What the fuck?" said Shane Duplass. There was a chuckle in his voice that reignited the rage in Ashley's chest.

"Back to class." She turned around and looked him in the eyes. "*Now*."

He stumbled back as if struck and put a hand on the door to the stairwell. Ashley turned back around.

Mary looked between Ashley and Greg Grabowski. First one. Then the other. Then back to the first. She formed her mouth into an O, an open pucker that preceded a question. The eternal question at this point:

"What?" Mary finally said.

"It's okay. It's okay." Ashley walked forward and put her hand on her mother's back.

"Is there…What's going on?" asked Greg Grabowski. He was a short man. Glasses. A dark brown bowl cut circled his head that was twenty years out of date and far too dark to be anywhere near natural.

Ashley shook her head.

"Nothing. It's nothing. Just go back to class."

Grabowski looked as if another question would spill from his mouth but he just held that expression and turned back to room 132.

"I need to get to class," said Mary. A slight tremor shook her hand. Mary continued looking between her daughter and the odd-looking man that receded into her classroom. "I'm late."

"It's okay, Mom. It's okay. Let's just go over—"

Ashley turned around. Her shoes squeaked on the tile as she grinded to a halt.

Shane Duplass let out a burst of laughter and almost dropped the phone he held in front of him.

"Hey!" yelled Ashley but Shane had already disappeared through the stairway doors. A new rage filled her. Murderous red blood bubbled out through the vents of the surrounding lockers, and she was too blinded by the fury to realize she was the only one that could see it. She felt a dull throb to her left and realized Mary was trying to move away from her.

"Let me go," she said. So Ashley did. "I'm tired."

Ashley tried to breathe out the fire inside her and the bubbling blood sucked back into the locker vents.

"Come on," she said.

Mary had known these hallways much longer than her. But it was Ashley leading the way to the teacher's lounge. She should have been taking this walk with that asshole Shane Duplass—she'd have to string him up for recording them earlier, but there was no time now—except they stopped maybe twenty yards away from the office.

The teachers' lounge wasn't a lounge. It was a shitty room with a refrigerator, soda machine, and vending machine the students couldn't drain. The lounge was roughly the size of her classroom and had most likely been an art room or something of the sort years before. Windows ran along one side but they started halfway up the wall. It was a design that hadn't been utilized since the 1950s and for good reason: It was depressing. Ashley always imagined the teacher's lounge would have velvet couches, tiffany lamps, and Persian rugs. She was wrong.

"Here. Take a seat." Ashley guided her mother to a plastic chair surrounding one of the four circular tables. Luckily, the room was empty.

Mary sat down and looked around. Her shoulders relaxed. She looked at Ashley with clear eyes. The hesitation of confusion had disappeared.

"I always loved it in here," said Mary.

Ashley held the phone in her hand but paused.

"Mom, what the hell?"

Mary shrugged. She offered a smile, but Ashley didn't believe it.

"Do you know where you are?"

Mary nodded. "I do now."

Ashley pulled out the chair on the other side of the circular table. The light aluminum legs gave a little as she sat down.

"Mom…" Ashley leaned forward. "What the hell?"

Mary took a deep breath and let it out slowly. "Do students still think of this as some sort of mythical place?"

Ashley sat back in her chair and set the phone on the table between them. She nodded.

Mary smiled. "I guess it sort of is. The decoration might be lacking but…I don't know. Having a place just for us. Just for the teachers. Somewhere we could swear and say what we actually thought of the students. Of the *kids*." She chuckled and Ashley believed it this time. "It's hard to remember they're just kids sometimes, isn't it?"

Ashley thought about driving her car over Shane Duplass' head.

"Sometimes," she said.

Mary stood up and walked over to the windows. She could see the end of the parking lot but that's about it. She turned around.

"What happened out there?" asked Ashley.

Mary looked around the room again.

"Some places are just better for me," she said.

Ashley followed her gaze around the barren room and tried to figure out what she meant. There wasn't even anything hung on the wall. It was objectively the ugliest and most depressing room in the entire school. Even the boiler room had more character than the teacher's lounge.

Mary walked back to the table and sat down.

"I'm tired," she said. Her gaze fell to the table and Ashley thought for a moment she might have fallen asleep.

She grabbed the phone and walked into the hallway to call her father.

28.

Sam Buys Some Lettuce

Driving around the neighborhood was pointless. They knew the neighbors. Greg was confident someone would give him a call if they saw Mary simply wandering down the road. And of course, nobody did. Not until Ashley did, at least.

Sam looked out the window from the passenger seat with his father behind the wheel. They sat at a gas pump. The tank was topped off and they were ready to go. All they needed was a destination. Aimless circles became overbearing. Each empty street that stretched before them after turning yet another corner became a punch in the gut. Sam was shaking, sweating, and shooting his attention back and forth so fast it made him sick. Greg Weber grew quiet the more they drove. Sam wasn't sure what scared him more—his mother's disappearance or his father's silence. Both felt like the edge of a cliff he didn't want to look over.

And then Greg's phone rang. The conversation only took a few seconds.

"Ashley? Oh thank God. All right. We're on our way."

Ten minutes later, they parked the car and quickly walked through the parking lot on the south side of the building. Mary and Ashley waited for them outside the door.

"Mary—" said Greg. He wrapped his arms around her.

Ashley and Sam nodded to each other but didn't speak.

"I don't really see what the big deal is," said Mary when Greg finally let go.

They spoke for a moment before Ashley said she had to go back inside and deal with something. Greg looked exhausted but insisted on driving. Sam didn't like the idea but what could he say?

And now here they were, driving away from school. But did it feel better than when they were driving there? The arrival was full of excitement, anticipation, and sure some nervousness. But now—what did it feel like now?

Sam looked to his left. Greg drove with one hand on the wheel. The other supported his head, bolstered by a crooked arm resting the elbow near the window. His eyes shone in the afternoon sun. Were they wet? Or just tired? The sun created shadows where the creases of his skin bunched together.

Behind them, Mary sat straight-backed against the seat with her hands folded neatly in her lap. Sam watched her in the vanity mirror attached to the visor. She looked young, but not in the way Greg looked old. It was her demeanor. Childlike. Innocent. This was a quality that people used all the time to describe somebody in a positive light. As if the world had yet to break them. As if they were able to rise above the pettiness of general society and maintain an idealistic view on the world.

But this wasn't how Sam saw his mother in the backseat. Straight-backed. Hands folded neatly. This wasn't the persistence of an old stalwart. This was a regression. This woman that at one time made students damn near bow down with respect. This woman that wasn't afraid to engage with the students everyone else thought were beyond help. This woman that had loved and cared for Sam and Ashley since they were born. Taught them how to ride a bike. Tie their shoes. Comforted them when the thunderstorms grew too strong.

A regression.

Childlike.

Now she was the one in need of reassurance. She was the one he felt had to be spoken to carefully to avoid unnecessarily upsetting her.

This switch in positions is bound to happen, Sam supposed. If he had taken the time to pay attention to anyone outside of himself he would have seen a version of this coming. Not this exact scenario—with his tired father struggling to get enough blood pumping through his weak heart and his mother sitting in the backseat with most likely no idea where they had just been or where they were going—but another one where he had to step into a role of responsibility. He would have to be the caretaker. He would have to recognize that these people that had an answer to every question he had ever asked weren't the statues of morality and knowledge he had built them to be. Every adult with aging parents must face this realization at some point. You can't ask your parents for help on your homework forever. A heaviness sunk into him. Into his chest, stomach, and around his shoulders. His sweatshirt became twenty times heavier and tears snuck their way into his eyes.

But this new realization also came with a recognition—he couldn't add to their problems. All of the help they had given him over the years, all of the support, it hadn't gone to waste. It still existed somewhere.

But the tears stayed in his eyes. He couldn't reason them away.

Greg finally eased on the brake and pulled into their driveway. He stopped the car before pulling into the garage and turned it off.

Nobody moved.

Greg took a deep breath.

"We're home," he said to the windshield and got out. He closed his door behind himself and opened the back door. "Come on," he said to Mary.

Sam got out but stayed next to the car as he watched his father and mother on the other side. Greg put his left hand across her back and looped his right hand onto her shoulder. She leaned into him. It was a scene from a postcard. A showcase of love that didn't have a beginning, an end, or a reason. It didn't need one. It existed on its own momentum despite the fact that many of the original building blocks disappeared long ago.

This happy scene.

Taken objectively, it was a pure personification of love.

But something about it was so fucking sad.

Sam lost his breath and turned around. He faced the street, the neighborhood, the houses.

What was the point of any of it?

Get it together, he told himself. He tried to recall any of the sentiments that flowed through him on the ride home. It was hard to put into words. It was hard to internalize. The only thing that remained—the most salient point of the whole ride—was that his parents were growing frail.

And one day they would die. Probably not at the same time. But it would happen.

He forced himself out of his own head and back into the neighborhood. The sun glowed yellow in the afternoon sky. The wind wasn't cold, but it wasn't warm either. He learned how to throw a football in the yard in front of him. He learned he'd never be good at basketball at the old hoop behind him. He learned that any ideas he had about his relationship with his family were outdated in the car right next to him.

Sam Weber walked around the car and followed his parents inside.

"There you are," said Greg. He walked up to his son. "Listen, just keep an eye on her. I gotta...I gotta go lie down."

Sam nodded. His father turned around and walked into their bedroom.

Mary sat at the kitchen table with a glass of water. Sam pulled out a chair on the other side.

"Really getting those steps in, huh?" he said.

Mary continued to look at the glass of water. Her hands formed a circle around the base of the glass.

It was quiet.

He thought about clapping just to see if it would make a noise.

He wasn't sure if it would.

Maybe she didn't even hear him.

Maybe his words weren't making it past his throat.

He stood up and went to the drawer next to the silverware. Loose envelopes, some pens, a pad of paper, various sizes of paperclips, and a deck of cards shifted from the movement. None of it made a noise. He grabbed the deck of cards, flung the drawer shut, and sat back down across from his mother.

"Play a game?" He slid the cards from their tiny cardboard box and started shuffling. The rhythmic slaps of friction were noticeably absent. Even tapping the ends of the deck on the table failed to register in his ears.

"Mom?" He tapped the cards on the table. Still nothing. He looked around the room but only saw the white walls and decades-old, framed family photos. Smiling high school versions of him and Ashley looked down at them.

Sam left the cards on the table, stood up, and walked around to the other side.

"Come on," he said and put his hands on her shoulders. Her eyes remained forward.

"Come on," he said again and took her by the arm. Mary finally started to move and he eventually got her standing up.

"Let's go to the store," he said. "I'm making dinner tonight."

Mary glanced at the glass of water before looking back to her son. She nodded.

He grabbed the keys from the key ring next to the garage door. A slight metallic *ching* rang out as he grasped them in his palm.

It was a quiet ride but that was just because nobody spoke. The engines of passing cars fought for his attention with the stereo that played pop songs from the nineties. There was no way Greg had left this station on the radio, but here they were.

The parking lot was mostly empty so Sam parked up front near the handicap spots.

He didn't have a plan for dinner, but he could figure it out with an entire grocery store of choices. So they walked. Up one aisle and down the next. He tried to ask his mother questions, but they didn't go anywhere. How could she be so coherent at the school and so quiet now?

Some places are better for me than others.

"Sam Weber?"

He turned around and saw a familiar woman his mother's age. Grey hair. Tall but not as skinny as she once was. Her chin came to a sharp point that he had still never seen on another living person.

"Hey Linda," he said. "How's it going?"

"Mary! How long has your baby boy been in town?"

They stood next to a corridor of bread, seven shelves tall. Cans of beans and tomatoes flanked the other side of the aisle.

Mary looked between Linda and her son but didn't say anything.

Linda waited for a few moments and finally gave up.

"You two…you two have a good one." Linda walked past them and patted Sam on the shoulder.

He had to get her home. He looked to his right and grabbed a bag of hamburger buns.

"Looks like we're grilling, Mom," he said.

He led her to the meat section where he grabbed a Styrofoam tray of preformed hamburgers in shrink wrap. They swung by the produce section for lettuce and headed to the cashier. Surely they had ketchup and mustard at home.

Their three items looked so lonely on the conveyor belt. Mary walked to the end and stood where a bagger would be if the store were a little busier. The lettuce wobbled a little as the items slid toward the thick man running the register. He looked down at the three items and back up at Sam.

He reached for his wallet. Did he still have a rewards card?

"Find where she needs to go."

Sam looked up. The man had yet to scan the items.

"Excuse me?"

The man returned his stare for a moment before dropping his attention back to the three items on the conveyor belt. He beeped them across the scanner and looked at the display.

"Seven eighty-seven."

"What did you say?"

The man looked back to the display and around again to Sam.

"Seven eighty-seven."

"No before that."

The man stared at Sam again, shrugged, and shook his head.

Sam ran his card through the reader but didn't take his eyes off the thick man in the blue apron as he shoved the three items into a singular plastic bag. The receipt spit out of the register which he snagged and dropped in the bag.

"Here you go," said the man as he handed the bag to Sam.

Sam stared at the man for another moment before he grabbed the bag and walked back to the car with his Mom.

29.

Mary Feels a Heaviness

Every bone in her body ached, but her legs burned particularly hot. Mary leaned forward on the couch and rubbed her calves. Little circular movements with her fingertips sent bolts of pain to the center of her legs. She hadn't gone for a run in—shoot, how long?—years. So why were her legs so sore? Each pulse of dull pain that rang throughout her legs tickled at a memory. She seemed to constantly be waking up from a dream she could *almost* remember. There was always a hint, a shadow of an image that refused to come out and show itself.

Just show yourself, damn it.

But of course, it didn't. The aches simply taunted her. Evidence of a memory without a link to reality.

So she was forced into the present. Darkness snuffed out the daylight sometime around when the TV program started. Mary watched with only half-interest. She'd given up trying to follow the storyline maybe halfway through.

The house smelled really good. She couldn't hear anyone else so she must be alone. Was a neighbor grilling? Is that what it was? A subtle smoky scent wafted through the room. Not unlike a campfire, but with a salty difference. The light in the kitchen was on so she stood up to turn it off. There was no need to be wasteful.

Her legs argued with her decision. They'd rather stew in their soreness instead of igniting it. Mary stepped gently into the kitchen.

The sliding door to the backyard opened with a *whoosh*.

"Oh!" The sound escaped her throat without a thought. Mary's cheeks started to burn, mimicking her tired legs.

"Almost done, Mom," he said and walked to the sink. An empty plate sat on the countertop with a watery red liquid pooled in the center. The spatula clanked against the plate as he set them down. A package of hamburger buns, an unopened head of lettuce, and a small stack of plates sat on the other side of the sink.

"Why don't you go sit back down? I'll let you know when it's ready."

Mary opened her mouth to offer help but the front door suddenly cracked open with the sound of a vacuum seal being broken.

"Hello?" A helium-high voice cut through the quiet house. An avalanche of footsteps quickly followed and then Noah and Sadie jumped into frame.

"Hey Uncle Sam!" yelled Noah.

Sam laughed. "Hey buddy. Say hi to your grandma."

"Hi grandma," the kids said in unison.

Ashley slowly walked into the kitchen with a strange man behind her. She waved and smiled.

Sam walked over to them and shook the man's hand. Should Mary know who he is?

Better not to ask.

"Hey Mom. Long time no see," said Ashley.

Mary smiled as if she knew what the hell her daughter was talking about. She continued looking at the man and something about him seemed familiar. He had yet to speak, but his soft, intentional movements felt familiar. He only moved when necessary, and when he did, it was a fluid motion. No jerkiness. He set a covered bowl on the table and it almost looked like a dance move. The kids liked him. They seemed comfortable.

A shadow of a memory refused to come out and show itself.

Just show yourself, damn it.

And then finally, the bedroom door opened and Greg walked into the kitchen.

"There's a bed in there." Greg tilted his head toward the bedroom. "You know, just in case anybody else doesn't want to get any sleep." Sadie walked over and hugged his thigh. He looked up at the man with Ashley and smiled.

"Well there's a surprise." Greg walked over and shook his hand. "Real good to see you, Darren."

Of course.

Of course.

Mary'd kick herself if her legs weren't so damn sore.

Greg spoke to Darren.

Ashley picked up Sadie.

Noah followed Sam outside.

And Mary stood near the refrigerator trying to follow just one of the conversations going on but her legs were screaming louder than anybody in the room.

"I have to sit down," she said quietly. The cackling conversation suddenly stopped.

Darren pulled out a chair from thin air. Greg lightly touched her elbow and guided her to it. Everyone stared down at her as she settled into the chair. Her legs continued to scream, but the volume had been turned down just a little.

Sam again walked through the opened sliding door with a plate of steaming hamburgers in one hand, the spatula in the other, and a smiling nephew right behind him.

"Alright here we go," he said.

The noise of conversation converted into movement. Chairs slid. Plates clanked. Plastic bottles were shaken. Glasses slammed onto the table. A plate of burgers sat next to the buns piled high on another plate. Lettuce was torn and placed in a bowl. Same with chopped onions. The bowl Darren had set on the table earlier was unveiled to be mashed potatoes. A larger bowl filled with chips acted as the centerpiece. Everything was ready. Everything was available. But nobody moved.

They all looked at her. It was as if the concern from earlier had only been paused. And now they wanted to make sure she wasn't cracked—wouldn't break into a million little pieces before their eyes. Even the children waited at attention.

Mary shrugged.

"Let's eat," she said.

And like the starting pistol before a race, her words caused an eruption of motion.

Plates were passed. Chips were scooped. Condiments were applied. Glasses were filled. Bites were taken. Conversations were started. People were interrupted. Children complained. Plates were emptied. Plates were refilled. Topics were forgotten. Stories were remembered. Adults complained. Questions were asked. Answers were given. Names were mentioned. Events were recalled. Chips were crunched. Glasses were emptied. Bowls were emptied. Plates were cleared. Dishes were cleaned.

And Mary just watched and chewed her way through her meal. She caught some mention about the school. It seemed like they were talking about her, but Mary just smiled and took another bite when someone looked at her. Greg stood up toward the end of the meal and seemed angry, but she couldn't fathom why.

The conversations moved too fast. She couldn't keep up. Plus all the distractions. First it was her legs—burning in recognition of a jog that couldn't have happened. Even her back felt as if she had carried something heavy over a long distance.

But that wasn't what caused her to block out the people around her. That wasn't what gave her something new to worry about—as if she needed something else.

It was the sensation in her chest. The heaviness. And although she couldn't see it, this heaviness felt dark as the night that surrounded the house outside the windows and walls.

She coughed.

The heaviness throbbed in recognition, as if taking credit.

Mary took a drink of water and then Sam asked if she was finished.

She nodded yes.

30.

Greg Watches the Video

As if it wasn't bad enough that his wife of almost 40 years went to a job she had been fired from two years earlier because she thought she was late. As if it wasn't bad enough that Greg had to relive one of the worst moments of his life with even more severe possible consequences. As if it wasn't bad enough that their income had dried up and their insurance went with it and he didn't know if he'd even have a cardboard box to eat for lunch in a couple months, some piece of shit kid recorded Mary when she was at her most vulnerable and just *laughed* at her?

"I'm glad I wasn't there," said Greg. He stood up from the dinner table. Any semblance of lethargy evaporated as soon as Ashley described that little shit laughing his way through the stairway doors at school.

"Come on Dad, sit down." Sam reached for his arm, but Greg ripped it away.

Dinner was over anyway. There were some chips left and Mary hadn't finished her burger, but it was basically over. He didn't need to sit down. He didn't want to sit down. That would give him an opportunity to feel the uneven pumps from his handicapped heart. Instead, he drew shallow breaths and tried to calm himself down.

Not in front of the kids.

Take a deep breath. As if that were even possible.

He grabbed his plate and set it in the sink. He watched the hamburger grease fight with the drops of water. Persistent brown circles rose to the top of the surface tension and refused to dissipate. He could feel an approaching body, so he looked to his left.

Darren carried a handful of dishes and set them on the counter next to the sink. He looked behind him for a moment before turning back to Greg.

"It's been a little while," he said.

Greg looked over his shoulder. Mary was almost done with her food.

"I'm, uh…well I'm sorry about—" Darren nodded behind himself. It was directed toward the entire table but Greg knew which seat he meant.

"You know I live with her. Every day. So it's been a gradual change. For me. You don't see your fingernails grow, you know? And then one day you look down and you've got claws."

Darren nodded.

"But for you—it's been, what? A year?"

Darren nodded again. "Ashley told me about it, of course. It wasn't a great surprise or anything but—I noticed. I can definitely tell something's different."

"Heads up," said Greg.

Noah and Sadie walked up behind them with a plate in one hand and a cup in the other.

"I'm done," said Sadie.

They gave their dishes to their father and returned to the table. Greg wished his kids were that well-behaved when they were that age.

"I just can't get over that…*fucking* kid," he said quietly. "Your wife has to be an absolute saint to put up with kids these days."

"Your daughter," said Darren.

"Yeah, well that too." Greg imagined the kid going back to the room while Ashley wrangled her mother. How long was she down there waiting for them? Fifteen minutes? More? That little punk must've shown everybody in his class. And everybody in the next class. And now everybody puts everything on the internet—

"Oh God," said Greg.

"What?"

"The internet."

Darren paused. "What about the internet?"

"That kid. He probably shared it with all his idiot friends." Greg turned to the sink and put his hands on the counter. A stack of plates accumulated in there and the persistent grease circles had been buried. His fingers tightened around the slightly raised ledge of the counter and he wanted to snap the whole damn thing off.

Darren sighed. "I'm sure this advice sucks but you just gotta forget about it. You gotta block that out."

He was right. But it felt wrong. Greg wasn't really one to just get over things. He straightened up and turned to Darren.

"I want to see it," he said.

Darren shook his head with a small, sad smile. "I don't think that's such a good idea."

"What's not a good idea?" Sam appeared over Darren's shoulder holding a glass in one hand and a couple plates in the other.

"It's nothing," said Darren.

"I want to see the video." Greg looked between his son and son-in-law.

Darren looked vaguely off to the left with that sad smirk on his lips.

Sam reached between them to put the glass and plates on the countertop. He wiped his hands on his pants and looked at his father for a moment.

"Give me a couple minutes," said Sam before he walked back to the table.

Ashley stopped by with the rest of the dishes from the table and went to find her kids who had run off in search of cookies. Greg didn't know why they'd look anywhere besides the kitchen. Darren started washing the dishes and Greg stood off to his right, waiting with a drying towel. His eyes stayed on his wife who had let out a few thick coughs but was sitting mostly quiet at the table.

And then Sam stood up and walked over to them with his phone in front of him.

"You sure about this?" he asked.

Greg set the towel on the countertop and nodded.

"Alright." Sam looked over his shoulder to his mother before turning back around. He hit the play button and held up the phone to face his father.

It was hard to hear. The speakers on the phone weren't that good, and the kid must have had his finger over the microphone or something. The image was shaky at first until the stupid kid felt comfortable enough that Ashley wouldn't turn around. The video wasn't long, but the sound cleared after a moment.

He listened as his wife explained to some short, weird-looking man that she was late. Ashley walked up and put her hand on her mother's back. He could see the tremors in her hands and arms. Just like when she got lost. A frailty. A fragility. And then they turned toward the camera and the video cut off. But just before it did, Mary's eyes stared out from the video. It frightened him. This was a woman ten years older than the woman sitting at the kitchen table. She looked tired. Confused. Scared. It took him weeks to get this look out of his mind after picking her up near the elementary school. And now here it was again. Staring him in the face. And on the internet for the entire world to use as a punch line. His eyes started to burn but he couldn't tell whether it was from pain or rage.

It was both.

He looked to the floor and noticed Darren was the only one of them wearing shoes.

Sam turned the phone back toward himself and pawed at it.

"Holy shit," he said. "It has a lot of views."

"Great," said Greg.

"Like, a *lot* of views."

Darren turned back around to finish the dishes.

A question bubbled into his head. He didn't want to know the answer, but he couldn't stop himself from asking.

"Are there comments?"

Sam hesitated. Then he looked up.

"On the video?"

Greg cocked his head and just stared at him.

"Um…" He pawed at the screen a few more times. Then his eyebrows slowly raised.

"What?"

"What do you think you'd say if you left a comment?" asked Sam.

"I'd say whoever posted this is an asshole and leave her alone."

Sam nodded and turned the phone around.

"Yeah, that's basically what everyone else is saying too."

Darren turned back around and craned his head next to Greg's. They read through the comments and didn't see one joke, one pile-on, one negative word about anybody besides the piece of shit that shot and shared the video. And then they came across a comment that identified Mary Weber followed by a link.

"Click that," said Greg.

Sam turned the phone around. "Click what?"

"That link. There."

Sam poked at his phone and audibly exhaled. He looked at Greg and Darren over the top of the phone.

"Holy shit," he said and turned the phone around. A picture of Mary sat at the top of the screen, followed by the video they shot in the backyard. Below that would be the explanation of her situation and the story Sam had written about going to the Grand Canyon. Below that would be the donate button. The status bar building from left to right barely had a blip at the end last time they checked.

But now it was full.

"We went viral," Sam said with a smile. "We're going to the Grand Canyon."

31.

Ashley and the Kids Walk Home

"It's still going?"

Darren kept his eyes on his phone and nodded slowly.

"I want a coffee," said Noah.

"Jesus. What's it at?"

"Five thousand."

Ashley leaned forward on the table. She put some folded napkins under it earlier but it still wobbled a little under her weight.

"Five thousand? Dollars?"

Darren finally looked up. A smile stretched his lips thin and he nodded.

"Are you gonna go?" he asked.

"The Grand Canyon?" Ashley sat back in her chair and crossed a leg. "No. No way. I'm not sitting in the car with them for 20 hours or whatever."

"Mom, I want a *coffee*."

"It's the middle of the afternoon, bud. You'll be up all night," said Darren.

"Alright, just a minute." Ashley stood up.

Darren caught her eyes. He mouthed: *Are you serious?*

Ashley smiled and walked up to the counter.

"Two lattes and a hot chocolate."

A barista, likely still in high school, nodded and told her he'd call out her name.

"So how long you been drinking coffee?" asked Darren.

Noah shrugged. "Forever, I think."

Darren looked at Ashley as she sat back down and shrugged.

It's not like Darren was gone for the last year. He wasn't on the other side of the country or anything. But still, he wasn't *there*. Not for all of it. He didn't know that Noah thought hot chocolate was coffee because she got tongue tied at the haunted hayride last year and accidentally lied to him. He didn't know that Sadie thought Ashley had to take her finger off at night in order to get the ring off. And he didn't know that Ashley had been thinking about all the things he didn't know because he was out of the house for a year.

But what he *really* didn't know was that she had been wondering about all of the things she didn't know because he had been gone.

Like how long had he been dating that woman?

Who was she?

And the thing that had snuck its way into her mind no matter how hard she tried to force it out, the thing that only grew in strength the more she ignored it, the thing that she knew she would end up asking because curiosity was becoming stronger than common sense:

Did he fuck her?

"Rebecca!" called the barista.

Ashley stood up.

"That's not your order," said Darren. He looked over his shoulder. "Somebody named Rebecca."

Ashley walked over to the counter and grabbed two lattes and one hot chocolate at the same time.

"You impressed?" she asked as she set them down.

"Yeah!" said Noah. His sister continued to busy herself with the prepackaged plastic thimbles of half and half.

"That you kept your real name from me all these years?"

Ashley shrugged. "Where's the harm?"

He took a sip from the white paper cup and burned his lip.

"Come on. Let's get out of here," she said.

Noah walked around the table and helped his sister down from her chair. Darren stood up and threw his coat over his shoulders as the kids walked out the back door to the parking lot behind the building.

"Did you really just get him a coffee?" he asked once the kids were out of earshot.

"Did you fuck her?"

The coffee shop was empty besides them and the barista. But somehow, the place grew quiet as if a crowd hushed all at once. It wasn't so much the silence of a noise going quiet, but more a recognition of the silence itself. Darren didn't move. He just looked at his wife and squinted his eyes.

"What?"

"Your…girlfriend or whatever. The girl you were seeing."

"Where the hell did this come from?"

A blast of steam erupted from the other side of the espresso machine. The barista stood facing them, bowing his head. Light, frothy gurgles replaced the hiss of the steam.

"Because if you did, I think you should tell me. Don't tell me like, everything about it. Don't paint me a picture. I don't need to know all of that. But I think I should know. I think I have a right."

"You have a right? You think you have a right to know about what I did after you kicked me out of the house for no reason?"

"I'm still your wife."

"This is ridiculous." Darren zipped up his coat, walked past the coffee counter, and out the back door.

Ashley replayed the conversation in her head and did not like what she heard.

"Did you need something else, ma'am?"

She turned to her left where the high school kid peered at her over the top of the espresso machine. His black beanie and brown eyes hovered without a body.

"No, no I'm fine." She quickly walked through the coffee shop and into the parking lot.

The kids sat patiently in the backseat. Darren waited in the driver's seat. And right before Ashley opened the passenger side door a thought flashed through her mind:

He didn't say no.

Ashley's hand tightened around the handle on the outside of the passenger side door. Yes, she had asked him to leave the house. And yes, if it were up to him things would have continued on like normal for the last year. But they didn't. They weren't living together, but they didn't get divorced either. They needed some time apart. They needed to figure some things out.

That wasn't a license to sleep around town.

Ashley pulled the door open and climbed inside. She kept her eyes on the glove box in front of her.

"This is good coffee," said Noah.

Darren backed out of the parking spot, pulled onto the side street, and turned onto the main road toward their house.

Ashley continued staring at the glove box. She didn't speak. She didn't look at her husband. She couldn't get the image out of her mind. Him. And her. Whoever she was. Together.

She wanted to scream.

And then a rapid series of pops echoed off the surrounding buildings, followed by a snake's hiss surrounding the car.

"Jesus," said Darren. Both hands grasped the wheel as it shook violently. He guided the car to the side of the road and eased it to a stop.

"What happened?" asked Noah.

"Not sure." Darren opened his door and climbed out.

Ashley watched him in the side mirror as he walked around and glanced at each tire. He opened the car door but didn't climb in.

"Tires are flat."

"All of them?" asked Noah.

Darren nodded. One arm rested on the roof of the car and the other on top of the open car door. He ducked to face the backseat.

"It must be some kind of record," he said. Darren stood back up and looked into the road. He said something but nobody could hear it.

"What?" asked Noah.

He turned back around.

"There's nothing in the road." Then he stood back up. "Weird."

Ashley opened her door, climbed out, and opened the door to the backseat.

"Come on, sweetie," she said and took Sadie by the hand. "Come on Noah."

Darren walked around the back of the car and the four of them stood on the sidewalk.

"Well—"

"You're going to have to call a tow truck," she said.

"Yeah I—"

"We're gonna walk home."

Darren moved his feet but didn't walk anywhere. He crossed and uncrossed his arms.

"You are?"

"How's that coffee, Noah?"

He held the cup in both hands and took a sip so fast there was no way it still had liquid inside.

"Great!"

"Okay good. Here honey take my hand."

Sadie reached up. Ashley's hand folded around hers.

"Um, alright I guess I'll let you know how it goes," said Darren.

But Ashley and the kids were already walking down the sidewalk. She raised her free hand as a backwards wave.

How far away were they? Couldn't be more than a mile. How long is that? A half hour? No way. Couldn't be that long. It couldn't be more than—

"Mom?" said Sadie. "I'm tired."

"It won't be long."

Ashley looked down at her daughter. Pink coat with a small hood hanging off the back. Black tights. White shoelaces, both slightly dirty. Was there any way she could stay the way she was? Not small. Parents always seemed to want their kids to stay small.

Little fingers. Tiny toes. Ashley didn't care about that. It was her daughter's calmness. Gentleness. There was something different about her. Noah hadn't seemed this coherent at three. His favorite game was to have Darren grab him by the ankles and hang him upside down like a bat. He gave himself black eyes from accidentally running into walls. He was a completely different species from his sister which made their bond that much more interesting. Weren't siblings supposed to fight?

Sadie's veneer would fade. The world wasn't exactly a nice place. And of course they approached the Oneida Street Bridge as this thought ran through her mind. She hated this bridge. The sidewalks were wide. The lanes were wide. You couldn't see the river from the middle lanes of the four-lane road. It would be hard to fathom that Josie Hammond took her last breath right before hitting the water about sixty feet below the wide lanes and wide sidewalks.

Josie was already a little off when they met in 7th grade. Her eyes never seemed to meet yours. Even her steps were quiet. Josie was scared. Of everything. Being called upon in class to offer her opinion or answer a question made her shake. Her words fumbled from her mouth and she'd sit with her head in her hands for minutes afterwards.

Everybody was shocked, but nobody was surprised when they heard she climbed over the railing on the Oneida Street Bridge. They found her body the next morning. Her name was in the paper that day. And it was all anybody talked about for an entire afternoon. But after that, it was over. A tribute page in the yearbook reminded everyone at the end of the school year of a sad little girl named Josie Hammond that nobody had known. Not really. Not enough to understand why the river was better than going to bed and coming to school the next day.

That was the question that stuck with Ashley: Why? What was so bad?

And now they were about halfway across the bridge—close to where Josie climbed over.

She looked down to her daughter who kept her eyes on the cars passing by to their right. What happened to Josie? What convinced her it wasn't worth it? And how could she keep that thought out of her daughter's head?

The first few raindrops were only a suggestion, but the downpour soon became a declaration: You better get moving.

"Come on!" yelled Ashley.

Sadie pulled her hand away from her Mom and ran. Noah kept pace next to her even though he could easily be a block ahead. Ashley trotted behind them. They became soaked. Immediately. There was almost no point in running but they continued anyway.

Over the bridge.

Take a left after the Chinese restaurant that used to be a bar.

A few more blocks and they finally came up to their house.

Kids have extra energy reserves somewhere inside. It's as if the multiple naps every day are storing some hidden battery cell. Their breath came in large puffs but it came out through smiles. Ashley, however, needed a moment.

She stood in the driveway with her hands on her knees. Her chest burned. The rain continued to pummel the back of her head. Her soaked jeans and sweatshirt clung to her body. Only now did she notice the cold air. She looked up and saw the second car—all four wheels inflated.

She imagined Darren standing on the side of the road as the tow truck loaded the hobbled vehicle. Cold. Wet. Alone.

And then like changing the channel she again saw him in bed with some nameless, faceless, shameless woman.

She walked to the back of the house where the extra key was hidden in a fake rock. She unlocked the door and the kids ran inside. She closed the door behind herself and turned the lock.

32.

Sam Keeps Hope Alive

The computer acted as a centerpiece on the kitchen table. Sam and his parents tried to wrap their heads around the attention that stupid kid's video brought to their campaign. He didn't want to say it out loud but Sam thought the incident at the school just might be about the best thing that could've happened.

"We did it," he said.

Mary smiled but didn't say anything. She'd been quiet besides the thick coughs that came out of nowhere.

"Five grand. And then some. That's more than enough for us to get there and back and to cover some bills." Sam smiled. Was this the first thing he had ever done for them? Ever *really* done? The pride in his chest threatened to burst through his t-shirt.

"Are you ready to see the Grand Canyon, Mom?"

She looked at him and smiled, but Sam didn't believe it.

Greg stood up from the table and grabbed a glass from the cupboard near the sink. He filled it with water and sat back down.

"Listen, Sam." He adjusted himself in the chair and looked at Mary. "I don't think we should do this. This trip."

"What?"

"That's a long drive."

"We'll fly."

Greg shook his head. "Your mother doesn't fly."

His parents were going to go on a vacation maybe fifteen years earlier. A real one. Not just to some other part of the state. They were going to fly to a Florida resort. The beach. The Gulf of Mexico. The middle of a Wisconsin winter can seem like you're repeating the same miserable day over and over for your whole life. Sunshine and warm sand became an unfathomable luxury and the Webers were going to immerse themselves in it for the first time. It was all they talked about for months. They'd have dreams about it.

And then the day finally came.

They packed their bags and had someone drive them to the airport and went through security and sat at the terminal and boarded the plane and clicked their seatbelts and then Mary started sweating. A lot. Strapped into a seat in a tube with a bunch of strangers and no open windows felt like someone wrapping their meaty hands around her neck and squeezing. Her breath came in frantic gasps. Her vision speckled white.

A flight attendant saw the woman in row 25 and immediately came over.

"Nervous flier?" he asked.

Greg looked up at the man. Mid-twenties with a perfectly manicured hairstyle.

"First time," Greg said.

"Well welcome aboard," he said with a smile. "You have nothing to worry about. Quick flight. We might hit a little turbulence over Chicago but that's totally normal and won't be a problem. If you need—"

And that's when Mary's blood pressure dropped, her head became a swivel—

"I don't feel so good."

—and she slumped forward in her seat.

The Weber family learned a few things that day. First, airlines don't take off after a passenger passes out. Second, Mary Weber doesn't fly.

Back in the kitchen with Greg holding his glass of water and Mary sitting silently at his side, Sam nodded.

"It's just with my heart, and you've heard this cough your mother has, I don't know if it's really the best idea to be in the car for a couple days."

"What if we go to a doctor and they tell us she's okay to go?" asked Sam.

"We don't have money for a doctor."

Sam slouched in his chair. The kitchen stayed quiet for a few moments. Finally, he reached forward and slid the computer toward himself.

"We set the goal at three thousand, which was already more than we needed," said Sam. "And now we're over five."

Greg shrugged his bony shoulders and nodded. "It's pretty crazy. I'll give you that."

Sam leaned forward. "You know, we can keep whatever money we get. Anything over the goal, I mean."

Greg didn't respond, but he also didn't turn away.

"We can use the rest of the money to pay for a doctor's visit. There's no way it'll be more than two grand, right? We can just pay it out of pocket."

His father looked over to Mary.

"I don't see why not at least try," she said.

Sam smiled.

33.

Mary's Diagnosis

Mary was really getting tired of going to the doctor. Being the constant center of attention is exhausting. But getting that attention because of a deficiency was downright embarrassing. And now here she was listening to another doctor talking about another thing wrong with her.

She sat on a stiffly cushioned table in a thin apron. They made her change her clothes so they could take an x-ray of her chest. It was cold and she wanted everyone to stop looking at her. Greg sat in a wooden chair in the corner of the examination room, a nurse held a clipboard and grabbed whatever the doctor asked for, and the doctor himself stood with his hands on his hips staring into the black and white image of the inside of her chest.

"Community-acquired lobar pneumonia," said the doctor. He didn't have to duck when he came into the room, but it was close. Mary didn't like having a tall doctor but she didn't know why.

"Community-acquired?" asked Greg.

"You said you didn't choke on anything, right?"

Mary shook her head.

"And you didn't have any hospital stays recently, right?

She shook her head again.

"Yeah, so that means she caught something out in the wild. It usually comes from a virus or bacteria." The doctor paused and turned to Mary again. "No flu anytime recently?"

She shook her head.

"So it's probably a bacteria then. Streptococcus pneumoniae is the most common."

"Strepto what?" asked Greg.

"Honestly, the name doesn't really matter to anybody but me. All you're going to see is shortness of breath, some gross coughing." He turned to Mary. "Have you been coughing stuff up?"

Mary looked to Greg. She hadn't told him about this part. She didn't want him to worry more than he already did. And telling him that she occasionally saw red in the tissue when she coughed would have sent him into a full freak out. But you can't lie to the doctor.

"It's not usually red," she said.

"That wonderful stuff is what we call sputum. It's a mixture of saliva and mucus. There can occasionally be some blood in it especially when the coughs really seem to come from down deep, but it's not a major cause for concern." He turned to Greg. "A lot of people think coughing up blood immediately means you're going to die. Don't get me wrong—it's not good." He chuckled. "I definitely don't recommend it, but it's not the end of the world."

Greg's mouth hung open as if he was going to say something, but he just sat there like that.

"So am I okay?" asked Mary.

The doctor shook his head. "Nope. No, definitely not. You have pneumonia. You see this?" he pointed to a vaguely hazy section of the x-ray. "This is fluid. In your lung. That's not good. It's localized to a singular lobe but that doesn't mean it isn't serious."

Greg sat forward in his chair. "So as far as a cross country road trip—"

"Sounds like a real nice time for somebody else. Just not you."

Greg nodded and sat back.

Mary watched the two men talking and hated every second of it. She was there. She was right there but they carried on as if Greg were acting as her proxy. She should have been used to it by now, but she wasn't. In reality, none of it really mattered. She tried to tell herself that as much as possible but she couldn't help the bubble of annoyance rising within her. It wasn't there often. At least not projected outwardly. Inward, sure. Almost all the time.

It wasn't a surprise that she wouldn't be able to go on the trip. The walls of the house were to be her coffin until she finally made it into an actual one.

Her chest burned. The coughs were only the crackles of the flames and the spit of the embers from the fire building within her ribcage. Breathing hurt. She sweat despite the chills that made her shake.

That final coffin probably wasn't all that far off, she thought.

The doctor and Greg continued blabbing back and forth but Mary didn't care to listen. She got all the information she needed: The Grand Canyon would remain a mystery.

The paper between her backside and the table crinkled as she adjusted herself. The doctor looked over.

"I bet you want to get dressed," he said.

She nodded.

"Alright, I'm going to grab my pad and get you some prescriptions. Now, all that gross stuff you've been coughing up? That's what we want. We want that stuff out. So you're going to drink plenty of fluids and get it all loosened up. Warm stuff. In fact, take some steamy baths and sit next to a humidifier. And rest.

You're going to just need to let your body take care of this so this is your excuse to have Mr. Weber over here waiting on you like a servant." He looked over to Greg. "Got that?"

Greg nodded.

"Alright. Great. We're going to get you some antibiotics and some pain killers to help you knock this stuff out. We'll throw in some cough suppressant for good measure too. I'm guessing those big whoopers hurt, eh?"

Mary nodded.

"Thought so. They sure sound meaty." The doctor turned and opened the door to the hallway. "Don't go anywhere." He walked out.

Greg stood up and walked over to the exam table.

"Here," he said and handed her a grey sweatshirt and a t-shirt. She threw the gown over her head and put them on. The exposure to the cold air, albeit brief, sent a wave of shivers through her body.

"Thank you."

They stayed like that for a moment. Her sitting on the table and Greg standing next to her. And then she turned to him.

"Greg?"

He turned and rested his hands on the table next to her thigh. "Yeah? You feeling okay?"

"Yeah, yeah I'm fine." She wasn't. "But listen, I still want to go."

Greg let out a long breath and looked down to his hands.

"We can't," he said without bringing his eyes up to hers.

She turned to face the door in front of her. The doctor would be back any moment. She knew she had to get there. She didn't know why, but that didn't seem necessary. Most things she did these days were done without knowing why. Maybe it was a thought that had passed and left a shadow of a memory. But just like being dragged to the store without knowing why, something pulled her to Arizona. Her chest throbbed in recognition and she coughed. It wracked her whole body. Every muscle from her waist to her hairline seized up.

"It's okay," said Greg as he gently set his hand in the middle of her back.

The cough scraped everything from her throat to the center of her body. It took a few breaths before her wind fully returned.

The door swung open and the doctor appeared.

"Alright. Here you go. Three prescriptions, three pills, three weeks. It should start to calm down in around ten days or so but it will take a bit to fully knock it out. Now I want you to be careful. Your age, your medical history, all of that makes this a dangerous position to be in. Honestly, if you had insurance, I'd put some serious thought into recommending a hospital stay until you're out of the weeds. But apparently you brought a sack of cash with you today like a couple of mobsters so that's not exactly an option."

He handed the pieces of paper to Greg who folded them up and stuck them in his back pocket.

"Now, if things get worse—at all—you just gotta say screw it and go to a hospital. Deal?"

Mary nodded.

"Okay good. Go lay down and let your body do its thing."

Mary stood up and followed her husband out the door, down a short hallway, and back into the waiting area. It had been full when they went in but now it was empty. A TV played the same loop of generic medical advice: Happy people doing jumping jacks while a voice over discussed the importance of heart health.

Greg paid.

They left.

He helped her into the car before walking around the other side and climbing in.

"I still want to go," she said after he turned the ignition.

The radio kicked in after a short moment of listening to the rumbling engine.

He seemed like he was going to say something. He looked at the gauges in front of him as if arranging a thought. And then he put the car in reverse, backed out of the parking spot, and headed home.

34.

Greg Puts His Foot Down

Sam waited for them at the kitchen table when they got home.

"Hey," he said. "How'd it go?"

"Pneumonia," said Greg. "She has pneumonia." He followed two steps behind Mary as they walked from the garage into the house. He closed the door behind them and waited for Mary to take off her shoes. "You should go lie down," he told her.

Mary ignored him and walked into the kitchen. Sam jumped to the side when a thunderous cough stopped her between the table and the counter. Each hack lingered longer than it should. It happened three times. She wiped her mouth and walked to get a glass of water.

"Jeez Mom," said Sam.

"Exactly." Greg pulled out a chair and sat at the table with his son. God, how he wanted to lie down. He felt like he could sleep for a year. His legs ached. His chest hurt. His breaths were thick and felt like they didn't really carry all that much air. It surrounded him. The lack of air. It seemed they had something special there for a moment when that asshole kid ended up doing them a huge favor, but that was over. There was no way they could take Mary anywhere besides the living room. Even that was pushing it.

"Pneumonia?" asked Sam.

Greg nodded. Mary sat down in the chair next to them. He looked over at his wife and forced a smile. It didn't seem to land. She only nodded and took another drink of water. It had to have happened during the walk. Some weird germ or whatever the doctor said crawled inside her and created this hack. This cough. It hurt just to listen to it. And the way she shuddered when the scraping exhalations forced their way out of her—it was downright terrifying to watch. He'd get the prescriptions tomorrow. She'd start getting better tomorrow.

Things would start getting better tomorrow.

Maybe one day that would be true.

"What do you think Mom?"

Mary took a drink of water and turned to her son.

"About what?"

"The trip. The Grand Canyon?"

"It doesn't matter what she thinks. Or you think. Or I think," said Greg. "The only thing that matters is what someone who holds a medical degree thinks. And he said we can't go anywhere."

"I want to go," she told her son.

Greg looked at the ceiling before closing his eyes. The light was still too bright, so he put his hands over his eyelids and pushed.

"I don't recall either of you going to medical school," he said with his face to the ceiling.

A twinkly song suddenly emerged from the tiny hallway leading to the garage. Mary's phone, muffled by the walls of her purse.

"I'm a nurse, remember?" said Sam.

"And we're all very proud of you." Greg continued facing the ceiling. "But this can't happen. She shouldn't even be in the kitchen. She should be in bed."

"Trust me, Dad. I know how serious pneumonia can be. I've seen it a few times. I probably should've been able to tell you that's what it was before you even went to the doctor."

"But you didn't." Greg let go of his face and opened his eyes. All of the shapes around him were nothing more than impressionistic blurs that represented kitchen items and family members. He faced the Sam-colored blob.

"Do you remember when your mother and I took a weekend up north for our anniversary?"

Sam looked to Mary for a moment before turning back to Greg. "Yeah," he said quietly.

"What happened?"

"Oh come on Dad that was—"

"What happened?"

Sam shuffled in his seat a bit. Mary's phone again sprang into song. Nobody paid much attention besides Mary glancing toward the garage.

"We had a small accident," said Sam.

And he was right. Sam was 17 at the time. He would be graduating high school in six months. Ashley had left by this time so he was going to have the house to himself for the first time. They considered it a dry run of Sam going off to college the following fall.

"This is your chance," Mary told him right before they left. "Prove to us you're an adult. That we can trust you."

She stared at him for a moment like she had to countless students over the years. He screwed up and told his friends that his house was going to be empty so of course they wanted to throw a party. He refused. He said it was a cliché. They said it was a cliché because it was such a good idea.

So in the end he told them the trip was canceled. Mom and Dad Weber were going to be in the house all weekend so don't bother coming over.

And then the boredom came. Being good lost its shine after a couple hours and all you were left with was the regret of a wasted opportunity and too much time to think about it. So he called Steve Bauer and invited him over.

They didn't drink. They didn't smoke weed. But they did get bored.

Sam had been sitting on the porch just flicking a lighter he found in a drawer. He didn't have a plan. Just grinding the sparkwheel and watching it flash. And then Steve took off his shoe.

"Hey check this out," he said. He grabbed the lighter, lit it, and held it up to his heel. A mesmerizing singular wave of flame engulfed his sock as it fed on the fuzzy lint and disappeared as quickly as it arrived. A smell of burned hair surrounded them before the wind took it away.

One thing led to another. Soon, they were grabbing random bottles from a storage shelf in the back corner of the garage.

"Do you think bug spray is flammable?" asked Sam. Steve shrugged so Sam held the nozzle, flicked the lighter and a burst of orange flame accompanied by a deep growl spit in front of them.

"What about WD-40?"

Eagerness quickly eclipsed intelligence and they forgot that these were moist sprays and not gasses. A gas would dissipate. A spray eventually lands on something. And even when it's set on fire, there will be particles that make it through the blaze to the other side, where they'll land on something until the flame finally reaches them.

Greg and Mary Weber came home two days later to find a corner of their garage stained black from the fire that almost engulfed the entire home.

"That was like fifteen years ago," said Sam. Mary's ringtone continued its chime near the garage.

Greg nodded. "Yeah, but the decision-making processes that almost burned the whole place down are the same."

"What are you talking about?"

"Why did you start burning things that night? You're not some weird pyro right?"

Sam sat back in his chair. "No."

"Didn't think so. So what was it?"

"We were *kids*."

"Kinda. You were basically the same then as when you went to college, right? That's pretty much the start of adulthood."

Sam shrugged.

"You started putting that lighter to bug spray because you wanted to see what would happen. You were curious. And that's fine, but your curiosity got in the way of seeing what the actual, concrete repercussions could be. There are consequences. There are always consequences. Focusing on the end doesn't mean the stuff in-between doesn't matter. Because it's that stuff that's going to dictate which version of the end you are going to get. So there you are, lighting things on fire and what did you want?"

"What did I want?"

"Yeah, what did you want?"

Mary's phone chimed again from the next room. She stood up but Greg hardly noticed. He stared at Sam, waiting for an answer. He wasn't mad. He wasn't yelling. But he needed his son to understand something.

"I don't know, I guess I didn't want to be bored anymore. I wanted something to happen."

"So you forced something to happen."

Sam nodded.

The sound of Mary's ring got slightly louder for a moment as she took her phone from her purse.

"Hello?" she said and turned toward the garage.

"This is the same thing," said Greg. "You're forcing an idea because you want something to happen."

Sam leaned his elbows on the table in front of him. He took a deep breath and ran his hands through his hair.

"Dad, listen. I'm a nurse. I can take care of her. There are hospitals everywhere just in case something goes wrong. She wants to go. You heard her. We can do this. We have the money. We have the time. We can make this happen for her before it's too late."

"It's already too late," said Greg.

Mary's muffled voice filled in the silence between them.

Greg hated his last sentence. He hated that it was the last thing to hang in the air of the kitchen.

Mary stopped talking and walked back into the kitchen, around the table, and back into her seat.

"Who was that?" asked Greg.

She sandwiched the phone between her hands on the table in front of her. She looked at it for another moment before she looked up to her husband.

"We have to go to the Grand Canyon," she said.

"What? Who was that?"

She cocked her head a bit before looking back down at the phone. Then back to Greg.

"Who was what?"

"On the phone."

She looked back down and let the phone drop to the table.

"I don't know," she said.

"You don't know?"

She looked at Greg. Her wide eyes jumped back and forth as they alternated focus on either of his. She shrugged.

"Mary, we can't—"

"I have to go," she said. "I'm tired and I'm going to lie down." She stood up and hovered above him. Greg caught a glimpse of the way those students must have seen her for all those years. Strong. Intimidating. In full possession of a firm authority.

"Mary—"

"Soon," she said. Her voice filled the entire kitchen despite its low volume. It seemed to come from within his head. He looked up to his wife and could tell she was exhausted, that she was almost shaky on her legs. But that hangover of previous authority never really left her. He found it difficult to hold her gaze, but he forced himself to meet her eyes. They stayed like this for a moment before he slowly nodded.

"Soon," he said.

35.

Ashley Makes a Decision

"Wow," said Ashley, looking down at her phone.

Darren set the box he was carrying through the living room of his small apartment on the arm of the couch.

"What?"

"They're leaving tomorrow."

"Your family?"

"Yeah."

"Huh." He stood up and grabbed the box. There wasn't much. Not like when they bought the house. But there was enough to make it a chore.

She slid the phone into her back pocket and watched as he carried the box out the door. The rented moving truck sat open in the parking lot on the first floor. She could see the top of it through the sliding glass door that led to his little balcony. Altogether it wasn't that bad. It's basically exactly what she would have pictured if someone told her to imagine a new apartment for a divorced thirty-something. In fact, that's exactly what she told him the first time she brought the kids over. Noah thought it was cool. Just like his room only bigger, he said. Sadie didn't like it but she only told Ashley after they left.

Well, they won't have to deal with it anymore.

It definitely had a certain amount of comfort to it. The brown rug and brown walls made it feel like a cabin on the inside. The dirty siding made it look like a flophouse outside.

Did she see it?

It was a dumb question Ashley couldn't get out of her head. What did she think the first time she came here? Had she come more than once? What did she think of the brown rug?

They didn't talk about it since the coffee shop. Embarrassment flooded her cheeks whenever she thought about it. What a terrible conversation. What a terrible image. What a terrible thing to do. She never wanted to talk about it again.

Darren walked back into the apartment. His forehead spit-shined with unwiped sweat.

"Did you sleep with her or not?" asked Ashley. She stood over an open box with a stack of forks in one hand. The four-compartment plastic silverware holder hidden inside, waiting.

He stopped walking but didn't look at her. He brushed a hand against the open door which slowly clicked shut. A deep breath seemed to fill the dark, brown apartment and he resumed his seat on the arm of the couch. Hands folded in his lap, he looked at Ashley and waited another couple breaths.

"I'm really excited to come home," he said.

"The kids are looking forward to it, too." And that was true. It was basically the only thing they wanted for the last year. They might understand one day, but that would be a decade or two from now. Maybe more.

Opening this door in her brain was one of the great accidental mistakes of her life. You never really try to have an idea. They just kind of arrive. If you're an inventor, they're a blessing. If you're navigating the confusing process of reassembling a marriage, they're a real kick in the ass. But you can't get rid of them once they're there. An idea is the only difference between a sane person and someone that needs to be locked away. A simple idea. It's not something you can measure, or guard against, or eradicate. It's there and you either have to figure out how to change it or exercise it until it loses all its power. Opinions are easier to change. Curiosities can only be seen to their end.

Darren stood up from the arm of the couch and grabbed another box. It was a clever attempt at conversational jiu-jitsu. Ashley set the forks into the box with a quiet *ching*.

He hoisted the box into one arm and grabbed the doorknob with the other. It didn't turn.

"What the hell?" he said quietly. He set the box on the ground and got a better grip on the doorknob. It refused to open.

Ashley crumpled loose pages of newspaper and set them on top of the silverware. The plates were next.

Darren again sat on the arm of the couch and pulled out his phone.

"I can't believe this," said Darren as he put the phone to his ear. He wiped his forehead with his free arm and then straightened up. "Hello? Yeah, hey it's Darren. Wolff. In 204. Yeah. Yeah, we're getting there. Listen, the door won't open. The front door. To the hallway." He looked over at Ashley and shook his head. "I don't know, the knob won't turn. Yes. *Yes*. I'm sure. An *hour*?" He closed his eyes and took a breath. "Alright bye."

"He sounds like a real treat."

"It's almost unbelievable talking to that man."

The electronics were already packed away. No stereo. No television. The couch and the kitchenware were the only things left in the apartment. Ashley still felt the question hanging in the air. She didn't need to repeat it. He heard her. He knew what she wanted. But here they were in total silence with no distractions and he could only analyze the doorknob. She wouldn't break the silence. That would only bury her question. Did she even want an answer or did she just want to ask the question?

Interesting.

Darren stood up and jiggled the handle a few more times. He didn't seem as acclimated to the silence.

"Have you ever watched one of those slaughterhouse videos?" he asked.

"What?"

He walked into the living room and looked out the sliding glass door.

"They don't allow cameras into them. The chicken houses and the slaughterhouses and all that. I mean, there's no real reason to bring a camera in there besides trying to make them look bad anyways. But sometimes an activist will sneak in or something and film, y'know, what happens in there."

"Why were you looking for that?"

"I wasn't. It just kinda came up."

"How the hell does something like that just come up?'

Darren pulled open the sliding door, walked out onto the balcony, put a hand on the railing, and jumped over.

Ashley watched from the kitchen and simply saw her husband disappear. She didn't scream. She listened. Soft crunching signaled his landing in the bushes directly below. The absence of a shout let her know he hadn't hurt himself—not badly at least. Next she heard stomps coming up the stairs. And then the door to the apartment abruptly swung open.

Darren poked his head inside. "I didn't want to wait an hour," he said.

"Did you sleep with her or not?"

He walked into the apartment and left the door open. The arm of the couch welcomed him back. He ran a hand over his face and through his greasy hair. A few green needles fell to the brown carpet below. A red scrape above his knee threatened to bleed but hadn't made it that far quite yet. He drew in a long breath and looked at his wife in the kitchen.

"Should I keep moving my stuff or not?"

Her heart sank. She slowly closed the box of silverware and dishes. She didn't tape it but let her hands rest on top. It took her a moment to steady her breath enough to speak evenly. The quiet apartment waited patiently for her response. She moved her gaze from the box in front of her to Darren on the arm of the couch in the adjacent living room.

"I'm going to the Grand Canyon."

She walked around the table of half-filled boxes and closed the door behind herself on the way out.

36.

Sam Feels the Topeka Wind

The first day of driving wasn't that bad. Not really. Sitting in the car for ten hours certainly wasn't great, but it wasn't terrible either. Greg drove most of the time. Sam helped out when he was allowed. Mary sat in the front seat, alternating between fitful naps and body-shaking coughs that exploded like shotgun blasts inside the car.

And now they were about to head out for a second day. Sam stood outside of the Motel 6 just off Interstate 70 in Topeka. It was his first time being in the absolute center of the country. People on the coasts always poked fun at these states. They called them fly-overs, boring, and farmland. He looked at the gas station across the street and then up and down the road that waited for him on the other side of the small parking lot.

He understood where those people were coming from.

In fact, the last five hours or so of their drive hadn't shown him much. They traveled the space between Des Moines and Kansas City after dark. But he didn't need the sun to know they were surrounded by vast, flat cornfields and farmland.

The goal today was Albuquerque. They'd clip the far ends of the Oklahoma and Texas panhandles before passing over into New Mexico. He expected it to be flat until then.

But now, at maybe eight o'clock in the morning, he felt refreshed. The bed had been surprisingly comfortable. The walls were surprisingly thick. And Ashley was surprisingly quiet in the bed just to the right of his. He could still occasionally hear the rough scrape of his mother's cough from the next room, though.

Ashley must be enjoying her vacation from the kids, he thought. Eight seemed like the equivalent of noon for her, but she stayed in bed as he showered, put on clothes, and walked out front.

The air was warmer here, even though it blew much harder. The general flatness of the area seemingly imbued it with a near-constant wind speed of at least ten miles per hour. But it wasn't cold. And it smelled like fresh cut grass.

They'd be at the Grand Canyon by tomorrow afternoon.

He heard the seal of the motel door crack open and turned around.

"Well good morning," he said.

Ashley shielded her eyes from the sun and waved. She took a barefoot step outside in an old t-shirt and pajama pants.

"It's cold out here," she said.

"Nah, it's just windy."

She crossed her arms and looked up and down the road like he had a few minutes earlier.

"When was the last time the four of us went on vacation together?" she asked.

"The Badlands."

She nodded. "Yeah. Wow. That was the last time?" She adjusted her arms and shifted the weight on her bare feet. They must have been freezing on the cold concrete. "I guess high school wasn't long after that. It'd be kinda hard to get us all in the same car."

"I can't believe they gave such a great name to such a boring place," said Sam.

"You think? You really think it was boring?"

"Do you remember being excited?"

"I don't remember being excited by all that much back then."

Sam nodded and again looked at his sister's feet.

"Aren't you cold?"

"I just told you I was."

"No, I mean your feet."

She nodded. "Yup. Those are part of me."

Another twelve hours in the car today. Albuquerque had to be warm enough for bare feet in the morning.

"You know, I'm surprised you came."

"Darren slept with somebody," said Ashley. And then she turned around and walked back into the motel room.

Sam listened to the wind racing the cars on the road for a moment.

It was only twelve hours.

The next door over cracked open and a thunderous cough exploded from the darkness. Then Greg stepped out and closed the door behind himself.

"How's she doing?" asked Sam.

"Worse." Greg had yet to crack a single smile since they left home.

"We can let her sleep some more."

Greg looked back at the closed door for a moment.

"She's gotten all the sleep she's gonna get in there." He started walking toward the office. "You're sure we can pay this off when we get home, right?"

"Well hold on." Greg stopped walking. "Let's see where we're at."

Sam pulled out his phone and poked it a few times. "Here. Look. It's still going up."

Greg leaned over and nodded.

"In fact…" Sam poked the screen a few more times and held it facing himself but toward Greg. "We should do an update."

"A what?"

"These people are donating so we can go on this trip, but they don't get their satisfaction from us actually going on the trip."

"What are you talking about?"

"They get satisfaction from *seeing* us go on the trip."

Greg crossed his arms. "So what am I supposed to grovel? Praise them for being so generous?"

Sam shook his head and dropped his arms to his side.

"No, it's not gratitude. Think of a reality show."

"Which one?"

"Any one. Any one at all. Why do people watch them?"

Greg looked out to the street for a moment before turning back to his son.

"Who cares, Sam?"

"Dad, come on. Why do people watch them? As opposed to other types of shows?"

He threw up his hands and shook his head.

"Because nobody's really that good of an actor. Even the professionals," said Sam. "They can get close, but it's not real. And yeah I know most of those reality shows aren't totally real either. I get that. But there's just something different about some poor sad sack in a nowhere town telling their story to a camera that isn't high definition."

"So what, they like how shitty it is?"

Sam took a deep breath of the passing wind. The scent of grass was still there but a semi-truck must have kicked up some dirt on the side of the road a little ways up.

"It's easier to connect with it. Crisp images of people with professional makeup and a full orchestral score is art, but it's not real. People like real." Sam flipped a hand toward the two closed motel doors and then pointed to both himself and Greg. "But this, this is real. I wish it wasn't, but it is. We're here, and it's only because of the people that got behind this silly thing we put online. Who would pay to send some old lady they don't know to a national park across the country?"

Greg shrugged.

"Exactly. It's weird. And weird is interesting."

Greg nodded. "So we're a freak show."

"Kinda." Sam smiled. "But we can use it to keep milking these donations while we have their attention." He raised the phone and aimed the camera at Greg.

"I mean, what am I supposed to say?"

Sam shrugged. "You're on."

The camera framed Greg on a small sidewalk between the motel and the parking lot. A dark strip of blacktop ran along the left edge of the frame. The cream paint of the building and intermittent double windows ran along the right. Greg's hair—normally combed over from right to left—blew haphazardly in the wind that had not quit once since they arrived the night before. Greg's eyes darted between his feet before hopping up to the camera and back to his feet. He tried to start speaking a couple times but never got over the first hump. Sam just held the camera and waited. Finally, Greg said:

"We're in Topeka."

And then he shrugged. Sam made a circle with the forefinger of his free hand.

"I, uh, it's been a while since I've seen my wife excited. Like, truly excited. I guess you just kinda get comfortable with someone after a while and before you know it, all the days run together."

He ran a hand along the back of his neck and then stuck both of them into the pockets of his jeans.

"And if that's true for me, it's double true for Mary. I guess you guys know what's been, uh, going on. And it's been hard, you know?" He smiled as he said this, but it wasn't a happy smile. "It's been hard. But everybody's got something hard to deal with I suppose. I don't think that makes us all that different. And this trip has been hard too, to tell you the truth." He nodded his head toward the closed door behind the camera. "She's not feeling the best. I know you saw her not feeling good on that other video but this is a little different." He shrugged again and looked directly into the camera. "But we're still going. Against everything that I know to be reasonable, we're still going. So here we are in Topeka, we have another day of driving to Albuquerque, and then we'll be there. The trip she had been wanting to take for fifty years—we'll be there." Then he looked into the parking lot and stared at something that was nothing. "I don't know why the hell it took this long, but we'll get there. Just one more day." He paused, still looking at that something in the parking lot. Then he turned his eyes back to the camera. "So, uh, thanks."

Greg nodded and shrugged.

"That was perfect." Sam slid the phone into his pocket.

The door next to him cracked open again and Ashley walked out in a light sweatshirt, jeans, and sneakers.

"Hey, shoes. Nice," said Sam.

Greg let out a long breath and clapped his hands in front of him.

"I'm going to check out." He turned around and walked down the sidewalk that had just acted as his backdrop.

"Where's Mom?" asked Ashley.

Sam walked to her door and knocked. A cough answered from inside. Sam and Ashley glanced at each other for a moment before he tried the knob. It opened.

"Good morning," said Ashley.

The thick curtains had yet to be opened, but the sunshine pouring through the door lit up half the room. They could see the beds off to the left and their mother's feet underneath the blanket.

They walked inside. Ashley grabbed the little plastic wand at the top of the curtain and pulled it open. Sam sat on the bed.

"Just about time to hit the road," he said.

Mary rocked back and forth as she got her hands beneath her enough to sit up. She tried to wipe the hair from her face but sweat caused a few errant strands to stick to her forehead. It took her a moment to keep from squinting at the light suddenly pouring through the window. She looked at Sam and then over to Ashley, but she didn't say anything.

"You okay Mom? You need anything?" asked Ashley.

"What are you doing here?" asked Mary.

Sam looked to his left at his sister. She didn't move.

Then Mary looked around the room, first with a slow murkiness that quickly sped up. "Where is this?" Her head snapped back and locked eyes with Sam.

The panic. The confusion.

"It's okay Mom," said Ashley. She walked over, pushed Sam out of the way, and sat on the bed next to her. "We're in a motel. We're going to the Grand Canyon!"

Mary looked again between her children, except now Sam stood and Ashley sat next to her. Her eyes softened and she nodded slowly.

"It's time to get dressed," said Ashley as she stood up.

Mary took the cue and swung her legs off the other side of the bed. Another cough erupted before she stood up. Her back hunched with each hack. Finally, she stopped long enough to slowly stand up and walk into the bathroom.

Ashley slapped Sam on the shoulder. "Come on," she said.

They walked out of the room and closed the door.

Back in the sunshine on the sidewalk next to the parking lot. They stood in silence for a full minute.

"I should've been nicer to her when I had the chance," said Sam.

Ashley nodded and slapped him on the shoulder again.

"You still do," she said.

Another full minute passed. Then Sam turned from the parking lot and faced his sister.

"There was a reason you wanted to get back with Darren, right?"

She tried to brush the hair from her face, but the wind did whatever it wanted.

37.

Mary Feels a Glow

It felt like they'd been driving for 15 years. The front seat's supposed to be the most comfortable seat in the car. And if that was true, the others must be in pure agony.

Mary had been on road trips before. Obviously. She'd seen long stretches of highway that never seemed to end. She'd heard the slow change in accents at gas stations. She was used to the idea that once you get on a highway and make up your mind to stay there for a while, time was going to blend together.

Speed limit signs look the same in every state.

And she should have been used to the idea of clicking in and out of contemporary reality by now. It had been happening for so damn long. But how do you get used to an idea you can't recognize? How can something you continually forget become familiar?

They were going to the Grand Canyon. She knew that right now. She forgot it a few times since noon, and would forget it again, but right now she felt good. Mentally. It came and it went. Right now it was with her as they drove straight down this unimpressive highway like they'd been doing for weeks and months.

Where were they? New Mexico. Everything was rocks. Everything was dead. It was hard to call a giant pile of boulders a mountain or even a hill, but she supposed that's what people did around here.

At least the scenery had changed, though. Driving through the never-ending cornfields of flat Earth in both directions as far as you can see gets old, even when you forget stretches of time.

The others must have been in pure agony.

But they kept their spirits high. They tried to, at least. Conversation was kept to a minimum but the radio filled in the gaps.

Speaking had become difficult. Each exhalation wanted to grow into a painful cough. She wanted to avoid that as much as possible. They were loud. They felt like someone taking an ice cream scooper to the inside of her chest. And worse than that, they made Greg look at her with that face.

That face that said, *Please don't die on me right now.*

There was a time and place for everything, she wanted to tell him. And this wasn't the time or the place for that.

But they couldn't stop. She knew that. She didn't know how she knew that, but it was clear. Maybe this was how clairvoyants felt. Not that she believed in that.

"Oh thank God," said Greg as they passed a sign reading *Albuquerque 10.*

"I can take over for you whenever you want," said Sam but Greg just waved a hand at him.

Greg turned to Mary. "How you feeling?" He moved that waving hand to her thigh and grabbed on. He didn't shake it, rub it, or move it in any way. He just held tight.

"Fine," Mary managed to say. Of course, this answer was always a lie. She hadn't been fine for years but it was all relative at this point.

Ashley lightly snored behind Mary's seat.

They drove another fifteen minutes before Sam directed his father to the parking lot of another Motel 6.

"You buy stock in these guys or something?" asked Greg.

"Hey, once they stop putting places to stay immediately off our highways, I'll find somewhere else."

It looked so desolate. So unsupportive of life. Even the roads seemed to cry out for rain.

"People live here?" she asked.

Greg laughed. "Plenty of 'em."

They pulled into the parking lot and Greg finally turned off the engine after they found a spot outside of the office. He stepped out. Sam and Ashley climbed out at the same time.

Might as well, thought Mary and followed them.

Greg disappeared into the building and the kids must have followed him. Mary took a few steps into the parking lot and felt a light breeze crawl across her skin.

It was warm. The sun was almost gone but it was still warm. She closed her eyes and ran her fingers over her exposed arms. No goosebumps. No sweater. She started to understand why people might live here.

She opened her eyes and walked to the edge of the parking lot. The road disappeared over a hill. Far beyond, the tip of a rock mountain peeked over the horizon, not quite ready to say goodnight. The road was free of cars. The parking lot had a couple of sleeping machines, but there were no engines, brakes, or tires battling the few bird calls she could pick out from the atmosphere.

Clouds spread throughout the sky like trails of smoke. They glowed red and orange from the setting sun behind her. She followed the flow of the clouds up above her head and behind her toward the glowing red ball. Maybe it was the angle, or maybe her eyes just didn't work as well as they used to—whatever the case, she was able to look directly at the setting sun and watch as it melded with the horizon. More rocks. More hills. More alien landscapes she had never seen and realistically, won't remember.

But that didn't matter.

Nothing needs to last forever. Not people. Not memories.

Not me.

She watched the sun flatten into the horizon and was confused as to why the light didn't dim. She looked behind her and saw the approaching darkness of night coming from the mountain at the end of the disappearing road. The shadow of the Earth quickly swallowed the smoke-like clouds and the city around her. It descended over her like a giant blanket.

But the light still didn't seem to dim at the center of the sunset.

"Mom!"

Ashley's voice cut through the air of the newborn night and sparked a quick flutter of Mary's heart.

A cough erupted from deep within her chest.

"Oh jeez. Hey, wow you okay?" Ashley trotted up and placed a hand on Mary's back. "We didn't know where you went."

Mary's throat screamed in red. She wiped the collected saliva from her lips. The streetlights kicked on and she could see red blotches on the ground beneath her, reflecting their orange light.

"Come on. Let's go to your room," said Ashley. She put her arm around her mother's shoulders and turned her toward the motel.

They walked across the parking lot where the doors hung open on two adjacent rooms. Sam walked out of the door on the left and leaned into the open car. Ashley hesitated.

"Everything okay?" asked Mary.

Ashley nodded and helped her mother into her room.

Mary stood in the doorway and looked at the two beds on her left. They were thinner than the hotel beds she had seen in the past, excluding the previous night. In fact, the room was remarkably similar to the room in Topeka. Mary's head became light and for a moment she couldn't be sure if they were in Topeka, Albuquerque, or anywhere else.

How long had they been here?

Is this where they live now?

"I gotta sit down," she said to the woman next to her. She felt a gentle hand on her back guide her to one of the thin beds. A man came out of the bathroom but Mary was too exhausted to be afraid. There was something vaguely familiar about them, but their faces were a blur.

She ran her hand along the grey comforter on top of the bed. It felt rough. More like a rug than a blanket. She wondered if the other side was softer. It had to be. She didn't realize beads of sweat had collected on her arms and forehead until the air conditioning made them feel like ice. The heat outside had been nice. Her insides seemed to be running cooler than the rest of her body lately. It was a cruel joke, really. Sweat cooled her down, but that was the last thing she wanted.

Nothing was recording. She could tell. Could she always tell? Focusing on the immediate sensory factors around her was the only way to stay in the moment. Engaging with that man now standing at the foot of the bed was impossible. There was a woman here a moment ago, wasn't there?

A harsh metallic scrape screamed from the curtains as the man threw them shut.

The small light in the distance might still be there. It had to be.

She didn't know how she knew it, but she did.

And then a muffled shout tried to pound its way through the wall behind her.

The man sighed and opened the door.

A debilitating lethargy enveloped her, but Mary stood from the bed and walked to the doorway.

The rush of fresh air eased the aches in her joints. The muscles of her legs stopped screaming and she breathed the night air in deep. She let it out in a long, slow breath and fixed her eyes on the horizon. The sun was gone. There was no reflection on the clouds above, no orange light warming the horizon.

But there was a glow.

It was faint but Mary could see it if she didn't try to look directly at it. Her peripheral vision detected a soft, white glow from the west. Not only could she see it, she could *feel* it.

Greg walked out of the adjoining room and Ashley came right behind him.

"Everything okay?" he asked.

Mary nodded and kept looking at the horizon. Greg glanced behind him to the west, and then back to her.

"What are you looking at?"

"Nothing," she said.

There were some things that just couldn't be explained. Only understood.

"I'm staying with you guys tonight," said Ashley as she walked past Mary and into their room. Greg followed behind her.

"What are you twelve? Just go back to your room."

You only notice certain parts of your body when something's wrong with it. Toothaches. Upset stomach. Sore muscles. They're there all the time but they blend into the background as your mind tries to find something to occupy itself.

And as Mary stood on the sidewalk outside of her motel room, her husband and daughter arguing over something, she became aware of everything.

Every bone in her body sang. Every muscle hummed along. The sickness in her chest throbbed with heat but not the familiar burn of the last few days.

And it didn't stop there. Mary could feel the tension in both of the motel rooms. Everyone was worried about something, but that was just life. A couple in the room above were on an anniversary trip to Joshua Tree. The manager at the front desk searched local job openings.

The bulb on the parking lot light closest to her had another week before it would blow.

The traffic light at the end of the block was about to turn red.

The glowing light on the horizon wouldn't be glowing at this time tomorrow.

Mary breathed deep and smiled.

Endings are the ultimate understanding.

38.

Greg Attempts Something Reasonable

Does the sun rise earlier in the desert? Does that make any sense at all? There was just so much less…everything. It seemed to Greg that the light from the morning sun could be seen a little earlier—that even though it was still on the other side of the Earth, there was just less stuff to get in the way of the light.

Did that make sense?

Greg stretched his elbows toward each other behind himself. His shoulder blades sang in recognition, but it was his chest that drew his attention. He was no doctor, but he could tell when something's wrong.

Just get there and get back.

It had become his mantra. His battle cry.

Just get there and get back.

Everything else could be figured out after that. But this trip—this stupid trip that he still didn't think they should be on—was his wife's last chance at enjoying herself. Of course, there was no way to know that. He couldn't tell how quickly things would continue to degrade. They seemed to be moving quickly but then, every once in a while, he could see Mary as she was when she terrified students. It was as if she were spying out of her own eyes.

Just checking in every so often to make sure things were going the way they should.

Of course, they weren't.

But this was it. This was the day. They were to leave early and get to the park a little after noon. They'd have a few hours to do whatever they wanted and then come right back here.

He'd have the same breakfast two days in a row.

He walked along the outside of the building until he turned the corner toward the office. A communal room sat just on the other side of the check-in desk where there was sure to be a terrible breakfast.

But hey, it was better than gas station energy bars.

"Good morning," said the small man behind the desk. Overnight jobs were never fun—Greg knew all about that—but working overnight while sitting was damn near impossible. This man must have taken a handful of naps since clocking in the night before.

And if so, he got more sleep than Greg.

Mary's pneumonia was a talkative beast even when she wasn't coughing. The fluid seemed to move directly into her air passages when she lay down. Each breath sounded like someone clearing seawater from a snorkel.

But that wasn't it. It was part of it, sure, but it's hard to fall asleep when it feels like you have to will your heart to move the sludge through your veins.

Just get there and get back.

Greg opened the door into the communal room. He expected the selection to be pathetic and he wasn't disappointed. A tray sat in the middle of a folding table with muffins stacked in a lopsided pyramid. A pot of coffee monopolized the scent of the room and beckoned to Greg's entire sense of being. He followed the vaguely chocolatey scent toward the machine and poured the scalding liquid into a Styrofoam cup. One packet of real sugar, one Splenda, and a shot of hazelnut half and half.

He set the cup down to wait for the steam pouring off the top to dissipate. Immediately to the right of the coffee pot was an intriguing machine that looked like something he'd find back in the paper mill.

Big metal handles made out of what looked like springs were attached to two flat pans. A large metal base anchored the front-heavy machine and kept it from spilling forward. A plastic Cambro container of batter sat to the right with a ladle leaning against the side.

He grabbed the spring handles and opened the mouth of the metal pans. A checkered pattern of raised cast iron grinned at him. He scooped the batter, dumped it into the bottom jaw of the machine, and closed it.

"I can never figure those things out."

Greg spun around as Sam walked to the coffee pot.

"You can't sneak up on a guy with a heart condition."

"Oh, sorry." He poured himself a cup of coffee. "How's Mom doing?"

Greg noticed his cup had stopped steaming so much so he leaned over and grabbed it.

"Honestly? Not great." He took a sip. It was still too hot but he swallowed it down anyway. Sam walked over to the tower of muffins and grabbed one off the top. "I just—I really don't think we should be pushing her like this."

Sam took a bite and nodded. And then, as if bit by bug, he started and set it down.

"Keep talking," he said through a mouth of muffin and pulled out his phone.

"Another one? Why?"

Sam chewed and nodded. "The struggle," he said. Then he pointed to his father.

Greg sighed and stared at the camera. He started to put voice to his breath but didn't have any words to make with it.

"Uhh…" He took another sip of coffee. "This is it." He set the coffee behind him. "This is the day. We'll be there by the—I don't know the middle of the afternoon or something." He wiped his hands through his hair, turned halfway around, and then back to the camera.

"I just don't want to do this," he said, speaking to Sam. "This—" He waved a hand to the camera. "Or this." He flipped his hand into the air. "It's a lot. I mean, I keep telling myself just get there and get back. Just get there and get back but y' know…"

He took a drink of coffee.

"Is there a back? What is there to get back to? Hospital bills? Surgeries I can't afford?" Greg put his hands on his hips and looked at the floor. The faded, purple carpet looked like it hadn't been vacuumed in years.

"But that's not the point, is it? That's not it. It's not to get—not to get in your head. You know? Especially when I can feel—" He fluttered his hand in front of his chest. "But that's not the point." He leaned against the table behind him and smelled a light waft of smoke. "The point is for Mary to—"

Greg tried to play it off like a cough, but a person's eyes don't squish together and leak when you cough. At least not unless the cough is trying to get fluid out of your lungs.

He took another moment.

The smell of smoke grew stronger.

"She needs to see this," he said. "If nothing else in the whole goddamn world she needs to see this place. I don't know how to make her happy anymore. I don't know how that works. It used to be the thing I knew best but here we are. In Albuquerque. And we're taking her to the Grand fucking Canyon because that's what she wants to do."

He held his hands over his eyes and felt the moisture push its way past his eyelids. He hated the way the corners of his mouth peeled downward when he cried. He hated how his voice sounded like he was driving over a series of speed bumps.

"So—"

"Dad—"

Greg opened his eyes and saw Sam walking toward him with the phone by his side. He reached forward and Greg braced himself for a hug.

But his hand went over his father's shoulder and opened the waffle maker.

"I told you these things were tough," he said as he fished out the black and smoking waffle from the teeth of the machine.

Greg took a few steps into the room, turned around and wiped his eyes.

"I'm sorry," he said quietly.

"What? No, no Dad that was perfect."

They stood in silence with five feet between them. Sam finally stepped forward and hugged his father.

"Grab a muffin," he said. "We got places to be."

They pulled onto the road in an hour. It took some time to get Mary up and moving. Ashley sat on the phone a little too long with the kids. But they didn't need to pack their things. They'd be back this evening.

Greg drove. It might not be until the sun was coming down in the direction they were currently driving, but they'd be making their way down this road later today. Familiarity felt good, even if it was in an unfamiliar place.

New Mexico was an interesting mix of barren landscapes quickly followed by forested hills. It was easy to forget they were in the foothills of the Rocky Mountains. Colorado seemed another world away even though it was just an hour or two north. Greg noticed a lot of the speed limit signs had bullet holes in them. Bored people or stupid kids, he thought.

They'd been driving for maybe two hours when Mary started coughing. This wasn't anything new until it wouldn't stop.

"Mary?" asked Greg. He looked to his right when he should have been watching the road.

Mary curled herself as close to the fetal position as someone could get while wearing a seatbelt. She leaned into the crevice between the seat and the door with a fist pressed against her mouth. But the fist couldn't cork the explosions in her chest and throat. She shook. Flecks of blood speckled her fist. One after another. It drowned out the stereo.

"Mary," Greg said again. But this time he kept his eyes on the road and pulled onto an offramp. "Mary please." He felt a burning in his eyes for the second time that day.

They reached the stop sign at the end of the off ramp. He whipped the car to the right and pulled into a gas station. The car shuddered to a stop and dust surrounded them like an old western movie.

"Find a hospital *now*," he said into the backseat as he jumped out of his door, ran around the car, and opened the passenger door.

Mary would have fallen onto the dirty concrete were it not for the seatbelt holding her in place. Greg watched his wife convulse with violent coughs. Panic sent electric bolts through each of his fingertips.

What can I do? I can't do anything. I can't help. She's going to die right here right now right in front of me and there's nothing I can do because I shouldn't have taken her on this trip in the first place but now we're in some nowhere town in the middle of New Mexico and Mary's going to die because I let myself get caught up in—

"Dad, move." Sam put a hand on his father's shoulder, moved him aside, and knelt down beside his mother. "Here, Mom, sit up." He pushed her on the shoulder until she sat upright in the seat.

"There's a hospital another five miles up the highway and a little off," said Ashley from the backseat.

Mary coughed into one hand and started waving the other.

"Back in the car," said Greg.

But Mary continued waving her hand.

"Here Mom." Sam handed her a bottle of water he had taken from the free breakfast back at the motel.

Her coughs didn't quit, but they occasionally took short enough breaks for her to get some of the liquid down her throat.

Greg ran back to the driver's seat and fired up the engine. Sam hopped into his seat in the back. Greg put his hand on the shifter and felt Mary's sweaty and cold hand on top of his. He looked over and she wiped a drop of blood from her lip. Strands of hair stuck to her forehead. She took another drink of water and everything stayed quiet for a moment besides the rumbling of the engine.

She shook her head side to side.

"We have to keep going," she said.

"What?" said Greg. "No way. We're going to a hospital. Now."

He put the car in gear and pulled back onto the road.

Mary took another drink of water and coughed a few more times.

Soon they were back on the highway.

"No," said Mary. "We have to keep going."

"Mom, it might not be a terrible idea to put it off for a day. Get checked out."

Mary drank the rest of the water and set the empty plastic bottle into the cup holder to her left.

She shook her head.

"We have to keep going." Her voice came out soft. Shaky. Raspy. But there was a glimmer of the old Mrs. Weber.

"But why?" asked Greg.

Mary looked at him for a moment but didn't say anything. She nestled into the seat and closed her eyes.

39.

Ashley Makes a Phone Call

They crossed the Arizona border and nothing looked different. Was everything in the southwest a patchwork of desolate deserts, piles of rocks, and roadside vendors selling colorful blankets?

And then Ashley saw a mountain. The highway looked like it would dead-end directly into the base of it. Ashley had spent most of the drive trying to sleep until Mary had the coughing attack just outside of Gallup. Nobody spoke much since then. Greg would occasionally mutter about someone swerving in their lane, but that was about it. There was no discussion as to whether they should stop at a hospital. They all felt it when Mary refused. There was something behind her words that filled the car and essentially scared everyone into obeying. They drove along the flat, dead Earth for a while after that. It was hard to say how long when you didn't have any markers. The only change was the sporadic frothy explosions from her mother's throat. They'd trade nervous looks. Her and Sam. But nothing was said. They were all thinking the same thing. They had to be.

This is fucked up.

And then she saw the mountain. Straight ahead. Looming on the horizon. She kept her eyes on it as they drove for an hour. Maybe more. And it never got any bigger. How could they be so far away from something to be able to drive toward it for an hour without seeming to get any closer? But she couldn't argue with physics. The world was the way the world was. People can do kickflips. Other people can climb skyscrapers. And this mountain was so big, and so far away, that you could drive toward it for an hour without seeing any noticeable difference.

The silence in the car splintered as her phone sprang to life in her purse. Sam glanced over as she unzipped the top of the black, fake leather bag sitting by her feet. She found the phone and looked at it as she sat up in her seat.

Darren.

She hit the ignore button, turned the phone over, and set it on her thigh. The bounce from the beat-up highway threatened to knock it to the seat or back down by her feet.

That wasn't going to be a quick, light conversation. Her head wasn't in the right space. Discussing your estranged husband's possible philandering while you're listening to your mother cough herself to death in a car with the rest of your family didn't seem appropriate.

It had somehow almost slipped her mind since they left Wisconsin. You'd think having about 24 solid hours of silence would give her nothing but time to dwell on it. To picture it. To imagine how he might try to explain himself. But she didn't.

So what had she been thinking about as she sat quietly in the back seat of her parents' car?

The wind.

Glacial movement snowplowing the Earth flat.

Corn's impact on the economy.

She saw what passed by her window and internalized it. And if she had taken the time to put together a hope for the trip before she left, this would have been it. To exist outside of the sphere of her confusing relationship with Darren Wolff, why she continued to shoot herself in the foot, and why she cared so much about something she had essentially caused.

But she hadn't taken the time to arrange that thought. In fact her reasoning for joining her family on this trip was almost exactly the same as her mother's:

I don't know why, but I feel like I need to go.

"Was that Darren?"

Ashley looked to her left. Sam nodded toward the phone struggling to keep its balance on her thigh. She exhaled sharply and looked back to the mountain that refused to grow. She didn't know why Sam wouldn't let this go but she was damn sick of it. She never should have told him about Darren and that other woman. Whoever the hell she was. It was all he would talk about. At night before they'd go to bed. When they woke up. During breaks at gas stations. She was just so damn tired of it.

She continued looking through the windshield at the mountain.

"I don't think I've ever been in love," said Sam.

She turned to her left. He looked back at her with his hands folded in his lap. All he needed was the white stick of a sucker hanging off his lip and he'd look just the way he did when he was ten.

"I've had girlfriends and relationships and all that, but I don't think I know what love is. Not really. I mean, I've heard enough about it to describe it. But you can describe a food you've never eaten. It's not the same."

The phone slid off her thigh, bounced off the seat, and landed by her feet.

"I think you should call him back," he said. "I think it's what you really want to do."

Ashley looked down at her feet. The phone sat between them facing the floor.

"Think about a year from now. Think about what it might feel like if you haven't spoken to someone you wish you did." He glanced toward the front then back to his sister. "I can tell you it's not a good feeling."

Ashley tried to cross her arms, but the seatbelt got in the way. She looked back to the front and saw the mountain had finally started to grow, if even a little. She leaned her head back into the headrest and took a deep breath. Mom coughed one long, wheezing breath and fell back into her seat. Ashley looked at the phone between her feet.

"I really think it's what you want," said Sam. "Just give him a call and see how you feel."

She wanted to tell her brother to shut the fuck up. To stay out of her business. That just because he's got regrets from his stupid decisions over the years doesn't mean he knows what's best for her. For her family.

But she didn't.

Instead, she looked at him for a moment. Held his gaze. It wasn't a stare down. Not a challenge. But a conclusion to the one-sided conversation before she leaned over, grabbed her phone, and called Darren.

She sat back up and put her phone to her ear. The phone started to ring but she didn't hear it at first. She was too busy frantically looking around the car at all the empty seats.

Nobody drove the car. Mom wasn't coughing in the front seat. And the rest of the backseat was empty besides the space on the passenger side where she finally tuned back into the ringing sound coming through her phone right before it clicked to an end.

"Hello?" came a high-pitched voice.

"Noah?"

"Hey Mom!" The joy in his voice almost hurt. It contrasted too heavily with the mood in the car. She continued looking at the empty seats surrounding her as she spoke.

"Hey bud. How's it going?"

"We built a fort! A big one! We're watching *Toy Story* and eating popcorn."

"He's making you watch that old thing?"

"He says that just because it's old doesn't mean it's bad. It's just old and that he's old so old things can be good too."

Ashley smiled. Always so damn logical.

"He's a smart guy," she said. "Are you having fun?"

"Yeah!"

Of course they were. Darren was great with the kids. Always had been.

"Is your Dad around?"

"Yup." The earpiece filled with static for a bit and she heard a muffled *Dad!*

Ashley looked ahead and noticed the car was still moving. It was still driving. The wheel turned slightly to correct for the poor alignment. The speed hovered around 75 but never exactly on it. She looked between the empty seats and let out a long breath. She slouched a bit and let go of the constant tightness in her chest that had built for the last couple days, even if it was only for a moment. And then the phone reported some more static before Darren said:

"Hey Ash."

People age. They change. But they always sound the same through the phone.

"Hey Darren."

"How's it going?"

She looked around the empty car and then out the windshield. The mountain continued to grow.

"We'll be there today. Pretty soon. Then we'll start heading back."

"Are you excited?"

"I'm excited for Mom to be excited."

They hadn't spoken beyond a few short sentences since she walked out of his apartment as he sat on the arm of the couch.

"You guys made a fort, huh?"

He laughed through the phone. "Yeah. And I gotta say, I'm proud of it. There are different rooms. And the TV's in there. And then your son suggested we put up some Christmas lights and it's nicer than the apartment."

Ashley smiled again and nodded even though nobody could see.

"Did you keep moving your stuff?" she asked.

"No."

The wind outside her window sounded like a whistle and a rumble at the same time.

"I didn't know what you wanted," he said.

She took a deep breath and looked around the empty car. Did she know what she wanted? Sam seemed confident. If only Ashley felt the same way.

"Listen," said Darren. He quieted his voice. "I didn't sleep with her."

"What?"

"Yeah. Nothing happened. Gary set me up with a coworker, we went on three dates, and nothing happened."

"Are you sure?"

He laughed.

"So why did you make me think you did?" she asked.

"I never said I did. You just assumed I did. And honestly, that's not really the greatest thing in the world."

"I just…" Her eyes searched the ceiling of the car as if the answer to the question she had been asking herself had been hidden up there the whole time. "I don't know. I just couldn't stop thinking about it."

"These things are supposed to be built on trust, aren't they?"

She nodded but didn't say anything.

"I'll be back in a couple days. Can we talk about it then?" she said.

"Sure."

She hung up and slid the phone back into the purse by her feet. She straightened up and noticed Sam looking at her. Mom was again cradled by the front seat and Dad had both hands firmly clamped around the steering wheel.

"So, how did it feel?" asked Sam.

She looked out the windshield and noticed they were finally coming up on the mountain. She expected it to be touching the clouds but it wasn't all that impressive up close.

"I don't know," she said.

40.

Sam Waits for a Moment

"Are you sure we have the right road?" asked Sam from the backseat. He looked out the window at the flat landscape stretching to the horizon. A barbed-wire fence held up by support poles that leaned at various angles sectioned off the grass on the other side of the road.

Arizona couldn't seem to make up its mind if it wanted to be an arid desert or a watered-down Colorado forest. He always thought of Arizona as it had been on the New Mexico border—hot, open, and unpleasant. But Flagstaff was surprisingly green.

And then they drove another hour. One road led into and out of the south entrance to the Grand Canyon. One lane in each direction allowed for the possibility of one unhurried driver to ruin everyone's projected arrival times. The traffic on the road seemed to suggest a destination at the end, but the lack of fanfare made it unlikely.

"This is what the thing says," said Greg.

Sam looked back out at the expanse of various shades of brown. Green bushes occasionally added small bursts of color, but that didn't dress up the absence of any form of a hill.

"I just kinda expected it to be more, I don't know, exciting," said Sam.

"Yeah well that's life," said Greg.

Sam looked to his right where Ashley stared at the phone in her hands. It had stayed mostly in her purse since they left Wisconsin besides daily check-ins with Noah and Sadie. But she stared at it pretty consistently since hanging up with Darren.

A coarse, thick cough exploded from Mary's mouth. They became more constant since they pulled off outside of Gallup. It hadn't been good this whole ride, but now they were worse. He believed she needed to be at a hospital. That she should have gone when they pulled over. But there was something about the way she demanded to get here. It seemed more important than anything else at the time.

And then they passed a national forest sign. It suddenly felt real.

They were at the Grand Canyon. They had made it.

As if summoned by the sign, trees began blocking the long, flat viewpoint of the land on either side of them. They didn't look like the ones back home. If anything, they resembled overgrown shrubs.

"Almost there," said Greg.

Mary hacked up a wad of something in response. Sam bent forward to get a look at her. Her sweat-covered forehead glistened in the sun. She leaned against the headrest with her eyes closed and her mouth open. She drew breaths in deep, wheezing pulls.

He reached over the seat and put his hand on her shoulder. He could feel her shaking.

"You okay Mom?"

She slowly raised a hand, extended her forefinger, and waved it toward the windshield.

Go, go.

He sat back and looked at Ashley. She shrugged and held the phone between her hands in her lap.

They continued along the longest, straightest, flattest road Sam had ever seen. Passing lanes occasionally opened up on either side of the double yellow. Frustrated drivers slammed on the accelerator to get even one car length closer to the Grand Canyon.

Sporadic trees. Tall shrubs. Different shades of brown.

They continued along Highway 64 for what was probably only a half hour altogether but felt like a week and a half.

And then the trees finally started to thicken.

"There it is," said Ashley.

A big stone sign reading *Grand Canyon National Park* zipped by them on the right.

"Almost there, honey," Greg said quietly.

Mary curled herself into the seat and tried to hold back another round of coughs. Her body rocked with each stifled expulsion.

The road split into four lanes, all leading to huts that resembled log cabin versions of a toll booth. They were only four car lengths back and made it to the window in about ten minutes.

"Single day pass?" A mustachioed man with sunglasses despite the shadow of the overhang sat just inside the window.

"Yeah," said Greg.

"Thirty-five."

Mary let out a long cough that went past the point where it seemed she could possibly have any breath left.

The sunglasses nodded to her.

"She okay?"

Greg handed him a debit card.

"She'll be okay," he said.

"If you say so." The man ran the card and handed it back with a slip of paper. "Put this in your windshield."

"Thanks." Greg pulled the car forward.

They drove deeper into the park and Sam pulled his phone from his pocket. He didn't check his messages. He didn't look at any websites. He just waited.

"Where's the big hole?" asked Ashley.

"Good question," said Greg.

Just more trees.

And more trees.

And then they finally saw a sign for the Visitor's Center.

"This is it!" said Sam. He hadn't expected to be nervous, but that was the only way to describe the sensation building in his chest. What did he have to be nervous about?

He looked between everyone else in the car:

Greg navigated the slight curves in the roads.

Ashley grasped her phone but stared out the window.

And Mary wrapped herself in her own arms and pressed herself into the seat. The coughs were just about every third breath at this point. They'd be lucky if she could walk.

"Here we are," said Greg. A series of parking lots spread before them. A cluster of buses took up an entire section.

"What is this, Disneyland?" said Ashley.

They drove up and down the rows of cars until finally locating a parking space. Greg switched off the car and nobody moved.

"Are we ready?" he asked. Nobody responded. He put a hand on Mary's leg. "Mary? You ready?"

She sat forward and wiped a hand over her face. She nodded and cleared her throat.

"Alright. Let's go."

Everyone climbed from their car besides Mary. Greg walked around and helped her out. Sam walked just a little behind the three of them and held his phone in front of him. It looked like a desert as they approached the park, but the air was far from warm.

They slowly made their way through the parking lot and up to the Visitor's Center.

"Just a minute," said Ashley. She ran inside.

"Anybody else gotta pee?" asked Greg.

Nobody responded.

Sam dropped his arms and let the phone hang in his hand. A series of sidewalks snaked around the Visitor's Center leading to different shops, informational booths, and concessions. Large groups of people pointed and talked and laughed as they walked between the various huts.

"Here Mom." Ashley snuck up behind them with a wheelchair in front of her.

Greg guided her toward the seat.

"Thanks, Ashley," she said and coughed.

"Good move," Sam said to Ashley. Then he pointed to the right. "This way."

He again fell behind the group as they followed the winding sidewalks. More people filed in as they went. Babies screamed from strollers. People from all over the world stood in front of the most mundane signs and posed for pictures. Sam continued framing the family in the camera of his phone, but he began to feel uneasy. Was there always this many people here? Was it always this crowded?

A line of bushes sat at the top of a short hill. The sidewalk ran between them. The breadth of the canyon spilled upon them like a sunrise as they crested the top of the small hill.

Ashley gasped.

Greg bent down and said, "There it is, Mary. You made it."

Sam followed behind and watched through the small screen before looking up and feeling the canyon overtake his senses. It was almost too big. It didn't look real. Maybe he had seen too many pictures that seeing it in person just felt like another image. But it wasn't. The ocean of open air spread before him and for just a moment he felt like the only person in the world.

For just a moment.

And then a toddler that had wiggled away from his mother tripped on a rock and screamed his way to the dirt. And then an overly excited teenager rushed past them, knocking into Sam's arm on the way. He dropped his phone on the ground and bent down to pick it up. He caught a glimpse of his Mom's face as he stood back up and couldn't believe it—she was shaking her head. He walked around in front of them.

"Mom?"

She gave her head a few more shakes.

"What's wrong?"

He had to lean in to hear her, but she said, "This isn't the right place."

Sam stood up and looked at his father. Greg rubbed Mary's shoulders as more people passed them on either side. He looked down, as if she'd stop breathing if he took his eyes off her.

"What do you mean this isn't the right place? This is the Grand Canyon."

She shook her head and let out a series of coughs.

"It isn't right," she said when she finally regained control of her breath.

"You gotta be fucking kidding me," said Sam. He turned around and walked toward the crowd growing along the guardrail. The time that went into the trip solidified and pressed itself directly into his forehead. He squinted his eyes and tried to squish the pain away by pressing his finger and thumb into the bridge of his nose.

There's only one Grand Canyon. And they had apparently gone to the wrong one.

"Sam," said Greg.

He turned toward his family and saw Mary hunched forward in the wheelchair, coughing toward her knees.

"We should go."

Sam held the phone in one hand and felt the fingers on the other start to tingle. He wanted to throw it over the heads of the swarm of tourists and watch it bounce its way to oblivion. But instead, he took a few heavy steps toward his family and said, "Okay."

Ashley, Sam, and Mary waited outside the Visitor's Center as Greg pulled the car around. They helped her into the front seat, Ashley returned the wheelchair, and they were off the way they came. Altogether, they were there for maybe fifteen minutes.

"What did you think?" asked Greg.

Mary just coughed.

Sam wanted to scream.

He stared down another two and a half days in the car with absolutely nothing to show for it. He tried to tell himself that they had done this for her and if she didn't end up liking it well, hey, at least they tried. A selfless act doesn't owe you anything.

Except it does. And it's not gratitude. That doesn't matter. But it should at least offer the satisfaction of enjoyment from the recipient of your effort. That's the bare minimum compensation one can enjoy.

And he didn't get it.

They wound along the roads, away from the Visitor's Center and every inch was a slap in his face. He pressed into his forefinger with his thumbnail. And he pressed hard.

Mary started coughing right before they left Entrance Road to get back onto Highway 64. She pointed to the stop sign at the intersection ahead.

"What?" asked Greg.

She continued coughing but tried to speak while catching her breath.

It was barely intelligible, but Sam heard her say, "Left."

"Dad, go left," he said.

"Here?"

"Yeah."

Greg flipped on the blinker, moved into the turn lane, and made his way onto what looked to be a service road that connected two different campgrounds. They drove along for a little bit and didn't see any other vehicles.

"Are you sure we're supposed to be here?" asked Ashley.

Mary coughed and waved her finger forward.

Go, go.

Trees blocked the view of anything beyond twenty feet on either side of the road. There was no way to tell if they were getting closer or further away from the canyon itself. Sam looked to Ashley who shrugged and looked forward.

The trees along the left side of the road thinned out and the multi-colored layers of the canyon bled through. And then the trees disappeared completely as the road grew wider for access to a small outlook.

Mary coughed and pointed, so Greg pulled over. She pawed at the door handle until it opened, but she didn't get out.

"Okay, hold on," said Greg. He turned off the car and ran around to her side. The kids got out in the back. Sam looked around and didn't see anyone else. In front of him, the Grand Canyon almost screamed its presence. He took a slow breath and tried to steady himself. It was intimidating, this giant weather-worn scar of Earth.

Greg led Mary up to the railing. She leaned on him so much he might as well have been carrying her. Ashley walked behind them and Sam behind her with his cell phone in his hand.

"Well, what do you think?" asked Greg.

Mary shuddered with a swallowed cough and gazed over the expanse of the canyon.

"It's beautiful," she said with a shaky voice.

Nobody else spoke.

Mary just looked left, and then right. And then left again.

"How does it feel, Mom?" asked Sam, holding the phone in front of him.

She coughed, but only a little.

"I've been thinking about this my whole life," she said. "What I missed out on. What it would be like. If I would ever get another chance to see something like this."

"And now that you're here?"

Mary turned around. Her forehead glistened with sweat despite the cool breeze. She tried to smile but the mechanics of tears don't always allow for a happy expression. She looked past the phone and into Sam's eyes. And then to Ashley. She opened her mouth to say something but nothing came out. Not even a cough.

People traveled from all over the world to look at the wondrous beauty of the canyon behind her, and Mary looked between the faces of her children and cried silently.

So did Sam. And Ashley. And Greg.

The absence of other people meant an absence of unnecessary sound—leaving only the brush of a constant wind, the occasional shriek of a distant hawk, and the rustling of the tree branches.

They could have gone on like this forever—with Greg supporting his wife, holding court in front of their children—but Mary nodded her head to the side. Greg began directing them back toward the guardrails and then Mary motioned to their left.

A paved walking trail seemed to go along the cliff's edge, and soon they followed it. Trees blocked out their view of the blue sky every so often. They left the road and the parking area behind until they found themselves with a peppered view of the canyon. A section of trees and dirt sat between the path and cliff. More trees filled in behind them and obscured the road. The path wound off in front of them to some unseen end.

They paused. Mary again looked at Sam and Ashley. Her eyes shone with moisture, but an additional brightness was there, too. She was there with them. One hundred percent.

I just seem to think better in some places.

"I love you guys," she said.

And then they heard the dog barking.

Greg held onto Mary with his left arm and couldn't help but swing her a bit as he looked around. Sam held the phone in front of him, but he looked into the woods as well.

"Oh my God," said Greg. He turned toward the trees and dirt and canyon.

Sam could only see his and Mary's back as they stared forward. Mary put her hand on Greg's shoulder and supported her weight on her own feet. Greg took a step forward off the path.

"Dad?" said Ashley.

Greg knelt down and Sam and Ashley could finally see what their parents had been looking at.

A small beagle walked toward them out of the line of trees.

"Al, oh my God," said Greg. The dog walked up to him and put its front paws on his knee.

He sobbed and wrapped his arms around his dog. The grey on her face had been replaced with the chestnut brown of her youth.

Sam looked at Mary, who only smiled and nodded.

41.

Mary Starts to Speak

It was just as beautiful as she imagined. Of course, she had seen numerous pictures over the years. The Grand Canyon popped up in television and movies and books countless times. But she knew it would be different. Pictures don't tell the whole story. They can show you the colors on the cliffs, but they don't surround you with a brisk wind that smells of a mixture of forest floor and the beach. They don't explain the breadth of the canyon—that you have to turn not only your head to take in the whole scene, but your whole body.

She had only been in the presence of a natural sight that had so completely overwhelmed her once before. The Atlantic coast of Florida made her dizzy when she was eight years old. Her family enjoyed a spring vacation away from the never-ending barrage of a Wisconsin winter. Her father had been haggling with a tour boat captain underneath a sign promising the adventure and great rewards of deep sea fishing. But Mary didn't listen to a word as she stood on the dock ten feet away. Her eyes remained transfixed on the miles of blue water in front of her. She imagined the underwater societies of monsters contained within the waves and started to cry. Her mother noticed first and assumed the arguing had upset her, but Mary didn't have the words at the time to explain that she was experiencing her first sense of insignificance compared to something as large as the ocean. And beyond that, the world.

And standing here at the edge of the Grand Canyon with Greg trying to hug an excited and jumping dog that was maybe five years younger than when he had last seen it, she was grateful for the memory of the ocean. Just like she'd be grateful for the memory of the Grand Canyon. Everyone knows you take something for granted until it's not available. But this doesn't really apply to memories. They're either there or they're not. And recognizing the absence of a memory doesn't make you long for it like you might for a vacation that had just ended. It makes you mad. It'd be like learning someone gifted you a car, but it had been stolen. It would be better not to know about the car at all.

There's no fear involved in memory unless it's the recognition of an absence of memory. Joy and pain can be derived from them, but the only action that can really be taken is to appreciate or regret a memory. They are ethereal, borderline magical, and essential to a happy and healthy life.

And this was the first time Mary felt like she could truly retain a memory in a while.

She took a deep breath and closed her eyes. The cool air bit into her throat and lungs as it absorbed into her body. Her lungs felt clean. The breath escaped without a hitch. No bubbling acid sprang up her throat. No irritating cough breathed fire from her mouth. Strength returned to her legs and she knelt next to Greg, who continued petting and crying over his dog.

"How could this be possible?" he asked. "How could this happen?"

Mary rubbed his back and felt the abbreviated breaths as he tried to calm himself down. The dog escaped his hands, walked around his knee, and sat in front of Mary. She stood up and looked through the trees to the canyon beyond. Of all the aspects to internalize, she couldn't help but notice the land above the canyon. Everything below was a collection of fluid colors and rock. The formations looked like whittled stone seats for the Gods. But the rim was consistent. In every direction she looked, the rim was the exact same height. There were no mounds, no hills, and no mountains above the canyon. It was flat. Completely flat from one ledge to another on the opposite side. It struck her funny how in a place where there were so many amazing attributes and formations to draw her attention, it was the one area with an absence of a point of interest that drew her attention the most.

It's these small details that make the strongest memories.

Greg finally stood up. Al stayed still. She always followed Greg but now she held fast to Mary's side.

Greg looked at Mary and wiped the tears from his face. He smiled through deep breaths. She leaned over and kissed him softly on the mouth. Then she turned to her kids.

Ashley's hands hung at her sides, and she looked back and forth between her parents every two seconds.

Sam held his phone between his hands in front of his stomach, but he looked her directly in the eyes.

"Well, Mom," he said. "How does it feel?"

She took another clean breath and glanced over her shoulder. The canyon sat patiently behind her. A cool wind continued to brush past her skin, but she couldn't hear the rustling of the leaves. The howling of the breeze racing through the canyon stopped as well. No birds chirped. No cars passed. The muted silence of a midnight walk after a fresh snowfall surrounded them. Another deep breath filled her lungs and exhaled smoothly.

She turned back to her kids.

"I always kinda imagined this is what death would be," she said.

"What?" asked Ashley.

Greg's hand found its way to her shoulder.

"Calm. Peaceful," said Mary. "No yelling. No anger. Just the breeze and standing exactly where I wanted to be with the people I most wanted to be with."

No one spoke. No one moved.

Mary looked down to Al who sat quietly with her mouth closed, staring forward and waiting. She patted the dog on the head once and stepped toward Sam. The dirt beneath her feet crunched softly.

"Sam," she said. "First of all," she lifted a hand and gestured toward the canyon behind her. "Thank you. We wouldn't be here right now if it weren't for you."

He smiled and nodded. The moisture building in his eyes grew shiny.

"I want you to do something for me, okay? Just take it easy on yourself. You have your own life to live. I know you blame yourself for moving out to Atlanta, but I don't."

Sam opened his mouth, but Mary only took a short breath.

"And I'm sorry. I know I got caught up with work when you were young. I assumed you knew how much I loved you, so I didn't feel the need to tell you all the time. It's a regret I can't control but it's one I can apologize for. You're my only son and nothing can replace that. You can move to the other side of the world, but you'll always be my son. I don't need to see your face every day to remember that, and neither do you."

Sam continued holding the phone in his hand, but he wasn't paying attention to where it pointed.

"Mom, I—"

She took a step forward and wrapped him in her arms. They stayed this way for half a minute before she finally took a step back. She looked up and noticed the sky turning the dull orange of early dusk despite the fact it was still early afternoon.

"Ashley." Mary took two steps toward her daughter.

"Thank you. I couldn't be more proud of the woman you've become, all that you've accomplished, and the work you continue to do. I wasn't sure how I'd feel with you going into teaching, but it's an absolute joy to know you are continuing on with the work that I cherished for so long."

The sky above transitioned closer to red than orange.

"And I'm sorry I couldn't be more of a help. I know I've been nothing but difficult lately."

"Mom, no I—"

"And I know you have a lot on your plate already. But just know that those kids of yours are off to a good start. Keep going the way it's been and they'll grow up to be as much of a gift to you as you two have been to me."

She wrapped her arms around Ashley for another half minute before stepping back and turning toward her husband and the dog he missed so much. The sky behind them glowed in a vibrant mixture of red and creamy orange. The wind regained its voice and howled through the canyon along with the chirps and calls of the birds. Her steps barely made a sound as she walked back toward the guardrail. Just beyond it sat about ten feet more of dirt and rocks, peppered with trees. Just before it stood her husband of 39 years. The man that had put her life and well-being before his at every possible opportunity. Not only would she not be here without him, she wouldn't be anywhere.

"Greg," she said.

42.

Greg Takes a Nap

He wondered how much of his weight he could put on the wooden railing before it collapsed. Then he wondered how much longer he could stand on this trail along the rim of the Grand Canyon before he collapsed.

"Greg," she said again as she came up close. Al sat by his left leg and looked up at the two of them. Tears formed in Mary's eyes, but her voice remained steady.

"The love of my life. The most patient man in the world."

Mary glanced down at the dog for a moment before looking back up to Greg.

"I'd be nothing without you. And I owe you everything in the world, but unfortunately…"

Her voice wavered and cut out. She turned her head to the right and gazed off into the canyon. Greg worried that maybe the cough would return but of course it would never come back.

"I owe you everything," she said again. "But I have nothing to give except a release."

The guardrail cracked behind Greg as he pushed himself off. It wobbled for a moment before the support beam fell into the dirt behind Al.

"What?"

Mary put her hands on his shoulders just as she had during the first dance at their wedding. Greg swore he could hear the opening chords of Neil Young's *Harvest* ringing out somewhere, but no speakers could be seen. The sky continued growing deeper shades of red. What time was it? What day was it?

What year was it?

"I'm not going back with you, Greg," she said.

He looked around at the trail leading along the canyon.

"So what you're just going to move out here?"

She shook her head again.

"This is the end of the road for me. Al was nice enough to come back to see me off, but I can't get back in the car."

"Wait, wait," said Greg. His shaking arms and hands tried to shudder out of her grasp, but she held onto his shoulders and stared into his eyes.

"Easy," she said. "It's okay."

"No it's *not*." He wanted to yell. He wanted his voice to echo throughout the canyon that this wasn't fair, it didn't have to end this way, and they didn't deserve an ending like this.

But of course he was wrong.

"I love you," she said. "I want you to know that I appreciate everything you've done for me. Everything." She leaned her head forward and looked directly into his eyes. "Okay? Every minute we had together was beautiful and I wouldn't change a thing."

Their last moments shouldn't be soaked in tears. He hated every one of them that rolled down his cheek. But he didn't wipe them. He didn't want to close his eyes even for a second.

"You've gone far beyond the vows of our marriage and I'll be grateful for everything you've done until the end of time."

"I don't want you to go," he said.

"I don't want to go either, but this isn't a choice."

Greg leaned his head forward and found her shoulder. They wrapped their arms around each other and felt the soft throbbing of sobs roll through each other's bodies. Finally, they pulled apart and shared another gentle, slow kiss.

"I love you," she said quietly.

"I love you, too."

And then Al barked for the first time since emerging from the woods twenty minutes earlier. Mary looked down to the dog, who barked again.

"Okay, okay," she said. And then to Greg: "I have to go."

Mary turned toward Ashley and Sam, who still held the phone in his hands toward them.

"Thank you two for everything," she said.

They told her they loved her, and she turned back to Greg.

"Goodbye," she said. And with a slight smile: "Don't forget me."

Greg shook his head and squeezed her hand in his.

"I love you," he said.

And then Mary looked down to the beagle sitting in the dirt at her feet.

"Alright," she said.

Al stood up. She started walking down the path with Mary at her side. Greg watched with Ashley and Sam as they wound along the path until they moved out of sight behind the trees.

"Wait!" yelled Greg. He ran up the path and felt his heart pounding against his ribs. The cold air scratched its way down his throat to lungs that refused to hold it. Saliva pooled in his mouth. He finally got around the corner and could see down a long stretch of the trail to find an empty expanse leading along the edge of the

Grand Canyon. The sky beyond the cliffs radiated a vibrant red in the cloudless sky. He tried to catch his breath but there was nothing to catch. He again leaned against the guardrail and tried to breathe through the sobs.

"Dad?"

He opened his eyes and looked to his left. Ashley stood about ten feet away.

"She's just…gone," he said.

And then Sam came up behind her with the damn phone in his hands.

"Really?" said Greg.

"Look." Sam pointed down the path.

Greg pushed himself off the railing, turned around, and saw Al trotting down the path toward them. He kneeled down and she again propped herself up on his knee and licked his face. Greg squeezed his eyes tight and thought maybe it wouldn't be so bad if the heart trying to beat its way out of his chest finally stopped once and for all.

"Dad, I think it's time to go," said Ashley.

He stayed on his knee for another moment until the flashing sparks that clouded his vision started to fade. And when he stood up he noticed the sky had reverted back to a creamy orange.

"Come on, girl," he said to Al.

The four of them walked back to the car in silence.

"You want me to drive, Dad?" asked Sam.

His breaths were still too short to fill the chasm of need in his lungs. The white spots had mostly faded but the occasional meteor could be seen from the corner of his eye.

"Yeah, that would probably be for the best."

He opened the back door and Al hopped onto the seat. Greg climbed in afterwards. Ashley took Mom's seat.

Greg watched out the window as they retreated down the road back to the main highway. And once they cleared the border of the park, he lay down across the seat and propped his feet against the window. Al curled up in the well behind the driver's seat.

He let himself drift off into sleep, uncaring of when or if he would wake up.

"Alright Dad," said Sam.

Six hours had passed. Greg slowly opened his eyes but didn't sit up. The fog of sleep clouded his mind and for a beautiful moment, he didn't remember that Mary was gone. It didn't last more than one shallow breath, but in that moment she sat in the front seat and would turn her head at any moment.

And then Al pressed her nose against the back of his hand. The afternoon rushed through him in an instant. He sighed and ran his hand over the dog's head. She looked up and licked the inside of his wrist.

Greg sat up and glanced through the windows at the Motel 6 parking lot. Mary's bag would be inside room 117.

"Let's go order some food, eh?" said Ashley.

"I'll be in in a minute," said Greg. He opened the car door and hesitated—he didn't have a leash for Al. But then he remembered the way she stuck by his side along the Grand Canyon.

"Come on," he said to her and climbed out of the car. She hopped down behind him.

The sky was again a mixture of orange sherbet and various shades of red. He could see the sun hovering over the horizon off to the west. The cool air that bit into his arms along the cliff's edge had returned. He rubbed his hands together and saw a bench near the entrance to the motel's office.

Greg walked across the parking lot. Al trotted by his side with her nose to the ground. He collapsed into the bench and she sat on the pavement, facing the parking lot.

This should be the time where he processed the afternoon. There was a lot to unpack and a quiet moment watching a New Mexico sunset with his dog was the perfect time to do it.

But he couldn't.

Not yet.

You can't process an event when you don't truly believe it happened.

Or don't want to believe it happened.

The old wooden bench hurt his back, but it was better than going back to the room with Mary's bags.

Al suddenly looked to the left and Greg followed her gaze.

"Hey Dad," said Sam.

Greg rubbed his cold hands into his eyes and looked back to his son. The red sky was blurry for a moment until he blinked a couple times.

"How are you doing?" asked Sam.

Greg shrugged. "I don't know."

"Listen, I'm sorry for recording at the canyon but—"

"I don't care about this internet thing. Okay? It doesn't matter. Not anymore."

Sam looked out at the glowing sunset. The sun, now a deeper red, had grown and rested just above the horizon.

"Can I show you something?" he asked.

Greg slid to his right and Sam sat down. He pulled out his phone.

"Sam I don't wanna see—"

"I started a new campaign."

Greg felt his heart thud in his chest. The beat wasn't constant but it did the job.

"You what?" he asked.

"A few days ago. I linked a new campaign off the first one. I figured we had the attention so we might as well make use of it. Here, look."

Sam leaned over and showed his father a picture of himself and Mary. *Help My Parents Retire* it said across the top. The goal had been set at $200,000.

"We were getting close to the goal this morning," said Sam. "And it's been going crazy since I posted the video of you and Mom at the canyon."

"You what?" Greg almost stood up but he was just so *tired*.

"It's gone completely viral. Celebrities are sharing it and everything."

"Sam I don't want—"

"Look here." He scrolled to the donations section where people could include personalized notes.

Greg pulled the phone close to his face and saw a comment from a hospital administrator outside of Chicago.

"Is this for real?" he asked.

"I just got off the phone with him. The hospital got some bad press when it sued low-income patients for outstanding bills. They need some good PR and this thing is completely blowing up." Sam started to laugh and said: "They're going to do your surgery, Dad. And you won't have to pay a thing."

Greg leaned forward and put his elbows on his knees. All the breath left his body and he worried for a moment he might pass out. Al scooted a bit to the side and sat between his feet. He rubbed her soft, floppy ear between his forefinger and thumb. He spent every night worried about how he could take care of Mary. How he could afford it. What he'd do about the surgery.

And just like Mary, these worries were gone.

He moved his finger and thumb from the dog's ear to the bridge of his nose as he started weeping.

"I just wish she could be here to see this." Greg stayed this way for a minute before sitting back and opening his eyes. The sun had completely set and all hints of red were gone from the sky.

43.

Two Months Later

Ashley Celebrates the New Year

"Can I really stay up until midnight?" asked Noah.

"Who said that?" Ashley set another giant bowl of chips on the kitchen table. This made three. And a spinach artichoke dip. And a beer cheese dip. That ought to be enough until the barbecue meatballs were done.

"Daddy."

"Oh. Well." Ashley tried to look around the corner of the kitchen into the living room but couldn't see Darren or Sadie. She looked back down to Noah. "Do you know where your suit is?"

He nodded.

"Well then go put it on. I'm putting you to work if you're going to stay up."

"Yeah!" He turned and ran out of the room, his footsteps pounding all the way to his bedroom at the end of the hall.

Darren walked in through the back door with Sadie right behind him. "What was that?" he said.

"That was our butler going to get his suit."

"The one from your mother's funeral?"

She nodded.

It was a small affair. Only close family. There had been massive interest with the success of the campaign and attention on social media, but they didn't want to turn it into a spectacle. Plus, without a body, it was more of a gesture than a funeral. They buried a cheap casket full of her clothes, pictures, and personal mementos from Greg, Ashley, and Sam.

Ashley put in her college diploma.

She expected it to be a terrible day. There wasn't a visitation at the funeral home. The absence of a body made it seem pointless. Instead, they met at the cemetery. A priest read something short, and then each of them had their chance to say something. Afterwards, Ashley had no idea what she said.

But nobody cried.

It wasn't that they didn't miss Mary Weber terribly, because they did. There was an unspoken understanding between them. Those who had watched the video had a vague concept of the idea, but it wasn't something that could be explained. In fact, they had never discussed it—her, Sam, and Greg. Not once since that day on the edge of the Grand Canyon had they spoken about what happened up there. What would they say? How could they put it into words? Emotions don't need to be spelled out to be understood. And that's how they left it.

So nobody cried as they lowered the casket into the ground. It was too surreal to be sad.

"Sadie could put on her dress, too," said Darren.

Ashley shrugged. "Why the hell not? Give her something pretty to fall asleep in."

He turned around and picked her up. "You ready to get fancy?"

She laughed and covered her mouth.

"You're going to be my New Year's kiss this year," he told her as they walked out of the kitchen.

As if on cue, Ashley's phone started to ring.

"Hey Dad," she said as she put it to her ear. She grabbed a chip and stuck it in her mouth, unconcerned about the crunch.

"I'm not gonna be able to make it," he said.

She leaned against the table and sighed.

"Dad, you gotta get out of the house once in a while. You're going to go crazy in there."

"It's Al. She's been throwing up."

"She probably just ate something she shouldn't have. Dogs throw up all the time."

"I don't want her to be alone when she's not feeling well. I mean, did you really expect me to stay up until midnight anyways?"

Ashley shrugged even though he couldn't see her.

"Alright Dad. Thanks for calling."

They said goodbye and hung up. That house became the silent waiting room it had been for Mary. She had hated every second of it, but Greg seemed to thrive. Ashley knew he was sad when Al was lost. Greg and that dog were always tight. But it had grown into something else. They were inseparable. And Ashley wasn't sure if he was looking after the dog, or if it was the other way around.

There was a quick knock at the front door and then it opened.

"I know we're early." Paula and Will Olson walked around the corner, both shrugging. "But we brought wine."

It wasn't long before the house grew thick with more people. Mutual friends, coworkers, friends of friends—these things tend to get out of hand quickly even in your thirties.

Sadie crashed on the couch around ten o'clock. Some band that had been popular in the early nineties played on the muted television. Noah surprised everybody by clearing drinks, bringing paper plates stacked with snacks, and chatting up the guests.

"How's it going, bud?" Ashley asked him as he piled chips and pretzel sticks onto another paper plate.

"Great!" he said. Midnight wasn't too far away and he looked like he had another few hours in him. "I've made twenty bucks so far!"

"Wait, what?" But he was already gone. She lost sight of his black suit coat in the thick crowd. Darren appeared to her left.

"He's quite the little charmer," he said.

"Well you know kids just imitate what they see." Ashley snuck a quick kiss on his cheek.

"I gotta ask you something."

Ashley turned toward the voice. She found a plump man that looked like a sagging water balloon being held by the knot. The drooping eyelids and half-smile suggested he had too many glasses of wine. Stained red teeth flashed behind his lips as he spoke.

"Hey Phillip," said Darren. Then to Ashley: "This is Phillip from sales."

"Well," said Ashley. "Let's get this over with."

She was already nodding her head when Phillip slurred, "That video."

"Yup. The video," she said.

"I just gotta ask...Is it real? I mean, it's just so convincing. And like, there's no way she just disappeared." Phillip placed a hand on the table and narrowly avoided putting it right into a bowl of dip. "But like, obviously something happened. So what was it? What happened? Really?"

It had mostly died down. This question. Maybe people thought nobody else had asked. Maybe they thought Ashley wanted to talk about it. The students at school were at least kind enough to only mention it behind her back. Adults shared the lack of shame, but with an additional lack of mutual respect. Her stock response was simply a shrug with a knowing smile. It's the same look a magician gives when asked how he managed to find the card in the middle of the deck. There'd be follow up questions but Ashley could always shrug and smile that "gee I just don't know" smile and they'd eventually give up. But it was getting late. And this Phillip was currently the last on a long list of people that had bothered her over something that she hadn't been able to process herself. The truth? The truth of it all?

"I have no idea," she said. There. There you have it.

"But—"

"Listen. Phillip from sales. Is your mother dead?"

A new song came on the playlist in the living room that was apparently quite popular. People cheered. The sound of shuffling feet grew louder.

Phillip glanced at the table for a moment before looking back to Ashley.

"No."

"Okay then. Do me a favor. Imagine her dying." Ashley put her hands on her hips like she was talking to Shane Duplass. Her heart beat a little faster. "Imagine your Mom dying right in front of you. You can't stop it. You can't help. All you can do is watch how much it hurts the rest of your family. She's dying and you know it's just about to be over and you have a chance to tell her that you love her one last time. You know it doesn't mean much in the grand scheme but at the same time it does. But for some reason, you just can't work up the nerve. And then she's gone. She's gone forever."

Darren took a drink of his beer and looked between the two of them but said nothing.

"I…I don't—"

"And then," said Ashley. "And then for months afterwards. For months after you saw your Mom for the last time random people walk up to you at the grocery store. Or at work. Or at a New Year's Eve party at your own house and they ask you to relive it for their amusement. Because they saw some video and found it interesting. Tell me, Phillip from sales. How do you think you'd feel?"

The song continued in the next room. Feet continued to slide. People continued to whoop.

"Excuse me." A little butler in a black suit coat and pants with a red tie pushed his way around Phillip. "Need a refill!"

Phillip again revealed his stained teeth but didn't say anything.

Noah disappeared back into the crowd. So did Phillip from sales.

Ashley turned around to Darren.

"Well," he said. "That was something."

"I couldn't help myself." She downed the last of the wine in her glass. "This might have something to do with it," she said, shaking her glass. "It was either that or I tell him Mom was attacked by a pack of coyotes."

"Jeez."

"Well she obviously killed every one of them with her bare hands and continues to live in the hills."

"Right," said Darren. He took a drink of his beer. "Obviously." He checked his watch. "Oh shit. Almost time."

They walked into the makeshift dance floor that had once been their living room. Darren turned the TV to a local station that had a live countdown on the screen.

"One minute!" said Darren. The group of drunks responded with whoops and shouts. It was a good thing Sadie had been on her feet until she was basically unconscious. She wouldn't be waking up any time soon.

Ashley turned down the stereo and quickly poured a little more wine into her glass. She wasn't much of a drinker, but they were going down easy tonight. It felt good. She hadn't had a real chance to unwind since the trip to the Grand Canyon. The uproar on the internet took over a month to totally settle down, but that didn't stop the locals from pointing. She needed a breath.

She just needed a deep breath.

But instead she heard a group of people in her living room begin counting back from ten. She walked into the small crowd and found Darren leading the countdown in front of the muted television.

Three.

Two.

One.

And then the lights went dark.

Happy New Year!

Everyone either thought it was intentional or played along perfectly because they all continued to whoop and shout as someone tried to sing *Auld Lang Syne* without knowing all the words. The rest joined in.

Should all acquaintances forget
That ever brought to mind!

Darren leaned down and kissed Ashley softly on the lips. They turned to the crowd and laughed at the exaggerated joviality of drunkenness despite the absence of light.

"What the hell happened?" asked Ashley.

"No clue," said Darren. "Even the streetlights are out."

"Let's go look."

She led him by the hand through the hallway and out the back door of the house. She didn't need a light to find her way.

It was freezing. The wind bit into their skin and each breath stung their lungs. There were no lights inside the neighbors' homes. No streetlights spilling orange all over the road. The only source of light hung above them in the sky. A waning gibbous moon hung in a nest of stars and reflected off the snow covering the yard.

"I'm cold," she said and took a sip of her wine.

She heard a soft crunch in front of her as Darren threw his beer into the yard. He wrapped his arms over her shoulders and crossed them just below her neck.

The wind disappeared. And with it, any communication of cold air with her skin. She felt as if she stood in the middle of her kitchen. Comfortable in both body and mind. He kissed the top of her head.

She turned toward him, careful to hold the glass of wine out of the way. He kept his arms around her shoulders except now his hands hung between her shoulder blades. She looked up at him and the moon reflected off his eyes.

"I'm glad you're back," she said.

A smile spread across his face. "I'm glad I'm back, too."

He kissed her again for a little longer this time. Then she turned back around in the warm comfort of his arms and looked at the snow stretching before them. It sparkled with a million tiny reflections of the moon above.

44.

Sam Goes to Waffle House

It was surprisingly chilly when Sam finally walked out of Emory University Midtown Hospital, especially for Atlanta. He zipped up the light coat he grabbed before his twelve-hour shift started at 7pm the night before. New Year's Eve was always an exciting night at the ER. He volunteered for it every year. Although that was more a result of a general disdain for New Year's parties than a desire to treat belligerent lightweights that can't handle their liquor.

He checked his watch and figured his father would be awake despite the time difference. He pulled out his phone and made the call.

"Dad?"

"Hey Sam."

"Happy New Year."

"Yeah, yeah you too."

"How was the party last night?" Sam found his black Honda Civic about halfway through the parking lot.

"What?" said Greg. There was some light rustling. "Oh, okay Ashley's. Right. Yeah well I didn't make it."

Sam climbed into the driver's seat, put the key in the ignition, but didn't turn it.

"Why not?"

"Al," he said. "Al wasn't feeling well so I stayed here with her. We were in bed by ten anyways."

"How's she doing now?"

There was a pause. It sounded to Sam like two pieces of fabric rubbing against each other but it was likely just Greg climbing out of bed.

"I don't see any new puke. So good, I guess."

Sam smiled. These daily check-ins never amounted to much. But even when you combine a whole lot of nothing you come up with something Sam didn't want to miss out on again.

"That's good. Alright Dad I'm gonna get some sleep."

"How was it?"

"What?"

"Work."

"Pretty much what you'd expect. Random people puking on the floor of the waiting room, few car crashes, the standard stuff."

Another pause.

"Alright we'll see you later," said Greg.

Sam slid the phone into his pocket and turned the key. The engine roared to life, the radio filled him in on the weather and traffic, and he closed his eyes. Sleep was going to be delicious, but he wasn't there yet. He didn't care what the people on the radio were saying but he didn't want it to be quiet.

He pulled onto West Peachtree Street and was about to turn right toward his new apartment in the Old Fourth Ward when he hesitated and missed the turn. It hadn't been a conscious decision but he wanted to get some food before turning in. A quick breakfast at the Waffle House would do the trick.

It took a bit, but he found a parking spot and walked into the small location just outside of the Georgia Tech campus. The dining room would normally be packed but most of the students had gone home for winter break. Plus, 7:30am on New Year's Day wasn't exactly a busy time for anything.

"Just one?" asked the woman working behind the counter.

He nodded and she showed him to a booth toward the back of the restaurant.

She offered him a menu, but he waved it off.

"Biscuits and gravy, a waffle, and hash browns well done," he said.

"Coffee?"

"Water's good."

He closed his eyes again and felt the backwards pull of his consciousness toward sleep. The salty and smoky scent of bacon wafted off the grill. Soon his hash browns started to sizzle and the waffle batter covered the iron.

He briefly flashed to the waffle iron in Topeka.

I can never figure those things out.

The trip felt like a dream. He had to ask himself multiple times if he simply imagined the whole thing. It made sense at the time. Everything that happened up there. But just like the most outlandish dream that seems perfectly plausible, a little distance helped him realize that none of it made sense at all. You can look back at a dream and laugh—some crazy gymnastics of the mind concocted a ridiculous scenario that couldn't possibly happen.

But this was different.

He couldn't dismiss that which had taken his mother.

Sam opened his eyes and glanced at the grill. The woman that took his order stood with one hand on her hip and the other on the counter to her left. She casually spoke with the man holding the spatula in front of the sizzling hash browns.

He continued looking around the restaurant and noticed a woman sitting at a table near the door. Had she been there when he came in? He hadn't seen her, but his sleep-deprived mind probably missed a few red lights on the way from the hospital, too.

The back of someone's head isn't exactly a fingerprint, but Sam felt like he recognized her. And this wasn't a vague notion. He knew exactly who it looked like.

This happened a few times since the Grand Canyon. He'd caught glimpses of people that looked like his mother in the grocery store, and at work, and now at Waffle House. Each time he knew it couldn't be her, but he couldn't help but think—

What if?

Why should things start making sense now? Events had been happening however they pleased for a while. It'd be a hell of a time for them to suddenly adhere to rationality and physics.

"Here you go, honey." The server slid a glass of water on the table in front of him.

Sam nodded his thanks and tried to unwrap the straw, but his shaking hands made it difficult to tear off the end. He finally butted it onto the tabletop, grabbed the exposed plastic with his lips, and dunked it into the water. He took a long, luxurious sip.

And when he looked up, he half-expected the woman facing the door to be gone.

But she wasn't.

"Oh," he said to himself and drew out the vowel sound. Would it really be that bad to say *Excuse me* and be wrong? You could always say it was simply mistaken identity. It's not like that would be a lie.

He stared at the back of the woman's head. He had to find out.

His scrubs *whooshed* on the seat as he slid to the left and heard the scream when he stood up.

"Oh shit!" yelled the server. She took a few steps back from the man that had just been holding the spatula. He now held his left hand in his right and wasn't making a noise. He simply stared at the blood running down his hand from where the top half of his forefinger used to be.

Sam stepped onto the seat of the booth and jumped over the partition. He kicked over some extra salt and pepper shakers on the other side but landed mostly clean on the rubber mat behind the counter.

The man turned to Sam with his eyelids peeled back. Sam saw the knife on the cutting board next to the grill and a small chunk of bloody meat in front of it.

"Do you have a clean rag?" he asked.

The man continued to stand there and bleed, but the woman reached underneath the counter and threw a white towel to Sam. She refused to take another step closer.

Sam wrapped the finger in the rag and told the man to hold it above his head.

"Do you have a first aid kit?

The server spun around and again dug into the storage cabinet under the counter. She threw a red, plastic box to Sam but he still had a hand on the towel.

"Ow! Shit!" he said as it bounced off his shoulder. Band aids and tiny packages of burn cream spilled onto the rubber mat. He let go of the towel and flicked open the small box. He found a roll of gauze and stood up.

"Okay. Ice? But just like, set it down this time?"

She disappeared.

Sam found some tape in the kit and began dressing the finger. He found a plastic knife on the counter next to the spilled pepper shakers and taped it behind the hand. It wasn't much of a splint but it was better than nothing.

The waitress came back with two containers of ice.

He nodded. Of course.

"Plastic bags?" he asked.

She grabbed a box from under the counter.

He filled one with ice and handed it to the cook.

"Here. Put this on top."

Then he grabbed another and walked to the cutting board. There was no time to find gloves so he simply grabbed the nub, walked it to the sink, rinsed it off, and dropped it into the bag.

"You getting dizzy?" asked Sam.

The cook shook his head no. Impressive.

"Alright…" Sam turned toward the front of the restaurant. Nobody had entered. And nobody sat at the table facing the door. Adrenalin had overtaken nervousness, but there was always room for disappointment. He turned back to the cook and waitress.

"Alright come on. I'll take you to the hospital."

The cook walked past Sam and he followed close behind, making sure the fresh amputee's blood pressure wasn't going to bottom out.

"Hey man, your waffle's on me next time," said the woman behind him.

Sam turned, smiled, and offered a short wave.

The drive was quick. He pulled up to the front of the ER, told the guy where to go, and left without going back inside.

Fifteen minutes later, he walked into his apartment. He moved everything out of storage immediately after signing the lease. In fact, he was a day away from selling it all and catching the first plane back to Wisconsin.

But he didn't.

Things were as close to normal as they were going to get. The internet quickly forgets. He'd get the occasional question at a bar, but that was about it.

He collapsed into the couch and thought about the woman in the booth. Would he have been more relieved if it was her? Or if it wasn't her? He couldn't be sure. Because even if he didn't understand what happened that afternoon at the Grand Canyon, there's nothing he would change about it. Of course, he'd never tell that to his father, but it was true.

Sam loved his Mom and he missed her every day. But when she turned down the path with Al at her side, she was content. She was at peace. She was happy. And if his last afternoon could be anything close to a scene as perfect as that, he'd be able to rest happy, too.

45.

Greg and Al Go for a Walk

A cold breeze perfectly matched the grey sky above. Al's nails clicked along the wooden path as they wound through the woods. Mary always liked this trail. The rainy spring season made the area beneath the raised walkways into a bit of a marsh—soupy, green, and spongy. It felt to Greg like walking on a never-ending dock, but at least he didn't have to worry about ticks. Not that ticks were much of a concern when the ground was covered in snow like it was now.

They went for a lot of walks. Greg and Al. Even when it was cold, he liked to get out of the house and just wander. Sure, the doctor set forth a light exercise plan after the coronary bypass surgery last month, but it was more than that. The walks calmed his mind more than anything else.

Al walked less than a foot away from his left leg. She hadn't needed a leash since she came back. The greatest gift in this whole crazy thing was seeing her again. And the fact that she was a few years younger than when she left meant Greg could add those years back onto her life expectancy. It was no replacement for Mary, but it sure helped.

God how he missed Mary.

He told himself it was for the best. She was sick. It was getting worse. And she was unhappy. Was it selfish to wish she were still around? Maybe. But he couldn't talk himself out of it no matter how hard he tried. His days started off with Al curled up on Mary's pillow next to him. They'd go for a short walk around the block before breakfast. Then they'd eat.

And that was about it.

Anything after that was the result of a reluctant *Oh I guess*.

Greg didn't need to return to work. He wouldn't be able to for another few months even if he did. Sam's secret fundraiser took care of that. It had been a while before Greg was comfortable with the whole world peeping into the strangest moment of his life.

Was it the worst moment?

It sure felt like it. But when he allowed himself to step back he thought no. It was best for Mary.

It was best for her.

It left him alone without the woman that had been his partner through everything since he could run two miles without hardly breaking a sweat. It sentenced him to live alone in their home, haunted by her shadow and her scent and her memory every single day.

But it was best for her.

And in the end, that was what he really wanted. He'd take a bullet in the stomach to save her a paper cut. So no, it wasn't the worst moment of his life. It was another difficult step that couldn't be avoided.

Greg dug his hands deeper into the pockets of his coat. The breeze picked up and blew a light dusting of loose snow across the wooden path. He was glad he put a sweater on Al. She continued sniffing the ground and following along beside him.

They came upon the halfway point of the loop. A bench marked the very back of the path and let you know you were again on your way back toward the parking lot.

The path had been empty.

The parking lot had been empty.

But as Greg rounded the corner he noticed a woman sitting on the bench and looking in their direction.

She smiled.

Greg's boots crunched on the snow as he came to an abrupt stop. Al, for the first time since being back, continued walking without him. And she kept going until she found Mary's leg and sat down.

"Hi Greg," she said.

He didn't move. He couldn't. The cold breeze continued blowing loose snow across the wooden path.

"Come on," she said and patted the open area next to her on the bench.

He forced his legs back into action. It was the first time he worried about his heart since the surgery. Wobbly knees made his slow steps uncertain. There wasn't a bog to fall into, but he didn't want to go off the edge of the path either way. In fact, all of his limbs tingled and seemed to turn into static. But finally, he made it to the bench and sat down.

It was her. And she looked just as she had on the rim of the Grand Canyon when she turned and walked down the path for the last time.

"Mary…"

"Hi Greg," she said again. "I miss you."

He wanted to tell her the same. He wanted to tell her how he thought of her every time he woke up, whenever he made a meal for one, and before he finally fell asleep at night. He wanted to tell her how the whole world was moved by her last moments. That it sparked a discussion and brought people together. He wanted to tell her so many things that they became caught in the back of his throat, all fighting to escape at once.

He wasn't worried about the tears freezing on his face.

"I miss you too," he finally managed to say.

She smiled and looked out into the snow-filled woods surrounding them.

"And I'm sorry."

She turned back to him. "For what?"

"I lost my patience. Sometimes. Like when—" He motioned to the dog. "I shouldn't have yelled." The tears became a flood and his voice stopped working correctly. "I shouldn't have lost my patience and I'm so sorry."

"Greg." She put a hand on his shoulder and it felt like a hot breath spreading beneath his coat. It warmed him. "I'm okay. And you made my life a dream. Every day." She smiled again.

Greg wiped his eyes with the back of his hand and stuck it into the pocket of his coat. He turned back to her and couldn't help another flow of tears.

"I just miss you so much. It's so much harder alone."

She scooted herself to the side, leaned her head onto his shoulder, and ran her hand along the inside of his arm until he took his hand out of his pocket. They interlaced their fingers and another breath of warm air spread through his coat. His fingers stayed warm despite the cold breeze. His breath puffed in front of him in a cloud of steam. No clouds came from Mary.

They stayed like this for a bit. Greg didn't know how long, but time didn't really matter anymore. A comforting heat surrounded him. Her fingers wrapped perfectly through his. He wanted to close his eyes and fall asleep but he didn't want to take his eyes off her, even if all he could see was the top of her head.

Finally, she let out a long breath and picked up her head. They looked into each other's eyes for a moment before she leaned forward and kissed him. Then she sat back and said:

"I have to go."

He nodded.

"I love you, Greg."

"I love you too Mary."

He stayed on the bench as she stood up. Al only turned her head as Mary walked back down the path the way they had just come. She left no footprints in the small dusting of snow that had started to cover the wooden walkway.

They didn't say goodbye.

It didn't feel like the right word to use.

And just like before, she walked around the corner and was gone.

But her heat still warmed the inside of Greg's jacket. He stayed on the bench for another minute before he wiped the tears from his face and looked down to Al.

"Well?"

He stood up and Al followed him. They continued down the path toward the parking lot. The woods were quiet besides the light howl of the breeze through the trees. However, it wasn't as cold as it had been on the way in.

They climbed back into the car at the front of the empty parking lot. He turned the key in the ignition but kept his foot on the brake. He looked to his right at the seat Mary had curled into on the drive to the Grand Canyon. Except now it held a small beagle wearing a sweater.

He put the car in reverse and pulled out of the parking spot.

He didn't turn on the car's heater. Mary's warm breath continued to flow within his jacket.

And for perhaps the first time since that day at the Grand Canyon, Greg smiled as he pulled out of the parking lot to head home.

About the Author

Josh Rank graduated from the University of Wisconsin - Milwaukee before moving to various cities around the country only to return to his hometown. His fiction has appeared in *The Emerson Review*, *The Feathertale Review*, *Hypertext Magazine*, and elsewhere. He keeps himself busy putting together ugly woodworking projects, cooking for his wife, and wishing his dogs were better behaved.

About the Press

Unsolicited Press is based out of Portland, Oregon and focuses on the works of the unsung and underrepresented. As a womxn-owned, all-volunteer small publisher that doesn't worry about profits as much as championing exceptional literature, we have the privilege of partnering with authors skirting the fringes of the lit world. We've worked with emerging and award-winning authors such as Shann Ray, Amy Shimshon-Santo, Brook Bhagat, Kris Amos, and John W. Bateman.

Learn more at unsolicitedpress.com. Find us on twitter and instagram.